WHERE THE OCEAN ENDS

PICT BY TIME
BOOK 3

MIA PRIDE

ARE YOU SIGNED UP FOR DRAGONBLADE'S BLOG?

You'll get the latest news and information on exclusive givcaways, exclusive excerpts, coming releases, sales, free books, cover reveals and more.

Check out our complete list of authors, too!

No spam, no junk. That's a promise!

Sign Up Here

www.dragonbladepublishing.com

Dearest Reader;

Thank you for your support of a small press. At Dragonblade Publishing, we strive to bring you the highest quality Historical Romance from some of the best authors in the business. Without your support, there is no 'us', so we sincerely hope you adore these stories and find some new favorite authors along the way.

Happy Reading!

CEO, Dragonblade Publishing

ADDITIONAL DRAGONBLADE BOOKS BY AUTHOR MIA PRIDE

Pict by Time Series
Where the Thistle Grows (Book 1)
Where the Stars Lead (Book 2)
Where the Ocean Ends (Book 3)

Irvines of Drum Series
For Love of a Laird (Book 1)
Like a Laird to a Flame (Book 2)
Maid for the Knight (Book 3)
How to Save a Knight (Novella)

Pirates of Britannia Series
Plunder by Knight
Beast of the Bay

CHAPTER ONE

S AMUEL WATCHED THE second hand move around the circular
analog clock on the wall across the room. Its rhythmic ticking
provided a steady, reliable comfort within the small classroom.
Students came and went, tests were passed or failed, and lectures
were learned and subsequently forgotten. Still, the second hand
kept pace, a constant companion reminding Samuel that he was a
prisoner of time, able to come and go but never truly allowed to
belong in one place.

Rubber sneaker soles squeaked against cheap laminate flooring as students anxiously shuffled their feet beneath old wooden
desks, carved with the initials of those who came before. Papers
rustled as test pages turned, and pencils scratched feverishly
against pristinely white test copies. Erasers left frenzied remnants
across desk surfaces, brushed to the floor by palms, or blown
away through puffed cheeks as his class scrambled to finish their
midterm exam.

Samuel observed these modern students while they worked.
They studied a civilization long since gone, scribbling their
answers to questions memorized from used textbooks purchased
for a discounted rate from the University's library. Samuel saw no
need to purchase updated texts, only to charge his students higher
fees. After all, despite his firsthand knowledge of the past,
contemporary archaeologists had yet to discover what Samuel
had learned during his time-traveling adventures. Much of the
information contained within these books was incorrect or

touched the truth, but just barely.

Samuel had often considered writing a textbook containing his knowledge of the ancient Pictish people, the ancestors of modern-day Scotland. But, how would he explain his intensely detailed understanding of events and artifacts that no evidence existed to support? There was simply no way around it—Samuel had no choice but to teach his students that which the University, and world at large, considered accurate Pictish history.

The second hand reached its destination just as the clock struck two in the afternoon. "Pencils down," Samuel said, locking his hands behind his back as he stood from his desk. A few students groaned, but it was the usual few who never seemed to finish on time, though Samuel understood their plight. Time never seemed on his side, either. "Remember that your mid-term papers on the discovery of King Brodyn Mac Cuill's remains and the techniques by which they were analyzed is due next Friday. But, I want you all to enjoy your weekend and take a deep breath. Your mid-term test is over, and that's the hard part. See you Monday."

Chairs dragged and screeched as students pushed to their feet, brought their tests up to the front, and offered Samuel half-hearted smiles before leaving the room.

"Mister Sullivan," Tommy Mullins mumbled as he handed him the test. "I studied so hard, I swear. I didn't finish the last three questions." His mouth formed into a frown as he looked down at his scuffed sneakers. This wasn't new for Tommy. The young man was bright but slow at reading, which wasn't something Samuel wished to punish him for.

Samuel looked at his watch, then the satchel full of Pictish clothing beneath his desk. He was anxious to leave campus and spend his weekend in the year 686, but he could spare a few more minutes. "Do you have time now to finish?"

Tommy's eyes widened as he nodded, his shaggy blond hair covering his eager brown eyes. "Yes, sir. Thank you, sir."

Samuel smiled and handed Tommy back his test paper. "I can

give you an extra fifteen minutes. Is that sufficient?"

Tommy nodded gratefully and hurried toward his desk. "Yes, Mr. Sullivan! Thank you, sir!" Samuel sighed and sat back in his chair while waiting for Tommy to finish, which luckily only took ten minutes. When his second-year student walked back up with the test with a broad smile, he said, "You're my favorite professor, Mr. Sullivan, and not just because you allow me extra time. I enjoy your classes and hope to be part of a future excavation with you. I've already finished my paper about King Brodyn! You led the team that found his bones?"

Rocking on his heels, Samuel nodded before swinging his satchel over his shoulder. Though he knew the bones found in that cave belonged to someone else, the world believed they belonged to King Brodyn. And so it must remain, for if the news ever spread that 1,300-year-old bones found buried three feet below the ground actually belonged to a modern man with tooth fillings and bone screws, it would cause a media sensation and possibly a ripple in time, for it was the discovery of Brodyn's bones that continued the time loop that saved Scotland from being torn into several kingdoms.

"I led the team, yes. But I am not the one who discovered the bones. My former students Emilie and Cait get that credit. So, keep at it, Tommy, and there may be a place for you on a team after graduation. One step at a time, okay?"

"Okay, Mr. Sullivan! Have a great weekend." Tommy flung his camo backpack over his right shoulder and disappeared around the corner.

Samuel glanced at the clock again before following Tommy into the hallway. The pharmacy closed in fifty minutes, and Samuel had to grab first-aid supplies before traveling back to Pinnata Castra. Existing between the years 2023 and 686 was tiresome, and Samuel often asked himself why he continued to do so. His role in this time loop had been to bring Caitriona Mac Murray—now Mac Cuill since she'd married King Brodyn—back in time through the cave since she was the *Savior of Scotland*, as

Samuel had dubbed her.

Nearly one and a half years had passed since Cait had entered the world of the Picts. She'd married Brodyn, united enemy tribes, and paved the way to a unified modern Scotland. So, why did Samuel continue to split his time between two worlds, belonging to both and neither simultaneously?

The answer couldn't be found in his mind, for there was no logic behind his actions. Instead, the answer resided deep within his beating heart. If Samuel closed his eyes and pictured his motivation, the answer came to him in the visage of the blonde-haired, blue-eyed beauty who'd plagued his life with her curiosity, intelligence, and fierce independence since the day he'd met her. But, he feared she would never be his, for this blonde beauty he dreamed of was Murielle Mac Cuill, the Pictish princess who must marry a king to strengthen *Pinnata Castra*, known today as Burghead.

Still, so long as she was unwed, Samuel would travel through the cave as often as possible, desperate to spend time in her all-consuming presence. And, after watching many kings come and go without a marriage arrangement, Samuel felt hope blossom in his chest. There was little chance that Samuel would receive King Brodyn's blessing to marry Murielle, but with her rejection of every available king, Samuel decided the time was now or never.

Shoving the stack of tests into his satchel along with his change of clothes, Samuel left his classroom and locked the door behind him before heading to the parking lot, where his trusty yet battered Jeep awaited him.

Mud splattered its panels, proof of adventures and extended trips through barren lands to reach new excavation sites. He'd had her since he first began his career and vowed he'd keep her until his final dig. They were bonded, he and Joplin, as he fondly referred to his Jeep. Janice's sultry voice had been the first to play on her radio when Samuel had bought the vehicle nearly fifteen years ago, so Joplin had become her name, now synonymous with adventure.

Pulling his keys out of the pocket of his worn jeans, Samuel flung his bag into the passenger seat and hastened toward downtown, where the pharmacy was. Emilie, who had taken over the care of the villagers since their healer, Anya, had peacefully passed in her sleep a few months prior, had requested Samuel grab antibiotic ointments, gauze, pain relievers, and first-aid products to bring back with him. She'd then disguise the items inside old clay jars or wooden trinket boxes to hide their modern origins.

Life at Pinnata Castra was not the same without the old healer scurrying about, fussing over everyone with her tender touch and sarcastic tongue. She'd passed through the veil of time in 1941 and ended up in Pinnata Castra while hiding in a cave during the Second World War as bombs destroyed her village. She'd lost everything that night but gained everything in the land of the Picts, where she'd met the love of her life, Edwin. Since then, she'd remained a staple of daily life for decades, raising King Brodyn and his siblings as her own.

Now, she was gone, and though he smiled, knowing she was finally with her beloved Edwin again, Sam's heart ached every time he traveled back and didn't feel her comforting presence. Her spirit had passed over, but he knew she and Edwin, soulmates in every lifetime, were starting anew somewhere else.

Walking into the small pharmacy, Samuel heard the familiar rattle of the door's overhead bell as he pushed through the door. Charles, the elderly pharmacist who owned the shop, looked up and grinned when he saw Samuel come through. "There ye are, me boy!" Charles said with his thick, Scottish brogue. "I was wondering if ye'd make it here on time."

"I had a student stay behind a bit to finish a test, but I'm here. Have you all the supplies I ordered?"

"Yes, yes." He patted a brown paper bag on the counter. "This new app where people can order ahead is taking me some getting used to, but I do like it. Anya, God rest her soul, used to come in here like a storm and pull things off the shelf so quickly. I had a hard time kenning what she bought during inventory. I daresay that whatever it was she needed all them supplies for has kept me in business all these years." Charles chuckled. "And, I do quite like seeing ye, Sam, but I'd lie if I said I dinnae miss Anya."

"We all do, Charles. But, the show must go on, and I will gladly take her place in buying these supplies for Burghead. We use them at the schools. The kids are very clumsy," Samuel said.

Charles laughed and handed him the bag. "Yer all set. I love the pre-pay feature of that app, as well. Ye ken, there is a delivery option if ever ye cannae make it here. Some nice young university kids swing by to grab orders. Helps them make a few bucks, ye see."

Samuel nodded, running a hand through his short, black, wavy hair, a gift from his Italian mother. His father had been Irish, lending him the quintessential Irish surname of Sullivan and a love for a good lager, but his dark hair, eyes, and olive complexion were all his mother. "Thank you, I will keep that in mind," Samuel said with a smirk. If only Charles knew there would be no delivery to Samuel's destination—unless a university student wished to travel back through time. It might not be worth the minimum wage pay.

With the full paper bag in hand, Samuel nodded to Charles, wished him a happy weekend, and headed back to Joplin, where he tossed the bag beside his satchel on the front seat.

"Pinnata Castra, here we come," Samuel murmured, wondering how much longer he could sustain such a lifestyle, spreading himself thinner than a crepe only to spend a little time in Murielle's company. It was futile, foolish, and no longer feasible. He had to pick his path and decide once and for all which time he'd call home.

He'd never made his feelings for Murielle known because she was destined to marry a king. It wasn't his place to interfere, nor could he risk ruining a potential alliance. But, every available king had called, and Murielle had sent them packing. As he approached the Moray coastline and prepared to travel through time, he also prepared to make the biggest decision of his life and ask for Murielle's hand in marriage.

As COLD WATER ran across her bare toes, Murielle stared into the horizon, tossing pebbles into the loch's glassy surface, watching ripples of water glitter in the afternoon sunlight. Her gray cloak rested atop a large boulder of similar color, the same color as all the wee pebbles littering the loch's shore. A few stubborn blades of grass pushed their way through the rocks, determined to add a drop of color to the otherwise bland shoreline. Just a few yards away, the landscape was littered with soft green grass, a shock of purple from thistle patches, and a spattering of yellow and white wildflowers. Murielle focused on the brilliant colors of the land, even if her mood resembled the bland, gray shore.

Lifting her blue tunic above her ankles, Murielle waded further into the loch, enjoying the enveloping chill of water against her flesh. This was her favorite place to be alone and think, but not for the reasons many would suspect. Aside from its vast beauty and wilderness, this particular strip of shoreline allowed Murielle a perfect view of the one dirt trail that led travelers toward Pinnata Castra's entrance.

From this vantage point, she could see every traveler coming and going without appearing to be anxiously staring at the road. Nay, to any casual passerby, Murielle simply enjoyed an early spring afternoon at the loch. Indeed, nobody knew that her eyes keenly scanned the road for any sign of a dark-haired traveler who came and went from her world like the passing of lonely days and nights. According to Samuel, he only came on what he called weekends, which were the two days of the sennight he didn't teach at the place he called a university. But the other five days lingered and spread into several more days as time passed differently on the other side of the veil. So, Samuel's five-day absence felt like an eternity to Murielle, but she'd paid attention, tracked his arrivals, and believed she'd figured out the pattern. If she was correct, Samuel's "weekend" would be upon him, and he'd be arriving soon, carrying medical supplies for the tribe, and regaling her with more stories from the year 2023.

A silver-scaled fish skimmed her ankle as it circled the water, following its friends as they swam through in a determined fashion, seeking algae or some other wee creature to eat. She was due back in town and hope of Samuel's arrival waned with every passing moment. A party of men had ridden past the loch an hour before, and Murielle was determined to avoid them as long as possible. She'd noticed the green, blue, and yellow standard, and though she hadn't recognized its origin from this distance, she knew it was the last available king in the land, traveling to meet her as a prospective bride.

Having sent away nearly a dozen thus far, Murielle didn't hold much hope that this king would be any more to her liking. They were all old, or toothless, or overweight, or evil, as evidenced by Arwyn ap Rhys, the last king who came calling. He'd been angry that Murielle didn't immediately swoon at his feet and declare herself his bride, so he'd abducted the king's son and her nephew, Lucas, and would have likely killed him had Emilie not run after them.

This new king had worked hard to convince Brodyn to allow him within Pinnata Castra's walls. Brodyn had finally agreed, granting only half a score of men to enter the village with him, and all must relinquish their weapons. Surprisingly, King Aldfrith mac Oswiu had willingly complied with all demands, so determined was he to meet the Pictish princess who'd sent away every other suitor.

She didn't send the kings away because her affections were given elsewhere. Nay, for as much as her heart belonged to Samuel, she knew he would never be hers. He was neither a king nor from this time. If her truest desire could be met, she'd marry Samuel and live in 2023 with him, damn the consequences. But the choice wasn't hers to make, and a lifetime of proper upbringing instilled the notion of a royal marriage whether she wanted it or not.

She did not.

"I fear 'tis time for us to return, me lady." Murielle looked over her shoulder and pouted at Ronan, her current guard. Ever since Arwyn's attack, guards were on Murielle daily.

She'd shuffled through a few, but Goodwin, her previous guard and greatest friend, was now married to Emilie and had a bairn to care for. He had little time to "prance around the land while she wandered aimlessly," as he so eloquently put it once before. Still, Ronan was a fine guard and pliable enough. So much so that she'd nearly forgotten he'd escorted her to the loch.

"Do we have to? Mayhap a wee bit more time?" she asked, wading back to the shore as water rivulets ran down her legs.

"'Fraid not, my lady. Already, we've overstayed. The king will be unhappy if ye dinnae properly greet King Aldfrith."

"What tribe is he king of?" Murielle asked.

Ronan shrugged. "I dinnae ken. There have been too many. But ye shall ken the answer soon enough." Ronan grabbed her horse's reins and walked him over to Murielle. "Ye must ready yerself," he said sternly as he mounted his own, sizeable, gray horse.

With a sigh, Murielle looked out to the horizon one last time, and without any sign of Samuel's approach, she knew there was nothing else for it. She had no excuses left and must return to the village and face yet another old, toothless, overweight warlord of a king.

In no rush, Murielle allowed her white gelding, Album, to meander up the hill at his leisure. Nobody would ever accuse Album of being motivated by anything other than food.

"I ken ye are wasting time purposely," Ronan said with a touch of exasperation in his tone. Murielle knew Ronan preferred being within the village walls, where he could spar and practice with the other warriors. She didn't mean to waste his time, but it wasn't her fault he'd been assigned as her guard.

Or perhaps it *was* her fault, for being so stubborn and unmanageable.

"Album is seventeen years old. He is slower than yer horse," Murielle offered as a consideration.

Ronan snorted. "My horse is eighteen, and she rides out with me just fine. Our horses arenae old, Murielle. Ye've simply allowed Album to grow fat and lazy with yer indulgence. What kind of name is Album anyway?"

"When my father gifted him to me, I was but six years old. I'd been busy studying Latin with one of the monks, and the horse was white, so I named him *Album*—Latin for *white*."

Ronan looked at her as if she was the oddest woman on earth, but he didn't say a word. No words were needed when a man had such an expressive face. Ronan wore his emotions openly, thus causing trouble in the past when he tried to woo Emilie, the last time traveler to join their village, though few knew her origins. Goodwin had already fallen in love with Emilie, but Ronan also wanted to try his fortune. It ended with Goodwin giving him a broken nose and bloody lip. Ronan had since admitted defeat where Emilie was concerned, but his opinion on her horse's name was difficult for him to disguise based on his curled lip and crinkled nose.

"What sort of name should a six-year-old give a horse?" she asked, raising one brow. "Could ye do better?"

"Thor."

"Thor? The Norse god of lightning? Ye would name yer horse *Thor* at the risk of offending our many Celtic gods?" she asked with feigned shock. But in truth, she was more shocked that Ronan should know who Thor was. He hadn't had the same education she and Brodyn received, though he was well-traveled.

"Ye would risk offending our many Celtic gods by naming a perfectly good horse after the color of his coat rather than one of them?" he asked in retaliation.

"Fair point," she sighed.

As they entered the gates and meandered toward the stables, Murielle saw scores of villagers huddled near the longhouse. *You'd think they'd all be accustomed to these shriveled old kings by now.* Never had she seen them so enthralled.

Handing Album's reins to the stable lad, Murielle turned toward her house, hoping to avoid this introduction for as long as possible. Mud from the loch's shore caked Murielle's blue tunic, and a morning spent in the furious autumn wind had tangled her long blonde hair into a chaotic mass. She didn't care about her appearance, but she knew Brodyn would wish for her to clean up.

She'd barely taken a dozen steps when her brother spotted her and reined her in. "Awe, there is the princess now," he exclaimed from the front of the longhouse. "Please join us, Murielle."

Pausing mid-step, Murielle froze as all heads turned toward her, and she resisted the urge to run quick fingers through her disheveled hair. *A princess does not groom herself before prying eyes,* her mother's voice whispered in her mind. Though her mother had died when Murielle was quite young, some lessons had stuck with her throughout the years.

Straightening her spine, Murielle approached the crowd, preparing to meet another toothless, wrinkled man. The crowd parted so she may ease her way to Brodyn's side. Several men wearing green, blue, and yellow plaids across their shoulders huddled together, but a quick glimpse didn't reveal any aging man wearing a crown.

"Murielle," Brodyn said with an unexpected grin, "I'd like to introduce ye to Aldfrith mac Oswiu, king of the Britons of Northumbria. He replaced his uncle, Ecgfrith, after the battle. But I am confident that his aim and goals as king are not those of his uncle."

A man appearing to be in his early thirties stepped forward. He wore a crisp, white tunic and fine leather trousers with the plaid of his people slung across his right shoulder. Little separated him from the men he traveled with except the finer cut and quality of his garments and the almost imperceptible silver circlet adorning his head. Thick, dark brown hair hung about his shoulders, and a smile full of teeth flashed as his soft, hazel eyes crinkled at the corners. A short, dark beard spread across his strong jaw, but she noticed matching dimples on either side of his smile. She sensed decency and kindness in his gaze and immediately felt ill-at-ease, for she understood all too well that he was the best match to arrive thus far, and her brother clearly held high hopes for this union.

Murielle bent her head and gave the man a small curtsy, hoping he paid little attention to her dirty tunic. He was a well-built man appearing to be lean yet muscular if his arms were any indication. He was handsome. There was no denying such a thing, which explained why every person in Pinnata Castra now hovered around, for none of the previous kings compared. Enigmatic energy radiated off the man, attracting every woman in sight.

"'Tis well to make yer acquaintance, King Aldfrith."

Slowly, the king stepped forward and gently took her hand in his, placing a soft, respectable kiss on her fingers. "The pleasure is mine. I have heard tales of yer great beauty, but I see it did ye no justice."

Swallowing her unease, Murielle forced a smile. She knew he meant well, and his compliments likely made most women swoon. Perhaps she too would swoon, if her heart did not belong to another. Still, she could not have the man she loved; this king, so far, appeared to be a great match. And, knowing that he replaced the tyrant king of the Britons her brother had slaughtered in battle, Murielle understood how crucial an alliance with him would be. The Britons and Picts had long been enemies, and nobody living remembered a time when the two kingdoms weren't at odds. Her marriage to Aldfrith would create years of peace between them, especially if she bore an heir.

If only Murielle didn't know how dangerous life as a king was. Brodyn had survived battles, but just barely. Murielle didn't wish to marry a man only to become a widow, and she didn't wish to birth an heir who would always be at risk of abduction or assassination. All she wanted was a quiet life with a man she loved. No battles to fight. No heirs to produce. No battles to fear. But being born the only Pictish princess in their kingdom sealed her fate.

"I'm certain ye are being kind, but surely my appearance is lacking and doesnae meet yer approval." Finally, Murielle relented and allowed her fingers to stroke her hair, wincing when she tugged on a tangle.

"Nonsense," Aldfrith said with a chuckle. "I quite enjoy this impromptu meeting and seeing ye after a fine walk along the loch. A woman unafraid of getting dirty is ideal, I assure ye."

He seemed not only kind but well-educated and reasonable, unlike many of these kings who wouldn't know a tome if it hit him upside the head. He seemed almost too good to be true, but it didn't matter either way. She may very well agree to marry this man for the sake of her people, but she'd never love him. Many would say love was not a consideration in a royal marriage, and perhaps that was true, but Brodyn had found a great love in his wife, and Murielle felt a sense of loss when she considered a life without that tender devotion.

"I'm sure ye are tired from yer journey," Brodyn said to Aldfrith. "My home is yers. Ye and yer men may visit the longhouse for a hot meal and fresh ale. My sister shall also rest and freshen up before we come together for the evening meal."

Caitriona, Murielle's sister-by-marriage, stood beside Brodyn with a sympathetic look for Murielle. She knew of Murielle's feelings for Samuel and yet also understood that this king was a likely candidate for a husband. Taking Murielle's hand, Cait walked with her toward the house just as Emilie, the queen's best friend, walked up and took Murielle's other hand.

Together in silence, the three women walked toward the house, and Murielle felt both their tacit support and sadness simultaneously. Murielle already knew it in her gut. She'd have to marry this man, and a life with Samuel would be nothing but a dream that plagued the remainder of her nights.

CHAPTER TWO

"I KNOW I am not your first choice for Murielle, but I am in love with your sister. No king has yet been worthy of her, nor am I. However, I have reason to believe Murielle loves me as I love her, and if you'd grant me your approval, I'd like to propose marriage to her."

Samuel practiced this speech the entire time he walked the distance between the cave and Pinnata Castra. Time was running out. Samuel couldn't continue living between worlds. He'd gladly give up everything in 2023 if it meant being Murielle's husband. If she preferred to live with him in his time, he'd consider that option. No longer could he live in the balance, pining for a woman he couldn't have. It was time to confess his feelings, and though he expected her brother would reject his suit, Samuel needed to confront this plague upon his heart so he may be freed from the agony of uncertainty.

Now wearing his worn tunic and faded trousers, Samuel walked along the coast, seeing Pinnata Castra silhouetted in the distance. He'd made this journey more times than he could count, and he wondered if this would be his last. His leather satchel hung over his right shoulder as he watched gulls circle over the glittering ocean water, looking for surface fish to have for dinner. Before he knew it, Pinnata Castra's gates loomed before him with their familiar wrought iron bars. Lawrence and Caeden guarded the gates, giving him a nod as they let him pass through. Aside from the medical supplies in his bag, he wasn't certain he served a purpose here any longer.

By the time he arrived, dusk was approaching, and the sky, blue only twenty minutes before, now glowed lavender and coral on the horizon. The usual sounds drifted to his ears as the villagers milled about. Many smiled and sent him greetings as they finished their daily chores. A scattering of cattle and sheep roamed freely as their owners slowly rounded them into their byre for the night, and chickens clucked as they pecked the dry ground for food. Samuel passed a bonfire, rounded a granary, and headed for Brodyn and Cait's home, steeling himself for the conversation he meant to have with the king.

"Oy, he is a finely made man, isnae he?" one plump villager whispered to another.

"Aye, and he seems quite taken with the princess, he does."

Samuel slowed and creased his brow. Surely, they weren't referring to him. Being slightly darker in features than the usual Pict, Samuel didn't consider himself handsome by their standards. He had always done well enough with women in his own time, even though he knew nothing more could be shared aside from casual encounters. From the earliest age, Samuel remembered every previous life he'd ever lived. He understood that his role in the universe was to secure Scotland's future by making certain King Brodyn of the Picts married a Scot's princess, securing peace among the tribes that would one day form modern-day Scotland. When that princess died en route to meet Brodyn, as she had in every lifetime due to this time loop they were stuck in, Samuel had to bring his student and friend, Caitriona, through the veil of time to fill her place. They were the same woman living different lives 1,300 years apart. Caitriona's destiny was always linked to Brodyn, and Samuel's destiny was always to unite them.

But, once his job was done, all memory of his past lives ended. Did he stay in Pinnata Castra or return home? Did he marry Murielle or remain alone for the remainder of his days before dying and starting this vicious cycle again? He had no answers, nor did he know who the village gossips whispered about. All he knew was he was at a crossroads and needed to make a decision.

When he entered the house after a polite knock went unanswered, Samuel dropped his satchel onto a bench near the hearth and looked around the house. "Hello?" Nobody answered, so he assumed they'd all wandered down to the longhouse for the evening meal. It was early for the village to gather, but something seemed different about this evening.

Reaching the longhouse entrance, he smelled the usual smoke from candles, the scent of wafting stew and ale, and heard the raucous laughter. There seemed to be many more men than usual in the room, not only evidenced by the unfamiliar plaids he saw draped across unfamiliar shoulders, but by the lassies swarming them like bees to a hive.

Had Brodyn found another king to consider an alliance with? After the danger King Arwyn brought with him during his visit, Samuel had believed—perhaps even foolishly hoped—that Brodyn had given up on the search. Knowing Murielle, she hid in the shadows, trying to avoid another overweight, elderly man with bad teeth.

Familiar laughter hit his ears from across the room, and Samuel's heart flipped against his ribs as it did every time he heard it. At this moment, Murielle sounded like she was enjoying herself, but surely, she was only being diplomatic.

Pushing through the crowd, Samuel maneuvered toward the head table, where he saw Emilie holding wee Anya as Goodwin sat beside her with his arm wrapped around her waist. When they spotted him, Goodwin smiled and offered him a seat beside them. Emilie looked over her shoulder and gave Sam a cringe face. He knew what that meant. There was indeed another king here.

"Have you seen Cait?" he asked. He preferred to find Murielle but didn't want to appear over-anxious.

"Cait and Brodyn are across the room with Murielle and King Aldfrith," Emilie said, emphasizing the king's name. "He is from Northumbria. Ecgfrith's nephew and successor."

"Oh." Samuel had not expected that the successor of Brodyn's sworn enemy would ever come calling, let alone be admitted within the gates.

"Aye, we are all as surprised as ye are," Goodwin said with a grunt. "Turns out, this king is nothing like his uncle, thank the stars. Dare I say he seems quite… decent."

That was a compliment coming from Goodwin, and it made Samuel's stomach clench. Still, decent wasn't enough to secure Murielle as a wife, was it? He'd read about Aldfrith in many of his books and had even idolized how the man ran his kingdom, but he'd never paid any attention to his wife's name. Samuel cursed himself for not studying that detail. Aldfrith mac Oswiu was a highly regarded, successful king of Northumbria. Well-educated, he'd traveled the lands learning theology, hoping to join the church. He was incredibly pious but also known to be fair, kind, shrewd, and diplomatic. He'd helped Northumbria reach a golden age of learning and growth during his reign. Shit. This was bad.

"Is he ancient?" Samuel asked with a small pinch of hope left in his gut.

"Nay. He isnae much older than we are. I'd guess he is close to yer age. The lassies seem to like him well enough from what I've seen," Goodwin said casually from over his shoulder. Emilie scowled at him and nudged her shoulder into his. "What?" he asked defensively before looking at Samuel and cringing. "Right. I forgot ye fancy Murielle. Sorry. For what it's worth, I dinnae believe he is her type. I hear he is pious and enjoys holy pilgrimages. Murielle prefers the pagan faith."

As if summoned by her name, Murielle laughed again, and Samuel followed the sound, spotting her standing beside a tall, dark-haired man whose eyes appeared glued to Murielle. Her head tilted back as she laughed, sending her golden waves of hair cascading down her back. She wore a royal blue velvet tunic that clung to every curve before flaring out at the hips. Did she choose that tunic to impress King Aldfrith, or was it simply her best tunic for entertaining royalty?

No matter the reason, she looked ethereal. Her lithe curves, her warm smile, her free laughter—all of it sent sharp pains straight to his heart. It sent other feelings to other parts of his anatomy, also, but Samuel did his best to ignore his damn libido.

At 23 years old, Murielle was older than most married women of her time but still innocent in the ways of men. She'd been carefully guarded her entire life by both Brodyn, as her brother, and Goodwin, as her guard. There had been a time not so long ago when Samuel believed Goodwin was in love with Murielle, but that theory dissolved when Goodwin fell in love with Emilie.

Perhaps Samuel's passive demeanor toward Murielle had been his downfall. She likely had no idea how he felt about her, though he had reason to believe she had feelings for him. Perhaps it was his overactive imagination or a desperate need for requited love, but he'd noticed her small glances, flirtatious smiles, and flushing cheeks often enough when they spoke.

He wasn't an amateur when it came to women. He'd had many in his time, and he knew the signs of attraction, but Murielle remained a mystery. Was something more profound hidden within the depths of her cerulean eyes?

He'd allowed himself to dream, to delve into that secret recess of his mind where Murielle was his, body and soul. He'd allowed himself to hope for more, prepared to face those feelings and seek more than just dreams and fantasies. He wanted Murielle to be his wife, and for one fragile moment, he'd allowed himself to consider that reality, even dared to hope for it.

But the man making her laugh in the corner of the longhouse served as a reality check for Samuel. Of all the kings, Aldfrith would make a fine match, not only for Murielle but as an ally to the Picts. The Britons of Northumbria were the greatest threat to the Picts, and if Brodyn could secure peace by marrying Murielle to their king, Samuel had to step back and allow it. Too much was at stake, and he'd spent far too much time correcting the timeline to risk destroying it.

Watching Murielle flush as she spoke to the handsome king of the Britons, Samuel decided to shrink back into the crowd, hoping to remain unseen. He wasn't a man with a giant ego, but he had pride and wouldn't interrupt Murielle if she was enjoying another man's company. He had no claim to her, even if his heart stopped beating at the mere thought of her with another man.

"Sam!" He closed his eyes and froze when he heard Queen Caitriona shout his name loud enough for the entire room to hear. Turning, he forced a smile, slowly moving toward her, even though she stood beside Murielle, whose glittering eyes settled on him in a way that—as always—made his stomach flip and his breath hitch.

"You made it!" Caitriona flung her arms around him in a strong embrace. Lucas rested in Brodyn's arms, looking even bigger than before. Time passed faster on this side of the veil, though Samuel never understood why. For every day he was back in his own time, it seemed several more passed in this time. It wasn't easy to tell the passage of time until he looked at the babies maturing and developing faster than expected.

"Indeed. I was delayed, but I just arrived." Murielle and King Aldfrith stood just behind him, and he didn't wish to appear rude, so he turned to address them, doing his best to hide any evidence of discomfort or heartache.

"Greetings, Murielle," Samuel said in a level voice before looking at the ridiculously handsome man beside her. Samuel bowed to the man. "You must be King Aldfrith."

"Indeed, I am," the man said pleasantly. "I daresay I've heard many things about ye already, Samuel, and I've only been here a few hours."

"Oh?" Sam raised a brow and looked at Murielle. Had she truly been speaking about him to this man, whose goal was to marry her?

"Och, aye. Queen Caitriona and King Brodyn speak very highly of ye."

"Ah," he said with a small smile. *Of course.* Why would he foolishly believe Murielle spoke about him to anyone, let alone this man, who could charm the pants off of even Henry VIII?

Surely, Samuel hadn't even crossed her mind since she laid eyes on Aldfrith. "Well, it's a pleasure to meet you, King Aldfrith. I will not take up any more of your time."

Samuel bowed again and turned to leave.

"Wait!" Murielle grabbed his arm as he turned. When Samuel turned to look into her eyes, his stomach flipped as it always did, but this time heartache accompanied the fluttering in his gut. "I've been awaiting ye."

"You have?" Samuel asked, looking down at her petite form. He was three inches above six feet tall, and she was about a foot shorter than him.

"Might we have a private word?" She pled with her eyes, but he forced himself to look away when he saw the handsome king watching her, waiting for her to return.

"We shall, but you have company right now. I don't want to intrude."

"You could never," she whispered, tightening her grip on his arm.

"I don't think he agrees," Samuel said lightly. "He's traveled far to meet you, Murielle."

"You've traveled farther than he," she reminded him.

He chucked and nodded. "True as that may be, I am not a king, not even close to being one. Go, Murielle. We shall speak tonight back at the house." He gave her hand a pathetic pat and turned to leave the longhouse before she saw the crack in his facade. He was a bloody coward. But what good would come of telling her or Brodyn how he felt now? Without knowing Aldfrith's spouse's name, Samuel couldn't know if he tampered with the timeline if he continued to pursue Murielle. What if she was destined to marry him and have multiple royal children who would one day become the Stewart dynasty? Imagine the damage he'd do if he stopped such a powerful royal line from existing. No, he couldn't risk it. It was one thing entirely when Murielle outright refused every king, but this time, it was different. If there was any chance whatsoever that she was meant to marry Aldfrith,

Samuel had to walk away.

He didn't know what Murielle was so set on discussing with him, but surely it could wait a few hours. Suddenly, Samuel felt like his decision to stay or go was being made for him. Caitriona was settled with her family, as was Emilie. If Murielle accepted Aldfrith's suit, there was nothing left for him here. He'd visit from time to time to see his friends and watch their beautiful children grow, but loneliness was a heavy burden on his soul, a weight dragging him down with every step. Though he'd love Murielle with his dying breath, Samuel needed to focus on his own life and his own future if he was ever to find happiness. Perhaps his future didn't involve a wife or family. He had his career, and with it came traveling to exotic lands, discovering lost history, and teaching the next generation of archaeologists, such as Tommy. He'd found enjoyment and fulfillment in his work for twelve years. Surely, it would sustain him for another twelve, at least.

The difference between then and now was a blonde-haired, blue-eyed Pictish princess who stole his heart nearly two years ago when he first arrived in this time, well before Caitriona ever stepped foot on this land. Months before it was time to guide Caitriona to Brodyn, Samuel began his mission, establishing himself as a messenger from a faraway kingdom so nobody knew the difference. He'd known Murielle in a thousand lives, but only as King Brodyn's sister. If ever a reality existed where she became more to Samuel, fate had cruelly erased those memories. Life after life, Sam was reincarnated without any memory of loving or having been loved.

Entering Brodyn and Cait's vacant home, Samuel sat on the bench nearest the hearth, placed his elbows upon his knees as he leaned forward, and stared into the dancing fire's depths. His future might be a mystery, but it was time to take it into his own hands.

AS THE TALLOW candles burned to useless nubs that would later be collected and remelted, Murielle watched as villagers left the longhouse, ready to take to their beds. For on the morrow, the chores would not complete themselves, and though King Aldfrith brought with him a gaiety their people quite enjoyed, the night had run overlong.

Aldfrith remained attentive the entire night, regaling her of his travels across Europe as he sought the favor of many different saints. She found that, while she didn't share his enthusiasm for the new religion, she didn't find his stories tedious or embellished. Aldfrith owned an intelligence and worldly view that she found refreshing, unlike the other kings who could only speak of their prowess in battle and how far their kingdom's power spread. Aldfrith didn't speak of politics, war, or money. Instead, he discussed art, religion, travel, and the delicious foods he'd sampled across the land. He was attractive and easy to talk to. So, why was she shifting her feet anxiously as she stood in the nearly empty longhouse, awaiting her chance to head home?

She knew the answer without putting much thought into it. Before meeting Aldfrith, it had been Samuel she awaited, Samuel she longed to regale with stories. Aldfrith could travel the world, but he hadn't traveled through time. But her attraction wasn't simply about Samuel's mysterious nature and easy conversation. It was about his mesmerizing brown eyes, how she could see secrets and perhaps even desire mirrored back in their depths, like a pool of wonders. His black hair, so unlike that of the other men of her village, made her think of a faraway land called Italy, where Samuel said his family originated. He spoke of olives, some unique type of food called *spaghetti*, and fine wine in a bright and sunny place called Tuscany in the land of Italy. She longed to see Italy and see it by Samuel's side because it was a part of his life and history.

Murielle wanted to be a part of everything that involved Samuel. His skin tanned easily in the sun, darkening in a most exotic way. Strands of white threaded through his dark hair, a sign of maturity and wisdom that Murielle found fascinating. So, while King Aldfrith kindly asked the right questions and showed interest in Murielle, she couldn't focus until she'd spoken with Samuel. The moment she'd seen Sam standing in the longhouse, her attention was solely his. And when he'd left, it took all of Murielle's willpower not to chase after him.

"Murielle." Aldfrith gently placed her hand in his, running his thumb across her palm. "I have quite enjoyed yer company. I daresay I havenae enjoyed a night this much in many a moon."

Smiling, Murielle dared to look into his hazel eyes. Beautiful as they were, she preferred eyes the color of the earth after a storm. "I verra much enjoyed yer company, as well." When he stepped slightly closer, Murielle froze, realizing they were utterly alone. Brodyn must have truly agreed with this match if he would leave her here unattended, unguarded. Panic overcame her. Thus far, few men had proved trustworthy while alone with her. Flashbacks of Arwyn's wandering eyes and eager hands made Murielle take a step back and close her eyes while she composed herself.

"Murielle, I have no intention of crossing any boundaries. I apologize if I drew too near."

Taking a deep breath, she felt herself flush with embarrassment. "I don't mean any offense, King Aldfrith. Ye've been a man of honor all night. I suppose I've met too many overeager kings during this process. My virtue is my honor, ye ken."

Aldfrith nodded with approval and smiled. "I do ken. As ye ken, before my uncle died a most deserved death, I studied to become a man of the cloth. While I've now become a king and require a queen, I still hold virtue in high esteem, and I wouldnae dare put yers in danger. King Brodyn has informed me of all ye've endured, especially with Arwyn of Gwynedd, who was a notorious lecher. He too met a deserved end. Men who disrespect women are the least worthy of them all."

Murielle nodded, relaxing slightly. He seemed genuine, and she knew she was safe in his presence. Still holding her hand,

Aldfrith cleared his throat. "I dinnae have much time to tarry here at Pinnata Castra, as much as it pains me. I'd enjoy spending another sennight in yer presence and getting to ken ye better, but having the entire kingdom of Northumbria thrust upon me has, oddly, consumed much of my time." He raised a dark brow and cracked a smile.

"I can only imagine."

"While ye are imaging that, I'd ask ye to imagine yerself ruling Northumbria by my side."

Murielle gasped and looked up at him. Why she was shocked, she didn't understand. The man was here for this very purpose, and she'd given him nothing but encouragement. Still, it wasn't that she wished to encourage him. Rather, she was hard-pressed to find a reason to reject him. The other kings were so foul, pompous, and disagreeable that she'd quickly accrued a mental list of their negative attributes within minutes of meeting them. With Aldfrith, Murielle sought any negative trait, but she only discovered that the man was nearly perfect. She was obliged to her people, and this man made it impossible for her to reject him without appearing uncooperative or disloyal to her brother.

Brodyn had done everything for her all her life. All he asked in return was that she helped him secure his borders through marriage. It seemed such a small request, yet it meant giving up everything that mattered most to her.

"Ye seem surprised," Aldfrith whispered, lowering his brow. "Do I not meet yer expectations?" he asked with all sincerity and not a hint of anger.

She shook her head. "I suppose I'm used to these meetings going terribly awry. I've come to expect every king who comes calling to be vile in one manner or another. Yet, ye havenae a hint of vileness in yer blood."

"I will take that as a compliment." He raised a brow and stared.

"Aye, 'tis a compliment," she laughed. "Doesnae this feel odd, seeking a lifetime with another person after only one meeting?"

"I agree this is not ideal. As I said, I had intended to join the church. Running a kingdom and finding a wife were not tasks I expected, but life is unexpected. Ye are unexpected. I truly enjoy yer company, Murielle. Yer intelligent, educated, diplomatic, virtuous, and beautiful. I'd like ye to consider becoming my wife and Queen of Northumbria."

He gripped her hand slightly harder. "I think we'd get on well, and mayhap, if we are the fortunate few, we will find love in one another. I willnae force ye to share my bed past begetting an heir. Though I seek the saints on pilgrimages, I cannae claim to be a saint myself. I have a healthy appetite, if ye ken my meaning. I'd welcome ye in my bed every night, yet I'd never force the matter."

Aldfrith shook his head, released her hand, and took a step back. "I apologize if I speak too plainly. I want ye to be my wife, Murielle, and I believe we'd do verra well together. I'd respect ye in all ways and give ye everything ye desire, including the freedom to seek adventure and truth, as I ken ye are eager to know the world as I do."

It was a fair offer. It wasn't one of love or passion but one of respect and companionship, which was more than she'd been offered with any other king.

"Have ye spoken to my brother about this?"

"I have. He has given us his blessing. Though, he made it clear 'tis yer choice. Ye shall not be forced, nor would I ever do so. I willnae make ye answer me now. I only ask that ye consider our suit. I must be away by morn, for the journey here took several days, and I must continue my pilgrimage, but should ye accept my proposal, I'll come back for ye within the next fortnight. If ye havenae made yer mind by morning, King Brodyn can send a messenger to me, and I shall ride back for ye."

"Ye are verra kind to offer me time to decide. King Arwyn stole Lucas when I didnae make a swift decision."

"I am nothing like him, Murielle."

"I ken that." Smiling, she squeezed his hand. "I will have an answer for ye by the morn. Ye've ridden far to be here, and I shall respect yer time. Please allow me time to consider it tonight." And speak with Samuel, she added to herself. She couldn't make this decision without telling Samuel how she felt about him. That may be unfair to Aldfrith, but as he said, this was to be a marriage of respect, not love, and she had matters to discuss with the man she *did* love.

Bowing his head, Aldfrith linked arms with her and silently walked her up the hill to the royal household, where he stopped just shy of the entrance. "'Tis been a pleasure," Aldfrith said, bowing again and taking her hand. "I shall await yer answer on the morrow." He gave her hand a gentle squeeze before letting go.

"Thank ye, King Aldfrith." Murielle curtsied with a small smile and entered the house, her mild reeling, and her heart throbbing. She very well could be formally betrothed by tomorrow. If her heart did not already belong to another, Murielle might have felt a hint of gladness and relief for finding a decent king to marry. But, instead, all she felt what an aching in the pit of her stomach.

Turning on her heels, she stopped short when she saw Samuel sitting on a bench, the hearth fire casting shadows across his features as his gaze landed on hers. He looked forlorn and contemplative, which struck her as odd. He was a disciplined man, often hiding emotions behind manners and silence.

"Samuel," she breathed, caught off guard by his unexpected nearness yet glad he was still awake. "Where is everyone?"

"They've all gone to bed. It's quite late."

"Oh." Her cheeks reddened when she realized how long she had stayed at the longhouse with Aldfrith. "I lost track of time."

"Time flies when you're having fun," he murmured. That must be yet another saying from his time, but she understood its meaning.

"I wouldn't say I was having fun, Sam. Just doing my duty."

He nodded and looked at the fire. Was he avoiding her? His

distant demeanor was both unexpected and hurtful. "Are ye angry with me?"

His gaze snapped to her, and he frowned. "No, why would I be? I just have much on my mind."

"Oh? Care to discuss it?"

"It wouldn't make a bit of difference." Samuel stood up and walked toward her, a solemn look reflected in his dark gaze as he towered above her with his great height. "How was your visit with Aldfrith? He seems like a decent man."

"He is, aye. Quite decent."

"Handsome, as well," Samuel added, scanning her features.

"Some may say so."

"But not you?"

Murielle shrugged. "He's handsome enough." She paused and chewed her lower lip. It was time to speak her heart's truth. She'd never have another chance to say exactly how she felt about Sam. Even if he didn't reciprocate her feelings, she could move on, knowing she was honest with him and herself. "He proposed to me tonight."

Some emotion flickered in his eye, and she wondered if it was disappointment or even sadness, but he schooled his features before she could adequately decipher it. "And you accepted?"

She shook her head. "Not yet. I needed time to think. Time to… speak with ye."

"Murielle, I'm returning home. For good."

She gasped, feeling all the air leave her lungs as her heart shattered. "What?" The fear of confessing her love was suddenly gone, replaced only by the fear of losing him forever. "Samuel… I want ye. I love ye." The words pained her greatly to say and yet freed her simultaneously. There was no going back, no pretending she hadn't spoken the truth.

"You and I simply cannot be, Murielle. You're meant for a greater man."

"There is no greater man!" she cried, rushing forward to take his hand, imploring him to listen. "I love you. Brodyn will understand! He wants only my happiness and—" She paused and swallowed her pain. "Or is it that ye dinnae want me? Och, I am such a fool!"

Murielle released his hand and turned to run from her humiliation, but Samuel wrapped his palms around her forearms and pulled her into him. The disciplined façade slipped from his face as his dark eyes narrowed and his lips turned downward. "Stop it, Murielle. You have no idea how I feel about you."

"Tell me! This is it, Sam. We have reached the point of no return. I must marry, and I dinnae want Aldfrith! I want ye! Am I so delusional that I've imagined ye own feelings for me? Have I been such a fool?" Tears slid from her treacherous eyes, and she hurriedly swiped them away.

"You've imagined nothing." Samuel closed his eyes and took a deep breath. "I'd be a liar and a fool if I said I don't have feelings for you—very strong feelings." He paused and looked at her with remorse. "The truth is, Murielle—I love you. I have since the day we met. But, my entire reason for existence is to fix the timeline, not change it. If you're meant to marry Aldfrith or any other man, I cannot interfere. The implications could be disastrous."

"I'm not meant to marry him!" she cried, pulling herself closer to him. His calm tone and stone-like demeanor hurt more than his rejection, yet her desperation demanded she continue her persuasion. He loved her, and that one truth gave her hope that he may change his mind. "It's ye, I ken it. If I tell Brodyn we are in love, he will agree to our marriage! He and Cait are in love!"

"He and Cait were destined to marry, to form integral alliances between tribes and unite the land," Samuel murmured, obviously struggling to remain logical, but Murielle needed to appeal to his emotional side.

"What about Emilie and Goodwin? She came through to save Lucas but marrying Goodwin wasnae her absolute fate. You didn't protest that!"

"Emilie was sent through time to save Lucas, yes. She had no choice. It just happened. Then her home burned down in our time, and she was declared dead. She was stuck here and couldn't return. That makes marrying Goodwin, or any man from this time, part of her timeline."

With an angry growl, Murielle shoved Samuel in the chest, turning away so he didn't see her cascading tears. Fool. She was an utter fool. "Ye are determined to push me away."

"No." She felt Samuel put a hand on her shoulder, but she shrugged him off. "Murielle. You have no idea how hard this has been for me, seeing all these men come to court you, knowing that I'm nobody in this place. I don't belong here. I haven't for quite some time. I kept coming to see you, be close to you. But it's a sweet torture. Do you know something?" he scoffed and shook his head. "I came here today to declare my feelings for you to King Brodyn."

Murielle gasped and turned to face him with a hand on her wildly beating heart. "Ye… ye were going to tell my brother that ye loved me? What's stopping ye? Go! He will be happy!"

Samuel shook his head again. "It wasn't meant to be. I see that now. I thought all the neighboring kings had come and gone, but when I saw Aldfrith here, I knew I had to walk away."

"Why would ye say such a thing? I hardly ken the man. He could be a tyrant in sheep's clothing!"

"He isn't, Murielle. I'm a historian from the future, remember? I know exactly who Aldfrith was… or is. He's a fine king and a good man. He goes down in history as a very pious king who brings enlightenment to Northumbria and peace with their neighbors. He erases all the damage his uncle created. You are a strong, intelligent woman, and this king will not only indulge that, he will embrace it. I wouldn't walk away from a chance with you if I wasn't certain that Aldfrith will make you a wonderful husband and secure the peace Brodyn needs to keep his people safe. His people are my people. I cannot do anything that would cause a rift between tribes. And, as I said, I don't belong here. I have a career at home and students to teach. If I stayed here, I could affect the timeline, and I can't risk it, Murielle. Not even for a life with you—the only thing I ever think about anymore."

"Have I no say in my own life?" she cried, no longer having any arguments to offer in her favor.

"No more than I do, it seems." Samuel pulled her close and wrapped his arms around her as she cried into his chest.

"It's not fair," she whispered, breathing in his comforting and familiar scent. "Ye are going to leave me here, and I shall die of a broken heart."

"Nonsense. You are the strongest woman I know."

Looking up at him, Murielle frowned. "Maybe I'm tired of being strong. Where has it gotten me? Can we not be weak this once and do what we want, not what others want?"

"Murielle, marriage is a bit more than simply doing what we want."

She shook her head and narrowed her eyes. "That's not what I mean. Dinnae ye ever wish to kiss me?"

"Every second of every waking moment, then every second of every dream," Samuel whispered, running his fingers comfortingly through her long hair.

"Then do it. Kiss me," she demanded.

"Murielle, you don't know what you ask of me."

"Tomorrow, I will accept Aldfrith's proposal, and I shall be a betrothed woman. Tonight, I'm still free. Kiss me, or ye shall never have another chance."

She felt pathetic, begging him to kiss her. She'd never kissed a man before. Sure, she'd had a few playful pecks with the lads growing up, but never a proper kiss with a real man. Never with Samuel, the man who plagued her every thought. Inside, her heart threatened to spill out of her chest. Samuel was leaving, and she'd be all alone. Perhaps he was right that Aldfrith would make her a fine husband. But, what if her destiny was in 2023 with Samuel? Why couldn't she go with him?

An idea began to form in her racing, desperate mind, but before she could put words to it, Samuel's strong arms pulled her to him, catching her off guard just before his lips touched hers.

The kiss was gentle at first, lingering, testing, as his hands rested on her hips; she gripped his biceps to steady herself. Murielle sighed, melting into him, taking a moment to memorize the feel of his lips, the taste of his tongue, and the scent of his skin.

Soon, Sam's gentle kiss grew possessive as he groaned and lost control of his carefully restrained desires. When his tongue slipped between her lips, Murielle moaned with the unexpected lust that thrummed through her body as he claimed her mouth. The sensations it pulled from the depth of her soul made Murielle cling to him, wishing this one moment could sustain her for a lifetime.

Something hard dug into her hip, and she knew what it was, smiling against his lips. He wanted her. And how she wanted him. But she was a virtuous woman and would not give herself away to a man who refused to marry her. Not even her love and desire for Samuel could push her that far. Aldfrith the Pious, as she now called him in her head, would expect her intact on their wedding night. Still, a little taste of passion couldn't hurt.

Slowly, she allowed her hands to wander over his shoulders and down his chest until she felt the long, hard bulge in his trousers. She cupped it, feeling the power in her hands. Samuel groaned and pulled away, ending the kiss. Confusion made new tears well in her eyes, but she held them back.

"I'm sorry, Murielle. You have no idea what you do to me." He panted as he caught his breath, and she did the same, feeling her heart beating fast enough to affect her breathing.

"I shouldnae have touched ye. I'm sorry."

"No. Murielle, this is on me. I want you to touch me. God knows I want you to touch me everywhere. But I'm leaving tomorrow, and you will become another man's bride. I have to live with this reality for the rest of my days."

Slowly, Samuel lifted her lowered chin with a finger, a look of grief contorting his face. "I shall remember our kiss for the rest of my life. I wish you a beautiful life, Murielle. You deserve it. I just wish I was the man who could give it to you. I love you." Leaning in, he softly kissed her one last time, turned, grabbed his satchel, and left the house.

With a wail of sorrow that tore from her very depths, Murielle stared at the door, praying he'd come back, but he did not. Running up the stairs to her chamber, Murielle slowly shut the door so as not to disturb Lucas. Her tears might go unattended, but his would wake the entire house.

As she threw herself onto her bed, two years of hopes and dreams disappeared, replaced by hours of tears and sorrow. On the morrow, she'd accept King Aldfrith mac Oswiu's proposal and become the future Queen of Northumbria. Nothing in the world could possibly make her more miserable.

CHAPTER THREE

THE NEXT MORNING, Murielle dragged herself down the stairs, eyes red and swollen, without having slept a wink. She hadn't even bothered to change out of her tunic, and now its beautiful blue velvet was wrinkled and crushed, but she couldn't care less.

The sun had yet to rise above the horizon, evidenced by the black void consuming the room. The fire was dead, just like her heart. With an unceremonious plop, Murielle sat upon the same bench Samuel had before, only this time, she stared at the charred remains of the fire that had raged while they kissed. Just as that moment had faded, so too had the flames.

A white piece of parchment rested on the tabletop, folded in half. Crinkling her brow, she looked at the rectangular item, thinner and more refined than anything from her time. Interest piqued, Murielle grabbed the parchment and scanned its length, her stomach flipping when she saw words scribbled across it in Samuel's language and his name signed at the bottom. Silently, she thanked Catriona for all of those English language lessons she'd taught her in secret. Although Cait had said Murielle would never need to use the language, Murielle was too intrigued by the future, desiring to learn everything. Much as Emilie, Cait, and Sam spent their lives studying the past, Murielle studied the future.

The letter wasn't directed at any one person, so Murielle felt no shame in reading it, for Samuel likely assumed she couldn't understand a word and only expected Cait and Emilie to find it. Quickly before anyone woke up, Murielle skimmed the letter, struggling to make out some details but understanding enough.

> *I've decided to return home early, and I'm afraid I won't be back for some time. I suppose I held onto foolish notions long enough, but I see it's time for me to choose my path, and there is nothing left for me here. I will continue to teach anthropology at Aberdeen University, where I can focus my attention entirely on my students and perhaps even find a life of my own, though it shall never be as I hoped it would. I wish you all well and will continue to think about you daily. Perhaps when University is on holiday, I shall visit. Take care of Lucas and Anya, and send Murielle my best wishes for her marriage.*
>
> *Respectfully, Sam*

Tears slid down her cheeks as she clutched the parchment to her bosom, her heart shattering as reality set in. How she wished Aldfrith had never arrived! Nay, she couldn't blame the man, for he'd been nothing but kind, but now Murielle had lost her chance at true love. Samuel loved her. That knowledge should be enough to sustain her through the years, yet she found it only to be a great torture on her soul.

"Murielle?" Caitriona stood before her, cradling Lucas with a creased brow and frown. "What is that?"

"'Tis a letter from Sam. He's left and may never return, and it's all my fault!" Holding the letter out with a shaky hand, she allowed Cait to read its contents.

"Oh, no." Cait lowered the letter and shook her head. "What could have made him leave so abruptly?" Her eyes widened, and she looked at Murielle. "Aldfrith? Did he propose marriage?"

"Aye, but I dinnae love him! I love Samuel! Och, I should have spoken up sooner! Samuel told me last night that he loves me, but he cannae get between my marriage alliance with Aldfrith! He said Aldfrith is a good man and that the Picts need this alliance!" Cradling her face in her hands, Murielle wailed, knowing she was pathetic but too distressed to contain her heartache.

"Oh, my…" Cait sat beside Murielle on the bench and placed a hand on her back. Lucas reached out and tugged on his Auntie Murielle's hair, but she paid no attention. Nothing could possibly hurt her more than losing Sam. "Sam isn't wrong about Aldfrith. He indeed goes down in history as one of the greatest kings of Northumbria, bringing peace, innovation, and prosperity to his people. But, I cannot recall who his wife was."

"That's what Samuel said!" Murielle looked up at Cait with hope. "Wh-what if he didn't marry me? What if he is destined to marry another woman? Can I possibly follow my heart and reject his offer? Is it too late?"

"Did you already accept Aldfrith's proposal?"

Murielle shook her head. "He said he must continue his pilgrimage, but should I accept his offer, he'd return in a sennight."

Cait frowned and shook her head. "I truly cannot remember his wife's name, nor can I guide you on this, for I'd dearly love to tell you to follow your heart, but Samuel is already gone, and Aldfrith awaits your answer. Brodyn has high hopes for this marriage. But Murielle, it's your life, not Brodyn's."

"Aye, but many other lives depend on me marrying a man I dinnae love! It wouldnae hurt so badly if Samuel didnae love me in return. How I wish he'd rejected me last night! It would have hurt, but I'd not spend a lifetime wondering what could have been."

"You don't want to spend the rest of your life feeling like the mother from *The Notebook*," Caitriona whispered.

"What?" Murielle pursed her lips and wiped her eyes.

"Never mind," Cait said, waving away yet another odd statement. Murielle was used to it by now. "Listen, I came down here to feed Lucas, but Brodyn will be up soon. Why don't you go clean yourself up and get dressed? We will figure this out together, all right?"

Murielle sniffled, removed Lucas's sticky fingers from her

hair, and slowly stood. Her eyes burned, and her knees shook. "I dinnae ken what to do with myself, but ye are right. I must gather my wits. Aldfrith will be calling this morning before he leaves."

"Maybe you will fall in love with him as I did with Brodyn," Cait said reassuringly. "Anything is possible."

Murielle knew it was impossible to love another man, but she remained silent. She had more thoughts than words and needed time to sort them out. "I'm going to my bedchamber to think and ready myself."

Slowly, Murielle dragged herself up the stairs, never feeling so worn down and heavy. Her numb limbs struggled to move. She wished to curl into a ball and disappear forever, but Aldfrith would arrive soon, and there was no way to escape the inevitable. Or was there?

Throwing open her door, Murielle stepped inside her chamber and slammed the door behind her, throwing the heavy wooden bar into the iron hinges. An idea developed, blossomed, and beckoned. Did she dare? Should she risk it? Pacing the small space between her four-poster bed and the hearth, Murielle chewed her lower lip, contemplating her greatest possible rebellion. It wasn't fair to Brodyn. He'd done everything for Murielle, but what was her life worth if she spent the rest of it in misery? She'd never love Aldfrith. It didn't matter how many years they were married or how wonderful a man he was. He was not and never would be Samuel.

Was marriage truly required to unite Brodyn and Aldfrith's kingdoms? Aldfrith was nothing like Ecgfrith. He wouldn't wage wars or reject alliances simply for his own gain. Nay, by all accounts, the man wished to create peace and prosperity for his people, which included allying with Fortriu—the entire Pictish kingdom. Pinnata Castra may be home, but Brodyn controlled vast amounts of land. Aldfrith wanted to join himself with Brodyn, and marriage wasn't necessary to achieve that.

The escape hatch beneath her bed called to her like a Siren's song. It had existed her entire life, set up by her father to ensure a safe route out of the village should an attack occur. Though she'd never used it and often feared the darkness and what lay waiting within it, that tunnel suddenly felt like a link to freedom. She'd slip away before anyone noticed, run for the cave, and try to enter Samuel's world. Of course, it was reckless to consider such a venture, yet she found herself wholly consumed by the notion of escape.

A knock on her chamber door made her shriek and jump out of her skin. "My lady, King Aldfrith calls for ye," Ronan muttered through the thick wooden door.

Closing her eyes and pursing her lips, Murielle took a deep breath and shook her head. Nay. Running away was cowardly, and she was no coward. But, in her heart, she knew she couldn't marry Aldfrith. It was Samuel or nothing. But she owed it to him and her brother to face them and call this off, even if Brodyn's neck vein bulged and his face turned red. It was her life, and she had to follow her own path.

"Just a moment!" Running toward her chest, Murielle lifted the latch, opened the lid, and hastily pulled out a crisp yellow tunic. She hoped this cheery color would help when she rejected Aldfrith's marriage proposal.

She pulled the tunic over her head, ran a comb through her hair, then looked into her beautiful compact mirror, a gift from the future given to her by Emilie. There was nothing for it. She looked frightful with her puffy eyelids and bloodshot eyes, but it only proved how hard this decision was to make.

When Murielle opened the door, Ronan stepped back and cringed when he looked at her face. "What happened to ye?"

"Oh, shut it, Ronan!" she shoved him aside, in no mood for his commentary. With her heart beating so wildly that she struggled to breathe, Murielle descended the stairs, frowning when Brodyn awaited her with Aldfrith in front of the fire.

Her brother shot her a warning look, and that only angered Murielle. She wouldn't be bullied into this match.

"Princess Murielle, ye look beautiful this morn." Aldfrith

flattered her, unlike Ronan, because he was a man with manners, but she knew he couldn't possibly believe his own words.

"I apologize for my lateness and appearance. I didnae sleep well."

Aldfrith nodded and folded his hands before him. "I ken this is a hard decision to make. Perhaps I was unfair in rushing ye. Should we take some more time to consider this match?"

He was a good man. Too good. He didn't deserve a wife who was incapable of loving him. Young, handsome, and educated, Aldfrith could have any woman he wanted—just not Murielle.

"Och, that willnae be necessary," Brodyn said, stepping up beside Murielle. "I'm confident my sister has made her decision. Havenae ye?" Again, he narrowed his eyes and towered above her as if he didn't know her at all. She'd never cower or be persuaded by intimidation. If she married Aldfrith, it was because she chose to. Her entire life, she prepared for an arranged marriage. But too much had changed. If the Picts were at war with the Britons again or if she even feared it was a possibility, she'd do her duty. But looking at Aldfrith and remembering his pleasantries the night before with Brodyn, she knew these men, these great warriors whose entire existence revolved around politics, would form an alliance regardless of her marital status.

"I have made a decision." Murielle paused, sucked in a deep breath, and looked Aldfrith in his hazel eyes. "I cannae marry ye, King Aldfrith. I am sorry."

Brodyn growled and grabbed her arm. "Are ye out of yer skull, lass?"

"Brodyn!" Caitriona stepped forward and scowled at her husband.

"I see. I am sorry to hear it, but I accept yer decision," Aldfrith said with a diplomatic nod. "Might I ask why?"

"There is no good reason why!" Brodyn shouted. "She is stubborn and insolent. Nay, worse! She is spoiled, and 'tis my fault! I've overindulged her every whim, but not this time! She will marry ye, Aldfrith. Ye have my word."

Aldfrith frowned and looked at Murielle when she wrapped her arms protectively about her waist, trying to hide her quaking limbs. "I am certain we can come to terms, King Brodyn. The Britons want nothing but peace with the Picts. But we dinnae need to force her hand."

She looked at Aldfrith again, this time with gratitude. How could he remain so calm and level-headed while Brodyn blew up like a volcano?

"We will come to terms through yer marriage," Brodyn said, scowling at Murielle again. "Consider yerselves betrothed. I'll have my monk write up the contract and have it ready when ye arrive in a sennight. Once the contract is signed, the marriage ceremony will commence immediately."

"King Brodyn, I cannae take a wife who doesnae want me."

"Please, Aldfrith," Murielle said, finding her voice. "This isnae about ye. Ye are a great match, and I'd be fortunate to be yer wife. But my mind and heart simply arnae in agreement, and I must follow my heart."

"Her mind and heart will be in agreement when next ye arrive, Aldfrith," Brodyn insisted, stepping in front of Murielle to block her out entirely while he flung an arm over Aldfrith's shoulder and walked away, discussing her life and her future as if she was not a part of it.

Anger, blood-boiling, stomach-churning anger brewed deep within her soul. She might be stubborn, but she'd always supported her brother. He had a wife he loved. Aye, he married her out of duty, but he immediately fell in love with Caitriona. He deserved happiness, and he had it. Murielle deserved it too, but it would not be found in Aldfrith's marriage bed.

"Murielle," Caitriona whispered beside her as she rocked Lucas to sleep in her arms. "I'm so sorry. I will speak with Brodyn."

Murielle spun on her heels, looking at her beloved sister-by-marriage, shaking her head. "Nay, save yer energy. He willnae be reasoned with, but I willnae comply. He wished to avoid war by marrying me off, but all he has done is wage war… with me."

Stomping off, Murielle grabbed Ronan by his tunic sleeve. "Come with me." Dutifully, Ronan followed, but she knew him well enough to know that he did so out of concern, not duty. Ronan was more than her guard. He was one of her closest confidants, and now it was time to share a little information with him and put him to the test.

When she stormed up the stairs and threw her chamber door open, Ronan scratched his head. "What are ye doing?"

"We are leaving."

"We?"

"Aye, Ye and me."

"Where are we going?"

"I'll explain it on the way," she murmured. Tunics, a hairbrush, a bronze hand mirror, a compact mirror, and other small items that may come in handy were hastily shoved into her large leather satchel. Feeling around the bottom of her chest, Murielle searched for the most important items. "Ah-ha!"

Ronan frowned and stepped closer. "Why are ye packing yer belongings? And what is in yer hand?" He tried to look over her shoulder, but she shoved Caitriona's ID, passport, and credit card into her satchel before Ronan saw it. Cait had given Murielle these trinkets from her past. She said they held no further use for her here, but in the future, they served as what was called identification, and somehow, the magic blue card with a silver strip across the back gave her access to coins. Murielle had no idea how they worked, but she had blonde hair and blue eyes like Caitriona and wondered if the ID would work for her.

Nothing about this plan was well-conceived. Murielle may be heading into danger or worse, but she had to get to that cave and seek out Samuel. She couldn't stay here and wonder how her life would unfold, left to her brother's machinations.

"Tell me what's going on, Murielle," Ronan hissed.

Standing up, Murielle kicked her full satchel beneath the bed and put her hands on her hips. "We are leaving." She ran to the closed door and barred it, knowing Brodyn would soon arrive, shouting like an ogre. But she didn't intend to be here to respond.

"If we are leaving, why are ye barring the door." Ronan's narrowed eyes suddenly widened in understanding. "Och, nay! Nay, nay, nay! Ye arenae leaving this chamber through the tunnel! After Arwyn used it to access the village, Brodyn ordered all the exits to be boarded up!"

"And ye are a strong warrior with a sword. We will break through."

"Yer mad!"

"Aye, I am! I'm mad at Brodyn, and I'm not staying here."

"Well..." Ronan crossed his arms and scoffed. "I willnae aid yer escape and betray my king."

"Ye betray yer king if ye dinnae guard my life everywhere I go, and I'm going. Are ye going to stay here and tell Brodyn I'm gone?"

Ronan growled at her and turned to the door, ready to lift the bar.

"Farewell, Ronan. Thank ye for everything." Murielle got onto her knees and crawled beneath her bed, grunting and coughing as dust tickled her nostrils. "Emilie did it. So can I," she whispered to herself.

Cursing, Ronan dropped to his knees to follow her under the bed. She felt horrendous, manipulating Ronan, but his duty was to guard her everywhere she went, and she'd need his protection where she was going. Besides, Ronan would be shunned if she disappeared on his watch. He was better off staying with her. When this was all over, Murielle would insist it was all her idea and that Ronan had no option but to follow.

The hatch cover lifted easily enough, and Murielle looked down into the dark abyss beneath her bed. A shudder ran down her spine. She slept above this space every night and did her best never to think of it, but now she imagined all manner of creatures lurking below.

She tossed her satchel down and heard an immediate thud.

The drop wasn't very far, and she maneuvered her legs to slide down first.

Ronan grabbed her and growled again. She assumed he'd be growing a lot during this journey. "I will go first and help ye down, ye meddlesome lass."

Ronan dropped down, feet first, just as her door's latch rattled and a banging followed. "Murielle!"

She'd run out of time. Brodyn was here to scold her, no doubt. Well, he'd need to catch her first. "Go away! I want to be alone!" she shouted just before dropping into the dark tunnel.

"Ye cannae hide forever. When ye come out, we will speak!" She heard Brodyn's distant shouting before closing the hatch and shuttering herself in the darkness as she clung to Ronan.

"Ye are going to get us both killed," Ronan hissed.

"This tunnel has been blocked off for months. Aside from wee critters, I dinnae think anything dangerous can be lurking," Murielle whispered, running her right hand along the wall to guide her through the darkness.

"I was talking about yer brother," he snapped. "Ye may be his blood, but I amnae. I dinnae have familial protection. I may face lashings or worse."

Murielle turned in the darkness and touched Ronan's face. She felt his stubble and the sharp point of his nose. "I willnae allow that to happen to ye. Ye are doing yer duty to me. Brodyn kens all too well that I tend to lead my guards astray. I'm sure Goodwin could tell ye stories."

"Och, the man was more than glad to step aside as yer guard. Ye leave disaster in yer wake."

"Not his time. Everything will be all right," she said more to herself. Her satchel hung from her left shoulder as she moved silently through the tunnel. Dappled sunlight shone through wooden planks, and Murielle gasped. "We made it." She kicked a board and heard it snap, but not enough to break through.

"Stand aside," Ronan said, pushing her back as he drew his sword and plunged its tip into the same small board she kicked.

When his sword lodged into the wood, Ronan put his foot on the board and pulled back, leaving a small hole but not much more.

"We need an ax," Murielle whispered.

"Och, sure, let me pull one out of my arse," Ronan shot back.

Murielle rolled her eyes in the darkness, kicking the board again. Ronan joined in, and soon, the small plank splintered and cracked enough for them to squeeze through carefully.

"We made it!" Murielle said with a thrill as Ronan stepped through, having a harder time squeezing through the small space.

"Aye, now that ye ken how the tunnel works, let's get ye back to Pinnata Castra." Ronan gripped her wrist and tugged, but she pulled away.

"I told ye. I'm going elsewhere."

"Yet, ye still havenae told me where."

Looking around, Murielle squinted into the blinding morning sun. Ancient trees toward overhead in tight clusters, blocking Murielle's view of the horizon. "Which way is the ocean?"

Ronan swiped webs out of his reddish-brown hair and scowled. "Why? All this so ye can romp in the ocean? We could have walked through the gates and made it there without issue."

"Where the ocean ends, my freedom begins," Murielle said with a grin. "Lead me there, and I shall explain everything."

"YE ARE OUT of yer mind!" Ronan shouted as they approached the cave. "Ye mean to tell me Queen Caitriona, Emilie, Samuel, and Anya were from the future, and they came through this cave? Did ye hit yer head while in the tunnel?"

"Look at these…" Murielle dropped her satchel onto the shore's rocky soil and dug through the bag until she found Caitriona's ID and credit card. "Do these look like anything that would come from this time?"

Groaning with frustration, Ronan ripped the objects out of

her grasp and stared at them in wild-eyed horror. "What sort of devilry is this? Queen Caitriona's likeness is trapped within this hardened parchment! And… the writing. 'Tis a different language and is printed like one of those tomes the monk once showed me."

"This," Murielle held up the ID, "was Cait's identification. In her time, everyone has to carry one, and this—" she held up the blue rectangle, "is currency. I have no idea how any of it works. She let me have them because I've been studying the future for a long time, Ronan. People have been coming and going right under your nose. I can read and speak the language. Samuel and Cait taught me. I've heard about things I cannae even describe to ye. They dinnae ride horses. They have cars made of metal that have the power of one-hundred horses! They have metal birds that fly people across the world! It's a wondrous place. I can use this ID to pass as Cait and use this card if we need to pay for items."

She paused and looked at Ronan, who silently stared at the strange cards while taking in her confusing words.

"Ronan." Murielle grabbed his hand and forced him to look at her. "I ken this is a lot to take in. But ye have to believe me, and I ken it makes sense if ye think about it. Cait and Emilie came from out of nowhere, speaking strangely. They came through this cave, along with Samuel. And Ronan… I need to find Samuel. I love him. He needs to ken I am not marrying Aldfrith!"

Ronan blinked several times as his mouth gaped open. "This is madness, is what it is. Brodyn and Goodwin ken all of this?" Murielle nodded, and Ronan ruffled his hair, letting out a puff of breath. "Och, I dinnae want to go to this strange land, Murielle. I've faced many battles, men with swords who'd slice me through without a thought. But this… this scares me."

"I'm scared, too. But I've heard enough about this place, and I think I can get us around enough to find Samuel and come back home. Please, Ronan. I need ye."

"I dinnae even speak the language!"

"I don't need ye to talk. Just stay by my side. Cait said that people speak many different languages around the world now. You can hop onto a metal bird, fly to another country within hours, and not speak the language. Nobody cares."

"I will go, but only because 'tis my duty to guard ye. Brodyn will chap yer hide for this, Murielle, but he'd chap mine worse if I let ye go alone. Is there any way to talk ye out of this madness?"

She shook her head. "I'm going."

Ronan sighed and looked at the ocean as the waves lapped peacefully against the shore. "I dinnae ken how this works."

"Nor do I, Ronan." She saw genuine fear in his eyes for the first time in her life, and suddenly Murielle's guilt overpowered her stubborn will. "I willnae force ye, but I'm going. Ye can stay here, and I will handle Brodyn when I return. Tell him I locked ye out of my chamber and left through the hatch. There wasnae anything ye could do to stop me."

Ronan shook his head but didn't look confident with this plan. "I willnae abandon ye. Not only would I worry for yer safety, I fear yer brother's wrath more than I fear the unknown."

Together, they approached the cave's entrance, and trepidation slithered up Murielle's spine as she slowly entered. Uncertain of what to do or what to expect, she pressed her palms against the cold stone walls, waiting for something to happen. Ronan raised a brow at her but did the same. "Ye ken, I am not happy ye all kenned about this cave, and nobody ever told me."

"Well, I just did. We cannae go around telling everyone that the Queen of the Picts came here from the year 2023."

"We are going nearly 1,400 years into the future?"

"Aye, if the cave allows us," she murmured, sliding her hands along the walls, desperately seeking a way to pass through the veil. Brodyn would know she was missing by now, and it wouldn't take him long to figure out where she went. Murielle needed to figure this out before her brother found her and dragged her home.

"Where is Taylor's grave? I ken he was buried around here."

Ronan crinkled his brow at her in confusion, and she elaborated. "Do ye remember when a man showed up who looked just like my dead brother Talorc, and Brodyn had him locked away?"

Ronan nodded. "That was Caitriona's former betrothed. He traveled here through the cave while looking for her in their time. Many of us have versions of ourselves living in different time periods. Cait is the future version of the bride that died on her way to marry my brother, and Taylor was the future version of Talorc."

"Ye speak about this calmly, as if it isnae the most ridiculous thing," Ronan said wearily.

"Ronan! There is another alcove! It's hidden just around this corner. Look!" Murielle ducked her head and entered the dark alcove where natural light ceased to shine. Squinting into the darkness, she noticed a burial site with a thistle growing from the top of the grave. It had been the discovery of a lone thistle growing from this alcove that had caught Caitriona's attention in 2023 while excavating. Cait had wondered how a thistle could grow in the cave's dark depths, and when she leaned down to touch it, she pricked her finger and was thrown backward into the year 685.

"Ronan, I think this is it!" She stepped aside so Ronan could enter. "Anya always planted a thistle atop grave sites. In 2023, Caitriona, Samuel, and Emilie excavated, believing Brodyn was buried here. It turned out to be Taylor's bones. It's a continuous loop in time. Cait searches for Brodyn's bones, gets thrown back in time, Taylor follows, dies, and is buried here. But over the centuries, the story is told that King Brodyn is buried here, sending Cait's team to discover the long-lost Pictish king's remains. And so it goes, over and over."

"So, this is where it happens," Ronan murmured, looking down at the soil. "In the year 2023, Queen Caitriona stands in this verra spot before finding her way to us."

"Exactly! Ye're catching on, Ronan."

"Murielle!" Her name echoed off the walls, sending chills of dread down her spine.

"It's Cait! That means Brodyn caught up with us! We have to go!"

"Cannae we simply speak with him and work this out, Murielle?"

"Nay! I'm going with or without ye!" she hissed.

"I willnae let ye go alone, Murielle!"

Footsteps crunched in the distance, and Murielle froze. "Ronan, on the count of three, we touch this thistle. Ready?" He nodded and prepared himself.

"One, two, three!"

CHAPTER FOUR

WHITE SPARKS FLEW from her fingertips, and waves of energy surged through her body as she was propelled backward, landing on the hard-packed earthen floor with a painful thud and grunt of pain. The hairs on her nape stood on end as a crackling sound surrounded her, almost as if she'd been a tree struck by lightning.

Scrambling to her feet and grabbing her satchel, Murielle looked around, wondering where Ronan had gone. Had it worked? If not, what had caused the sparks and pulsing waves of energy that threw her backward? Swiping dirt off her tunic, Murielle cringed and hissed when residual energy snapped at her fingertips, biting her flesh.

"Ronan?" Murielle stood still and looked around. The thistle was gone, and the gravesite was disturbed. It didn't look how it had when she first arrived. Caitriona's voice no longer called to her, and the footsteps no longer approached.

"Cait? Ronan?" Ducking her head, Murielle left the cave's alcove, following the light toward the entrance. Murielle saw the faded Pictish symbols on the cave walls and noticed a few more engravings that hadn't been there before. It had worked. She knew it in her bones. But she was alone. Had Ronan been rejected by the cave, or had he decided not to participate in this wild scheme of hers? She knew she asked too much of Ronan, and guilt niggled at her. But, he wouldn't have left her alone. So, where was he?

Without the thistle, she had no idea how to get back to her time to find Ronan. Oh, by the gods, what had she done? Panic swelled in her chest as fear trickled down her spine—or perhaps that was the remaining energy flowing through her bones.

Brodyn was right about her. She was a stubborn, spoiled lass who never listened to his guidance. Now, she was lost and alone in a time and place she didn't belong.

Approaching the cave's entrance, Murielle paused and cried out in shock when she realized she was trapped. Waves crashed against the cliffside, their angry white, foaming fingers invading the cave's entrance. Murielle slowly stepped closer, wondering why the tide was so much higher now. Even at high tide in her time, there was plenty of shoreline left to walk along. The cave was always accessible by land. Now, she saw water in every direction, no shoreline or way out.

"Oh, God." Murielle dropped to her knees and folded her hands the way the Christian priest had taught her when she was a wee lass. She'd never truly known which deity to worship, for her Celtic ancestors believed in many gods and goddesses, yet the Christians believed in one almighty creator. Too afraid to anger any god, Murielle preferred to simply live a good life and hope that, wherever she ended up when her time was over, it wasn't Hell or Purgatory.

"Please, help me!" she whispered with her eyes closed as a small pebble dug into her knee.

"Murielle!"

With a gasp, Murielle looked over her shoulder and felt relief flood her veins. "Cait!" Murielle clamored to her feet and hugged her sister. "I ken I messed up. Dinnae lecture me! I didnae listen, and I ran away to find Samuel. Now I'm trapped in this cave and cannae escape! What have I done? Where is Ronan? Is he all right? I will never forgive myself if he's hurt because of my foolishness!"

Cait gripped Murielle and let her sob into her shoulder for a moment before releasing her. "Ronan is fine. He couldn't pass through. But, I couldn't let you go through alone, so I told Ronan to run outside and tell Brodyn I was going after you."

"Oh, nay!" Murielle wailed, feeling her limbs grow numb as reality struck her. Her actions had now caused Caitriona to leave her family. "Ye had to leave wee Lucas because of me? Brodyn is going to kill me!"

"Breathe, Murielle," Caitriona whispered. "Once we discovered you were gone, we knew exactly where to find you. Brodyn brought me down here and told me to go through and find you. He also said it was evident by your actions that you truly love Samuel, and he encouraged me to help you find him."

"He... he did?" Murielle asked, wiping her tears away as she hiccupped.

"Yes, but don't get your hopes up. He isn't releasing you from your betrothal. I didn't have enough time to yell at him about that before we discovered you were missing. He wants me to help you resolve this and deliver you back home."

"Am I a terribly ridiculous lass?"

Caitriona chuckled and shook her head. "Of course not. You're a woman in love with a man who lives over 1,300 years in the future, and you have a way to find him. Combined with your obsession with my time, I'm not at all surprised you did this. But, Murielle, Samuel will not change his mind if he believes he may affect the timeline. Still, there is an easy solution to this."

Murielle perked up. "Oh?"

"We have something called the *internet*. A simple search will tell us who Aldfrith married... or marries. I suppose the tense there depends on which timeline I'm referring to."

Murielle crinkled her brow, unsure of what Cait referred to, but half the time, she didn't know what her sister-by-marriage was saying.

"However," Cait added, "Much history has been lost. There may be no record of his wife, and if that's the case, we won't know if you're meant to marry Aldfrith. I want to help you. Brodyn is determined to see you marry Aldfrith. I agree that he is a great match. But, if we have proof that he didn't marry you,

you should be free to marry whomever you choose."

"Oh!" Murielle launched herself at Cait, nearly knocking her backward. "Thank ye, Sister. I dinnae mean to be a selfish woman, and I dinnae wish to ruin an alliance between our people and the Britons. I only thought, well, Aldfrith is nothing like Ecgfrith. He seems like the kind of man who'd accept peace without a marriage."

Cait nodded. "I agree. Brodyn is set in his ways. He wants to do what's best for the masses, not just one person. But I'm hoping we can have our cake and eat it, too."

"I dinnae understand that."

"It means we can have it all if everything works out. But let's not get ahead of ourselves. We have no money, and money rules the land in 2023. I haven't been back in almost two years, but I can contact my parents and borrow money, then have Samuel pay them back with my account. It's still active. I wasn't declared dead like Emilie was."

"Uh…" Murielle dug into her satchel and pulled out Cait's cards. "I may have taken these to help me. Ye didnae need them, and I thought I could pass for ye." Murielle handed Cait her belongings and hung her head in shame. She'd done many terrible things in the past few hours. Aside from rejecting Aldfrith, she'd taken Cait's ID and credit card to use in a way Cait had not intended. Then, she ran away and forced Ronan to go with her. She was glad the cave didn't let him through. Ronan deserved to be where he belonged. "I also told Ronan the truth about everything," she said, making a cringy face.

Cait pursed her lips, holding back a smile. "Murielle, love drives people to do things they usually wouldn't do. I'd do far worse to find my way back to Brodyn. I'm actually impressed. You listen when I talk. Those items will literally save us on this journey."

She took them from Murielle, who smiled widely and began to calm down slightly. Looking outside, she pointed at the water blocking their path. "How are we to get out of here? What happened to the shoreline?"

"Over the past 1,300 years, the sea level has risen, which means there is less shoreline here than in your time and, at high tide, this cave entrance gets blocked. But don't worry. It will lower, and we will be able to leave. We just can't come and go as readily as we can in your time. We must wait for low tide."

Murielle nodded, in awe of the earth's changes and its mysteries. She was anxious to get out of the cold, barren cave and see the world beyond it.

"Cait? Why do ye think I was able to pass through the veil of time, but Ronan wasnae?"

Caitriona shrugged. "I honestly don't know. Samuel explained it to me in a few ways. One, he believes the veil allows you to pass if you are serving a greater good for the timeline, if the reason you wish to cross is, in fact, meant to be. The second factor is whether your soul exists within another body here. Our souls live on even when our bodies die. I was pulled through the veil because the body containing my spirit died, and she had unfinished business that was crucial to the timeline. Luckily for me, that business was marrying your brother to secure important alliances that won him a war and secured Scotland's history. If your soul already occupies a body in another time, you cannot cross over."

Murielle scrunched up her face as she tried to understand. "So, ye mean to say that my soul isnae in a body in 2023? That's why I was allowed through?"

"I believe so. I cannot be sure. Honestly, it still confuses me. Either Ronan's soul already exists in my time, or there was no benefit to him crossing."

Murielle gasped and grabbed Cait's arm. "Do ye think this means Samuel and I are meant to be together? Why else would it allow me through?"

"I cannot say, Murielle. I'd suggest we make this trip as quickly as possible. Time passes faster in your time, and every day here is two or three days there. Brodyn will be worried if we take too long."

The tide had already begun to recede, and Murielle looked at Cait, feeling guilty for forcing her to leave her family. "Ye should go home, Cait. I will be all right."

"Murielle, there's a lot you won't understand. It might as well be another world entirely. In fact, it *is* another world for you! You need me here, and I'm happy to help. Besides, it's nice to be back, even if for a while. Maybe we can rent a hotel room and take hot showers!"

"Oh, ye told me about those…"

"I'm going to make this worth our while! And…" Caitriona looked at her credit card. "This card doesn't expire for another five months! So, we will be just fine."

Cait stepped up to the cave's entrance just before the waves lapped against her leather boots. "In about another thirty minutes, I think we will be able to leave the cave, as a little shore will be visible. Then, we will get to town, rent a room, clean ourselves up, and start looking for Samuel."

Murielle threw herself at Cait, gratitude lodging in her throat. "Thank ye, Cait," she whispered as she embraced her sister.

She was here in the future. She'd finally made it.

SAMUEL'S FINGER ITCHED to press the "enter" button as he stared at his screen. Instead, he shut his laptop and balled his hands into fists, slamming them down onto the highly polished oak desk in his office. It was mid-afternoon on a Sunday, which meant the University was mostly vacant. He'd seen one student walking her pug as she chatted on the phone and another skateboarding in the parking lot, but other than that, Samuel was utterly alone, as always.

He'd only come to campus to grab his laptop and look up King Aldfrith Mac Oswiu. But now, he couldn't bring himself to look. If he saw Murielle's name listed as his spouse and a list of their children's names, he'd be devastated—more than he already was. Walking away from her had been the hardest decision of his life, especially because he'd left his office Friday afternoon intending to propose marriage.

With Cait and Emilie gone, Samuel was well and truly alone here. He wondered what Murielle was doing in her time, and it sickened his stomach to know that he was in love with a woman whose unmarked grave was somewhere near his small flat in Moray. The drive to university took about ninety minutes and was longer than he preferred, yet he couldn't bring himself to move farther away from the place where he knew all his loved ones lived, even if that was over 1,300 years ago.

A knock on his office door startled Samuel. He hadn't known anyone else was in the building. "Come in," he croaked, trying to mask his angst.

Professor Johansson peeked inside with a smile, her red hair falling to her shoulder in waves. "Hi, Sam. I thought I was alone in the building today until I heard a loud bang from in here. I wanted to make sure everything is okay."

"Oh, hi, Eva." Samuel watched his co-worker and former fling walk in wearing a burgundy pencil skirt with a cream-colored blouse and matching heels, her hair and makeup done as if she had plans for later that night. "I just wanted to catch up on work. I left in a hurry Friday and forgot my laptop," he explained.

"You do seem to leave in a hurry quite often," she said with a grin. "You're quite the mystery. Many of us go out for drinks together on weekends, but you're always missing."

He knew she was fishing for information, but he couldn't exactly tell her he spent his weekends in an ancient Pictish village. "Maybe I will come the next time you all go out," Samuel said half-heartedly.

"We are all going out tonight, actually. We're meeting at Shelly's Pub at seven. Care to join us?"

"Uh..." Samuel cleared his throat and looked at the clock

mounted on his wall. It was five now. He'd have no time to run home and change. "My flat is over an hour away, and I… well you… you look lovely. I'm afraid I'll be underdressed."

Eva looked down at her outfit and cringed. "Oh, I had a meeting earlier." She looked over her shoulder and down the hall before quietly shutting the door behind her. Swaying her hips as she moved closer, Eva leaned over his desk with a conspiratorial look in her brown eyes, as if ready to spill a dark secret. "Between you and me, I'm up for another position at the University of Edinburgh."

"Well, congratulations. You went all the way to Edinburgh and back today? That doesn't seem likely."

She laughed and shook her head. "Oh, no. I met with her here. She was in the area."

"Ah." Samuel tapped his fingers against his desk. Being alone with Eva made him uneasy. He suspected that Eva was still interested in him, even though they'd only had a brief physical relationship two years ago. And though she was beautiful, his mind and heart belonged to a woman he'd never have.

"What do you say, Sam? Meet us at Shelly's tonight? Seven?"

He didn't want to go. He wanted to drive home, sit inside his small Moray flat, and surround himself in the darkness that reflected his constant mood. Being around laughing people who couldn't possibly understand where he'd been or what he'd lived through was a daunting thought, but he didn't have any grand excuses to offer. Instead, he sucked in a resolved breath and nodded. "I'll be there."

"Great!" Eva smiled and patted his hand that rested on the desk. "See you then."

She swayed out, her four-inch heels elongating her legs as she stood at least five-foot-ten in them. Samuel still had about five inches on her, not that it mattered. She wasn't for him. Nobody on this earth was.

Eva shut the door behind her, and Samuel let out a frustrated growl, running his hands through his hair. He'd hoped to pack up and leave, but now he had two hours to kill before meeting them at the pub, and his office no longer felt like a sanctuary. He'd wanted total privacy to dwell in his thoughts. Now, he'd have to force himself to be the ever-smiling, people-pleasing Samuel Sullivan that everyone expected.

"Snap out of it, Sam," he whispered to himself. After all, life was for the living. He hated cheesy sayings, but this one was true. It was the year 2023; he'd made his choice and left Murielle behind in 686. There was no going back. She was dust now, but he still lived. He couldn't spend the rest of his days in anguish over what might have been, cursing this time loop that continued to pull him back to Murielle lifetime after lifetime, only so he could fall in love and suffer the consequences.

He remembered every lifetime, but only up to the point where he successfully reunited Caitriona with Brodyn. Beyond that, it seemed the universe erased all memories of his life. Samuel had no recollection of ever being loved. Oh, but he had memories of being in love, for in every life, Murielle captured him immediately upon his arrival at Pinnata Castra. But did they ever end up together? He didn't know, but in this lifetime, he was certain—it was not meant to be.

Samuel opened his laptop again and decided to focus on grading papers to keep his mind occupied for the next two hours—and his eyes from wandering over to the internet to search for Murielle. Taking the last sip of his cold coffee, Samuel tossed the cup into the bin and got to work.

When he next looked up, the clock read 6:30 PM, and Samuel shut his laptop with a sigh as he slid it into its leather carrier. "I guess it's time," he lamented. It would be easy enough to pick up his phone and text Eva that he wasn't coming after all, but a lifetime of being reliably passive stopped him. He'd go, have a drink or two, chat with some colleagues, and go home. How bad could it be?

When he arrived, the jukebox in the corner played a familiar song as patrons chatted loudly over the music. Samuel sometimes wondered what purpose music played in such a place when everyone simply shouted over it, adding to the chaos. Identical, round tables were scattered across the pub, each surrounded by patrons sitting in red-painted chairs with pints of beer leaving water rings on the tables' highly polished surfaces. A table of familiar faces waved him over, and Samuel slid on a smile as he slowly pushed through the crowd.

"Hey, Sam! I never thought to see ye show up here!" Arnold shouted, patting the open seat between him and Eva.

"Eva cornered me. I couldn't say no," he said with a chuckle, and thankfully, everyone else laughed.

"Had I known that's all it took to get you here, I'd have done it a long time ago!" she responded before taking a sip from a fancy-looking pink drink. "Would you like one?" she asked. "I can order another Cosmo for you." Eva winked playfully, and he smirked.

"I'm an ale or whiskey guy and nothing in between."

"Spoken like a true Scot!" said Charles, lifting his snifter of whiskey in salute. "Except ye arnae a Scot. Where ye originally from, Sam?"

"California," Samuel shouted when the music somehow grew louder. A waiter stopped by to drop off a sampler platter, and Samuel ordered a single malt whiskey, neat.

Soon, the conversation delved into archaeology, which was to be expected given that the group taught that subject at the University. Samuel listened and downed his whiskey, one glass and then another. He stopped after he realized he'd had four drinks, knowing he'd need to drive himself home in a while.

A hand gripped his thigh under the table, and Samuel sucked in a breath, looking at Eva, who leaned forward to whisper in his ear. "Has anyone ever told you that you look like Raoul Bova, only with dark eyes?" She batted her lashes at him, and he shifted uncomfortably.

"Yes, I've been told that a time or two."

"It's a good thing," she purred, tightening her grip on his

thigh.

"Thank you," he said, clearing his throat and straining to hear what Charles and Arnold discussed, hoping to jump into their conversation and avoid Eva.

Looking at this flashing cell phone, Arnold grumbled and downed the last bit of whiskey before slamming the glass onto the table. "The wife has sent me the baby signal. Time for me to head out."

"The baby signal?" Charles asked, raising a brow.

"Yeah, like the bat signal, only it's a crying baby emoji. It means I need to get home and help with our infant son or else..." Arnold slid his pointer finger across his neck and chuckled as he stood from the table. "As always, it was nice to see you all. Great hanging out, Sam." Arnold gripped Sam's shoulder and smiled. "Until next time." With a dramatic flourish, he headed toward the exit. With a stretch and a yawn, Charles pushed to his feet. "I suppose I should head out, too. I don't have a wife or baby waiting on me, thank God, but I do have a stack of mid-terms yay high to grade." He lifted his hand above his over six-foot frame.

"Bye, Charles!" Eva said, and he waved goodbye before leaving Samuel alone with her.

"Wanna get out of here?" she asked Samuel, her hand still on his thigh.

"Yeah, I do need to get home. It's a decent drive."

"Why drive home just to turn around and come back in the morning? Stay at my place. It's just up the road."

Samuel shifted in his seat, trying to think of a kind response. "I'm used to the commute. It's a nice drive. I don't mind it. Besides, I need to feed my dog." He was lying. He had no dog, though he might consider getting one now that he'd be home more often.

"Oh." She pouted and removed her hand from his thigh. "You know, Samuel." She tapped her well-manicured, red nails on the highly glossed pub table. "I've tried to catch your attention many times. I'm sorry if I laid it on too thick tonight. But I was hoping you might be open to something between us again. We are both single adults, and I know as well as you that we are very compatible when tangled in the sheets." She eyed him seductively, sliding her tongue up the length of her straw before suggestively sucking out the remainder of her drink.

Samuel felt her hand slide closer to his crotch, and he shifted, clearing his throat. "Eva, you're an incredible woman. Brilliant, kind, beautiful. But—"

"But you're not interested. Got it." She mindlessly toyed with the straw in her empty glass, pouting her red-stained lips.

"Eva. I'm in love with someone else," Samuel said. "Someone I have no future with. I need to move on, but now isn't the time. I'm sorry. I know it's cliché to say this, but it's really not you."

She nodded and sighed. "I understand." She stood from the table, and he did as well. "I just thought… don't you ever get lonely? I know I do. I'm not looking for anything long-term. But what's the harm in a little playtime?"

"No harm in it at all, and you deserve that with someone who is emotionally and physically available. I'm just not that man right now."

"Fair enough. Walk me out?"

Samuel nodded and walked out of the pub with Eva by his side, realizing that his vision was blurred, and his body swayed. Perhaps he'd drunk one too many and should sit in his car until he was ready to drive. The night's chill had a bite to it, and he saw her shiver. Removing his black leather coat, he draped it over her shoulders. She smiled her thanks and kept walking toward the street, stopping in front of a red BMW. "Well, this is me. Here." She handed him back his jacket. "I have a sweater in here and can use my heater now. Thank you." She unlocked her car and opened the door but paused before sliding in behind the wheel. "You know, Samuel. You are a true gentleman. I'm not sure who this woman is who you love but have no future with. It's not my business, but I hope she knows what a great man you are."

"Thank you, Eva. I appreciate that. Please drive safely. I'll see you on campus on Monday."

"Sam?" Eva stepped away from the car and closer to him, dragging her nail across the shadow of stubble gracing his jaw. He froze and stared at her, wondering what she was waiting to say. He stared at her lips, waiting for her to speak, but before he could react, those lips were on his, coaxing him to respond. Despair clawed at him, his heart and mind warring for purchase as he felt her tongue glide along his lower lip before slipping inside his mouth. He didn't want this, and he should pull away. But after four drinks and knowing that a lifetime of loneliness awaited him, Samuel felt himself giving way to the need for affection— anything to numb his constant pain.

But when her hand slid down his hip and cupped the bulge in his jeans, Samuel snapped out of the moment, gently removing her hand and stepping back a pace. "I'm sorry, Eva. I'm not ready for this."

With a nod, Eva moved back to her car, slid inside the passenger seat, and winked at him. "You know where to find me when you're ready." She reached for the handle, slammed the car door, then started the engine and sped out of the nearly empty lot.

With guilt tugging at his stomach, Samuel looked at his watch and realized it was close to ten at night. He'd not get home before midnight. He was sure now that he'd also drunk one too many whiskeys, and based on his poor decision-making, he knew driving home wasn't an option. A small *motel* sign flashed across the street, and Samuel decided it was best to book a room. He kept spare clothes in his trunk for such purposes, so he retrieved those and his laptop bag and proceeded to the motel, where he checked in for the night.

His head ached, his heart throbbed, and his groin, angry at Samuel for refusing a much-needed romp in the sheets, tightened. He was only a man, after all. Still, despite his need for release, Samuel wasn't the sort to slake his lust with a woman who clearly wanted more than he could give. Eva had claimed to want a casual tryst, but he'd learned from his previous experience with her that she always wanted more than she let on. If he'd taken her up on her offer, he'd have a stage five clinger on his hands.

Opening the motel's door, Samuel looked around the small space and sighed, plopping his bag on a worn blue, upholstered chair. A single bed with pristinely white sheets rested in the center of the far wall with a nightstand on either side. An open door on the right showed off a small shower stall and a smaller countertop.

Setting his laptop on the little table in the room's corner, Samuel dropped into the chair beside it and tried to talk himself out of what he wanted to do. But he lost his self-control. He could blame it on the whiskey, but the truth was, he couldn't stand not knowing if Murielle married Aldfrith. He typed in the king's name, scrolling through his Wiki page. When he saw Aldfrith's spouse's name, Samuel's heart flipped in his chest, and his breathing hitched.

Aldfrith had married a woman named *Cuthburh*, who later became a saint. He didn't marry Murielle…! But…why? Did she reject him? Did he change his mind? After all, he was quite pious, and it made sense that he'd marry a pious woman. Murielle had her beliefs, but she knew too much about the world to follow any one religion.

But then again, why did he even care? There was only one thing that mattered to Sam. "She didn't marry him!" he shouted, jumping up from his chair and making it fall back to the floor with a thud. He cringed, hoping he hadn't disturbed whoever was below him on the floor below.

He needed to get back to Murielle right away.

He cursed himself for having drunk so much that he couldn't drive home. If he were home, he'd pack his bags, jump into Joplin, head toward the cave tonight, and wait for the low tide. But he was determined to make it back to Murielle as soon as possible. If she wasn't destined to marry King Aldfrith, nothing else would stand in Samuel's way—not even her brother.

He'd find Murielle, and he would marry her.

CHAPTER FIVE

"A RE YE SURE this is his… *flat?*" Murielle asked as she stood in front of a black door on the third story of a large, stone building.

"Yes. I'm certain. I wonder where he is. Usually, he drives to work, lectures, and comes right home."

"Mayhap he went out with companions?"

"Samuel doesn't have many of those. Traveling back and forth through time to correct the timeline so the earth doesn't implode doesn't leave much time for a social life. Maybe he went on a bender."

"What is a *bender?*" Murielle asked.

"Never mind. It's getting late. We need to find a place to sleep. Tomorrow, we will try to find him."

After finding a ride into town from the cave, Murielle and Cait had awaited Samuel for hours. Caitriona had considered getting a ride to Aberdeen University, but the cab bill would be a lot of money, and though she still had money in her savings to pay off her credit bill, she couldn't recall exactly how much she had, and she didn't want to spend it all on a potentially fruitless endeavor.

Caitriona had no phone, which meant no internet to look up the closest motel. Together, they wandered the streets of Moray looking for a place to stay. A few people stopped to stare at their odd clothing, but nobody said a word.

"I find it strange that nobody has called us witches for our unusual state of dress. If ye showed up in my time dressed like half these people, a pyre would be built."

"Yeah, well, in this time, pretty much anything goes. You can dress however you want. People may think we are part of a renaissance fair. In fact, I think they do have one in town this time of year."

"I dinnae ken what that is, but if people are dressed like we are, we should go!"

"One thing at a time, Murielle." Already, Cait had had to answer a million questions while they were in the car. It was only an eight-mile drive to Samuel's flat from the cave. The driver didn't question their clothing or why Murielle seemed so intrigued by his Mazda. "How does it move? Why does it go so fast? What is horsepower, and why does anyone need 190 horses to get anywhere?" That was only the beginning of her questions, but Caitriona patiently answered them all, knowing how many Murielle answered for her when she crossed over.

Caitriona flagged down a man in a suit. "Excuse me. Where is the closest motel?"

"Just down that street and to yer left."

She nodded and thanked the man, dragging Murielle away before she asked another question. They were both cold, filthy, wet, and exhausted. Cait didn't care how bad the motel was. If it had a hot shower, she was there.

Finding the flashing motel light, Cait brought Murielle to the check-in desk, requesting a room with two beds. The man swiped her card and handed her a key to a room, all the while eyeing them both like they were slightly insane. Murielle's wide eyes as she spun around the lobby blinking at the lightbulbs and rifling through tourist brochures didn't help.

"Let's go, Murielle," Cait said with a chuckle, dragging her sister-in-law toward the lift. "We are going to go up an elevator. Don't freak out."

"I willnae! Why, what is it?"

"It's a metal box that has buttons. Do not push the buttons."

"I don't even ken what buttons are!"

This was more complicated than Cait even expected. It was a good thing she was here. "Let's just use the stairs."

Shrugging, Murielle followed Cait up a flight of stairs, and they stopped at room 237, where Cait tapped the keycard on the door, opening it when she heard the click.

"That was the lock?" Murielle asked. Her question was forgotten when she entered the room. "This is... wondrous!" Squealing, Murielle ran full speed toward one of the beds and plopped down, stomach first, with her arms spread out. "This bed is stuffed with clouds! It is, isnae it? Ye've figured out how to capture clouds and stuff them into mattresses. Brilliant!"

Cait bit back a laugh, not wanting to hurt Murielle's feelings or stifle her excitement. "It sure feels that way, but it's just a combination of wood, metal springs, and fabric cushions. Nothing fancy. Come with me into the bathroom. You must have to go."

"Oh, aye. So badly," Murielle nodded and followed Cait into the bathroom, exclaiming with excitement as she flicked the light switch to illuminate the small space. She quickly explained how the toilet, sink, and shower worked, turning the knobs until a perfect temperature of water flowed.

"I am never, ever going home!" Murielle shouted.

"This is for your hair. This is for your skin. Just take your time and enjoy it. I'll be just in here," Cait said, pointing to the main room. "Oh, and don't go to the bathroom in the shower."

"Ach, why would I?" Murielle asked, curling her lip.

Cait shrugged. "You'd be surprised what people do." Even an ancient Pict had better shower manners than Cait's old roommate, she thought as she shut the door behind her, leaving Murielle to her first hot shower ever and wondering where the hell Samuel was. She may not have a cellphone or a computer, but she had an old phonebook that rested atop the wooden table beside the room's rotary phone. Had this motel room also traveled back in time? The brown and beige plain curtains, dark wood paneling, and laminate flooring spoke of an era well before Caitriona was born. At least it was clean.

With a sigh of exhaustion, Cait flipped the book open and searched for Samuel. There were five Samuel Sullivans in Moray, but only one in Elgin, which is where they were. Dialing, she perked up when she got his voicemail, pleased that Samuel was so old-fashioned that he kept a landline and an answering machine.

"Sam! Sam, It's Cait. Don't freak out, but Murielle and I are here. She ran off to find you, and I had to pass through with her. I will explain more later. We waited outside your apartment all night. Where are you? I don't have a phone, and we won't be in this motel room after checkout tomorrow. Please call the Marigold Motel in Elgin if you get this by tomorrow morning. We are in room 237."

Flustered but hopeful, Caitriona claimed the other bed and sighed when her back hit the modern mattress. She never thought she'd sleep in a real bed again, and though she missed Brodyn and Lucas like crazy, this was a fun adventure. She'd take a shower in the morning. Her eyes drooped, and sleep threatened to carry her away. Besides, Murielle was singing loudly in the shower, and Cait didn't expect her to finish any time soon. Rolling over, Caitriona rested her head on the cool, fluffy pillow and rested her eyes.

"It really does feel like clouds, though," she sighed before falling asleep.

Sunlight streamed into the room through a crack in the dark curtains, illuminating the motel room as Murielle stirred awake. As her eyes fluttered open, she recalled where she was and immediately hopped out of bed.

Cait was in the shower, and Murielle took that moment to look around the room and observe the modern items Cait explained to her last night before bed. A coffee pot sat on the counter near a sink, and Murielle wondered how anyone took indoor plumbing for granted. No trips to the well. No stagnant water. Her shower last night had been one the most incredible experiences of her life, and apparently, people bathed daily in this time. Even now, she smelled mint and something floral wafting in her hair after using the shampoo and conditioner, which made her hair softer than it had ever been.

She never wanted to leave this time. And, if she could find Samuel and convince him they were meant to be, maybe they could live here together. Images of her and Samuel holding hands while she cradled a dark-haired bairn made her heart flutter.

A knock on the door made Murielle jump. "Room service!" she heard a man call from the other side of the door. Crinkling her brow, Murielle grabbed her overtunic and slid it on before creeping to the door and cracking it open as she looked through the small slit.

A man in a red vest smiled back at her. "Good morning, Miss. I have yer breakfast! May I bring it in?"

Murielle saw a wheeled cart carrying plates covered with clear lids. She had no idea what room service or breakfast was, though she could figure that one out based on the name. Standing aside, she opened the door and watched the man wheel the cart inside.

Cait stuck her head out the bathroom door, a large towel wrapped around her head. "I ordered food. We need a good meal before we start our day. Tell him I'll add a tip to my room's bill. I don't have cash."

The man heard her and looked at Murielle with a smile. "Much appreciated. Thank ye, and enjoy yer meals."

When he left, Cait came out of the steamy bathroom wrapped in another towel, lifting the lids off plates of delectable food. Murielle's stomach growled when the smells reached her nose.

"Scrambled eggs, toast, fruit, and bacon. A little bit of everything. These are jams to spread on the toast," Cait explained.

Together, they ate, and Murielle hummed and groaned with every bite. These foods were also common in her time but prepared here in a way she'd never seen. There were no bits of gravel in the bread that might chip her tooth, and the citrus fruit, despite the autumn season, was sweet and fresh. Black specks covered her eggs, and it was a seasoning called pepper, not bugs. The jam, something she'd never had before, was sweet and delicious on the buttered toast.

"I could live like this," Murielle murmured.

Caitriona frowned and put her fork down. "That's exactly what I'm worried about. Murielle, you still need to return to your time. We are only here to seek closure for you and Sam… right?"

Murielle chewed her lower lip and looked at her lap, deciding how honest to be. She found she could not lie to Cait, who'd already sacrificed so much to help her.

"Nay. I didnae come all the way here to say goodbye to Samuel. I'm not marrying Aldfrith. If Samuel won't have me even after knowing I turned Aldfrith down, then I shall die a maiden."

"Murielle. This world… this time—it keeps records of people from birth. You have no birth certificate, no identification, no social security number, and no place of origin that still exists. How will you live here, make money, or do anything? You need identification to get anywhere in this time."

Murielle frowned, her excitement forgotten. Even Cait was giving up on her. "I don't know. I just want to find Samuel."

"I do, too. I called his flat last night—using one of these—" Cait explained, pointing to the old phone on the table. "But he didn't answer and never called back. I don't think he ever came home last night."

"What does that mean?" Was he out with another woman or injured? Murielle stood up and began to pace the room.

"He's fine. I'm sure he was working late and got a place to stay for the night. I think we should spend our day doing some research while we wait for Samuel to get home."

"What sort of research?"

"Don't you want to know if you marry Aldfrith or not?"

"I already ken I dinnae. I need not look it up." Murielle turned her head and straightened her back as she crossed her arms. She would not bother looking it up. She knew the truth in her heart.

"Okay." Caitriona sighed and looked at the time on the clock beside the bed. "If only I had a cellphone. If you don't want to do research, I won't force it. But we have about six hours until Samuel should be home... if he works today. I'm not even sure what day it is. I don't have much money to work with, and I need to return home by tonight, or Brodyn will be worried. Checkout is in three hours, so we can't stay here, nor do I think that's the best use of our time while you're here. Let's head out and discover some things while we wait for Samuel."

Murielle nodded, guilt weighing her down. She was being stubborn, and poor Caitriona clearly wanted to get home. "I'm sorry, Caitriona."

"Don't be sorry. I'm just sorry I have limited resources right now. Would you like to visit Pinnata Castra in this time? It's a small town called Burghead now. Most of the Pictish fort is gone or buried beneath the earth, but the well remains."

Murielle shook her head. "Seeing my village's remains doesnae seem like a good idea."

"None of this is a good idea, but here we are," Caitriona huffed. Murielle felt Cait's agitation.

Perking up, Murielle said, "On those brochures in the lobby, wasnae there information about what ye call a *museum*?"

"Oh, yes. I'm sure we can find our way there and spend some time until heading back to Samuel's flat."

"I appreciate ye being here, Cait." Murielle grabbed her sister's hand and squeezed. "I ken I am a stubborn woman. I will do exactly as ye say, and if we dinnae find Samuel by tonight, I vow I will return home. I willnae marry Aldfrith, but I will return home so ye can see Brodyn and Lucas."

Caitriona smiled and stood from the bed. "Thank you. Let's

ask the people at the desk for directions to the museum. But first, we need coffee. And not this motel room garbage." Cait grimaced at the odd-looking item near the sink. "If I'm in my own time for one day, I need the perfect mocha latte."

When they arrived at the museum, Murielle's eyes widened as she looked at all the exhibits. "Look, Cait! They have one about the Picts! Are these photos of Pinnata Castra? Why does it call it Burghead? I ken that's its name now, but dinnae they ken what it used to be called?"

"Nobody was ever certain what the Picts called the village. Romans had names for it, and so did other tribes. The kingdom was called Fortriu, but the smaller village names were unknown."

"We should tell them! Oh… this is also not accurate. It says the bull symbol depicted our father, but it was Brodyn's symbol! And ye are the thistle, not my mother!"

"Murielle… I know this. But we cannot interfere. Samuel knows all the same information but hasn't corrected modern scholars."

"Well… why not? We have the chance to tell modern people all about the Picts!"

"Because, Murielle…" Cait sighed and pulled Murielle aside. "Without evidence in any historical record, there is no proof or way to validate our information. We would be dismissed outright. Archeology is a science, which means everything remains a mystery or theory until proof is discovered. That's why we do what we do. We literally dig for evidence. We have theories and hope what we discover proves them. Until two years ago, we all believed Brodyn was buried in that cave because a legend said so. We had no proof it wasn't him until we were able to access the cave and dig. What we found was not Brodyn. But we cannot just walk up to people and tell them everything without evidence. I know it's frustrating."

Murielle swallowed her discomfort. How odd it was to see information and images depicting her people, yet so much of it was incorrect. How easily she could correct it all and let modern people know how Picts truly lived.

If she stayed in the future, she'd find a way to teach people about the Picts. The images depicting them as dirty, simple-minded warriors and farmers did little to convey the truth. Her people were innovative, intelligent, hard-working, *and* they bathed!

Murielle suddenly knew what she had to do. She had to make it her life's work to teach the modern world exactly how the Picts lived and what the symbols meant. She wasn't sure how she'd do that, but she would find a way.

SAMUEL MADE IT to the university with little effort since his motel room was just down the street. His first class went by quickly enough, but as the morning dragged on, Samuel grew anxious to leave and head for the cave. He debated stopping by his flat to grab another change of clothes and a quick shower, but he'd already be very short on time if he was to make it to Pinnata Castra, find Murielle, deal with Brodyn, and make it home before classes began tomorrow morning.

When the clock struck noon and his last class filed out, Samuel wasted no time packing up his belongings, leaving his classroom, and locking up before anyone stopped him.

He headed toward the stairwell, taking two steps at a time before reaching the first level and pushing through the double doors to get to the parking lot. Hopping into his trusty Jeep, Samuel sped off down the road, heading toward the coast like his life depended on it. To him, it did. His life was meaningless without Murielle. And now that he knew she was not Aldfrith's wife, he had to find her.

Rain pelted his windshield as an October storm brewed. According to the weather station he followed, the low tide should occur around two in the afternoon, which meant Samuel could make it to the cave with no time to spare if there was no traffic. He'd have to run to Pinnata Castra, handle his business, and return to avoid high tide and becoming stuck in the cave overnight. High and low tides in his time didn't always align with the tides in 686. He could easily cross through on one side and be stuck on the other until the tide changed. It wouldn't be his first time, and he'd often considered storing some personal effects inside the cave for such purposes. Because the cave was mostly hidden from shore, few if any people ever entered.

Mile after mile passed, and the sky darkened as he drew closer to the coast. Traffic locked up, a car spun out, and two lanes shut down. Samuel looked out of his window as police lights flashed and vehicles came to complete stops.

An hour passed, but it felt like an eternity as Samuel leaned his head against the glass, watching the sky go black as rain flooded the road. Once cars began to move again, Samuel's hope of making low tide vanished.

Just as he was about to give up and head home, Samuel roared his frustration and punched his steering wheel. He didn't have time to waste! Murielle may have already accepted Aldfrith's proposal, and Brodyn would be busy preparing a wedding! Samuel had served others his entire life, always putting himself and his needs last. He couldn't do that this time. He'd never forgive himself.

Knowing Murielle wasn't listed as Aldfrith's wife wasn't enough to calm Samuel. He knew that things could change in every timeline. Mayhap Murielle rejected Aldfrith in the last time loop but accepted him in this one because Samuel left.

He'd call in a sub tomorrow at work if he had to. Yes, his career and those students meant everything to Samuel, but so did Murielle. His students would be fine with a TA filling in for him for one day, but Samuel's entire future rested on him making it to Murielle in time.

The cave might not be accessible when he got there, but Samuel had to try. The moment traffic broke up, he hit the gas, determined to make up as much lost time as possible. Samuel finally arrived at the cliff overlooking the cave, two hours behind schedule. He drove his Jeep as far down the narrow trail as possible before hopping out and running the rest of the way. Mud caked his brown loafers and splattered his jeans. His button-down shirt was plastered to his chest as rain soaked through his clothing, but he refused to be slowed down any more than he already had been.

Reaching the shore, Samuel stopped and panted, watching violent waves crash against the cliffside, covering the cave's entrance. He cursed and bent over to catch his breath. He was too late but he wasn't deterred. High tide had another five hours left. He'd go home, clean himself up, get some sleep, and come back here to try again.

Slowly, Samuel trudged back up the muddy trail, his shoes slipping in the thick mud with every step as his frozen hand gripped his flashlight to guide the way. It was time he took his life and destiny into his own hands, but he couldn't control the roadblocks of nature.

Despite failing to make it to the cave in time, hope bolstered Samuel. Now that he'd made a plan, determination drove his every step back to the top of the cliff.

Hopping back in his Jeep, Samuel headed home, which fortunately was only a thirty-minute drive. Parking his car beneath his designated overhang, he grabbed his laptop case and headed up the old steps leading to his small flat.

Rounding the corner, Samuel stopped and looked down when he saw two figures huddled on his porch. Murielle rested her head on Cait's shoulder as they both shivered and leaned against his door, apparently asleep.

"Cait? Murielle?" Alarms rang in his mind, along with a million questions. "What are you doing here? How?" He kneeled beside them and touched their arms, making them both awaken with a start. Murielle's eyes widened when she saw him, and she lunged forward into his arms.

"Samuel!" She shook as she clung to him. "We found ye! Caitriona! We found him!"

Cait looked up and wiped her eyes. "I was hoping you hadn't moved. We were here last night waiting for you, and you never came."

Samuel held Murielle against him, his mind reeling. Of course, on the first night in years that Samuel decided to stay out late, Cait and Murielle would cross the veil of time to find him. "I was out late with some co-workers and decided to rent a motel room near the university." Remembering his kiss with Eva, Samuel closed his eyes and gritted his teeth against the sudden onslaught of shame and remorse. Murielle had been in his time, desperately seeking him out, and he had been drunk and kissing another woman.

Slowly, he stood, bringing Murielle up with him. She quivered as the wind blew and rain slanted down from the sky, nearly reaching his porch despite the overhang. "Come inside. We'll get you dried off and warmed up, and then we can figure out what's going on."

Digging his keys out of his pocket with a shaky hand, Samuel opened his door and let the women enter. Cait plopped down on the couch with a dramatic sigh, but Murielle stood in the middle of the room, spinning in a slow circle as she took in every detail of his home with wide-eyed wonder.

"What the hell happened to you?" Caitriona asked. Samuel looked down at his destroyed clothing, soaked through and caked in mud.

"I planned to go to the cave immediately after work but got stuck in traffic and missed the low tide. I tried anyway, but it was too late. I was going to change and try again tonight."

Murielle spun to look at him. "Why were ye going to the cave?"

Samuel stepped closer to her. "I was coming to find you."

"Me? But, ye said ye couldnae be with me."

Cait stood up. "I'm going to give you two some privacy."

"You don't need to go anywhere, Cait. You look like you've been through an ordeal, too. I'm sorry I wasn't home last night. Had I known..." His voice faded off, and his head throbbed. Murielle was here, in his home, and he wasn't sure why or what to do or say next.

"Let me put on some tea and turn up the thermostat." He needed to keep busy while he processed this. What he wanted to do was take Murielle in his arms and kiss her passionately, then confess his undying love and ask her to marry him. But, until he knew why she was here, he decided to rein in his desires and wait for Murielle to explain the situation.

Forcing logic to stifle his emotions had always been his method of choice, but he found it nearly impossible to remain logical while Murielle watched him move around his flat. Her hair was damp and frizzy, and her tunic was dirty and torn at the hem, but she was still easily the most beautiful creature on this planet.

With the kettle on and heat pumping through his vents, Samuel wiped his hands on a dishcloth and went back into the living room, standing in front of Murielle, wondering how she could be so beautiful even while covered in mud. Despite the millions of questions running through his mind, he couldn't ask one—he wasn't sure where to start. And it was enough, really, to just look at the woman he loved, in his home, 1,400 years from where she was supposed to be.

"Murielle turned down Aldfrith and snuck out of her escape tunnel to get to the cave. She wanted to find you," Cait finally blurted out, cutting through the awkward silence.

"What? How?" Samuel looked at Murielle, both impressed and angry that she'd risk her safety. "Murielle, any number of awful things could have happened!" He gently took her hand and looked into her distressed blue eyes. "You could have become lost or worse."

She swallowed, and he saw her chin begin to quiver. "I... I wasnae thinking about anything but finding ye! Ye left me!" She pulled her hand away from his and spun around, crossing her arms.

Samuel looked at Caitriona, unsure what to do or what to say. He had left her because he couldn't risk changing the timeline. He couldn't allow people to vanish in a puff of smoke if she'd had a line of descendants created from her marriage to another man. So why couldn't Murielle understand his decision? She knew the consequences well enough.

Caitriona stood from the couch and cleared her throat. "I'm going to run to the store for milk."

"I have milk."

"I need almond milk." She walked to the door without looking over her shoulder.

"You drink a lot of almond milk at home?" he asked, raising a brow. He knew what she was doing. She wanted to give them space, and though he was desperate to speak with Murielle alone, he couldn't just let Cait run back outside in the rainstorm.

She turned and gave him a dangerous look. "Obviously not. But I like it, and I miss it, and I want it in my 2023 tea since my 686 tea doesn't have it."

Samuel bit back a smile. She was as stubborn as they come. "Whatever, Mac Murray," he said, calling her by her maiden name as he used to when she was his student. "But take Joplin and some cash from my wallet."

"I have my credit card. Murielle brought it and my ID with her."

Samuel looked at Murielle and shook his head. "I'd forgotten you gave those to her."

"I didn't forget," Murielle said, raising her chin proudly. "Ye all may believe I'm reckless for coming here, but I've been planning it for a long time. This is where I belong... with ye, Samuel."

"And... I'm out." Caitriona grabbed a five-dollar bill from his wallet on the table, snatched his keys, flipped a peace sign, and left the house.

The kettle whistled, making him and Murielle jump at the

same time. He rushed over to the kitchen, turned off the heat, and removed the kettle. Walking back to Murielle, he took her hand in his and smiled. "I am so glad you are here, Murielle. Please don't think otherwise. I was trying to get to you, but a car accident on the road made me miss the low tide. I would have passed through the veil and walked all the way to Pinnata Castra to find you missing!" he said with a grin, trying to ease her mind.

"We went to a wonderful place today called a museum. I saw many things, and many of them were verra incorrect."

He nodded and chuckled. "Yes, that's quite right. Unfortunately, your people didn't leave enough written records behind."

"Samuel…" Murielle stepped closer to him, looking at him with her worried blue eyes and thick, dark, sweeping lashes. "Are ye mad at me for coming here? Did ye not wish to be with me? Mayhap ye were only being kind when ye said ye loved me because ye didnae expect to see me again?"

"That is absurd." Samuel slipped his hands around her slim waist and looked down at her. "You know why I had to leave. It was the hardest thing I ever did."

"And yet, ye were coming back for me tonight?"

He nodded, scooping a lock of wavy blonde hair behind her ear. "I was."

"What changed yer mind?"

"Google."

She wrinkled her brows in confusion, and he laughed, leaning down to kiss her furrowed brow. "I tried not to look you up, but I broke down. You aren't listed in any historical record as Aldfrith's wife."

"Because I amnae his wife, and I will never be! Samuel, I've loved ye since the moment ye showed up in Pinata Castra dressed like a messenger from Dal Riata. From that moment, my heart was yers. Ye say that ye live the same life over and over, stuck in this time loop, but ye only ever remember up to the battle where Brodyn was thought to die, is that right?"

Samuel nodded, looking into her eyes and watching her

sweet lips as she spoke. How he wanted to carry her into his bed, beg her to marry him, hear her say *yes*, and then remove her clothing so he might finally see the tempting flesh beneath her tunic and claim her as his *forever*. He tried to be different than the men in her time, relying on his modern sensibilities and respect for women. But, his primal need to possess her, to ravish her and make her his, clawed at his heated flesh as the blood left his head and swiftly traveled south.

"Do ye remember me in those memories?"

"Yes, I do. I may not remember anything after the battle, but I always remember you. I always remember loving you."

"Then it makes sense that we are always in love, and I always reject marriage to Aldfrith for ye. Doesnae that make us meant to be?"

"Perhaps. I've always been so concerned with making sure Cait married Brodyn and fixed the timeline that I only remember private thoughts of love for you and sadness deep in my soul."

Murielle put her hand on his cheek. "Ye dinnae need to be sad, my love. I am not meant for Aldfrith. I'm meant for ye. I ken it down in the depths of my soul. I wouldnae have traveled here if I didnae ken that. And, I was allowed through the veil! That must mean something! The cave wouldnae allow Ronan through."

"You tried to drag poor Ronan through?" Samuel could only imagine the man's face when Murielle told him the truth.

"Aye, he is my guard. I couldnae go alone, and I kenned Brodyn would have his head if I slipped away. It was for his own good, as well. But Brodyn noticed I was gone and kenned exactly where I was headed. He and Caitriona rode down to the cave and found me just as I crossed over. When I passed through, and Ronan didn't, my brother told Cait to follow me through, help me find ye to say goodbye. He expects me back, Samuel. He demanded I marry Aldfrith and told him to return in a sennight for the wedding!"

She shook in his arms, and he pulled her closer. "Everything will be all right. We have time to figure this out."

She looked up at him with narrowed eyes and that stubborn tilt of her head. He knew she was ready to do battle, and he loved watching her determination flair. "I have already figured myself out. It seems ye are the one who hasnae. Ye say ye love me. Ye say I am not Aldfrith's wife. Here I am, in yer home, in yer time, and ye want time to figure it out? Mayhap I misjudged ye."

She turned away from him, but he pulled her back, growling with frustration as he looked down at her. "I want you more than my next breath, Murielle. You have no idea how much and for how long I've suffered. Why do you think I was prepared to cross back through and find you tonight?"

"I dinnae ken! Ye tell me!" she shot back, her cheeks flushing with frustration in a way that made Samuel wish to tear away her tunic and make desperate love to her.

"Because I want you to be my wife! I want you to marry me! Not Aldfrith, and not any other man!"

"And yet, ye havenae asked me." She crossed her arms which only served to push her breasts together. Even through her modestly cut tunic, Samuel saw the roundness of her ample bosom as she heaved for breath.

What she didn't know was that Samuel was fully prepared to propose. After all, he'd been on his way there. Turning away from her, he walked into the dining area and opened his laptop bag, looking around for the small diamond ring he'd been carrying around. He'd expected to ask Brodyn for permission first, but that wasn't a possibility, nor was he certain Brodyn would approve. But, they were in Samuel's time, and Brodyn's rules didn't apply here.

"Sam?" Murielle whispered his name, sadness lacing that one word. Turning around, Samuel walked back and stood before her, soaking in every perfect detail of the woman he loved. Her long, dark lashes, petite frame, and powerful presence. She chewed on her bottom lip with anxiety, and her eyes watered with unshed tears.

Slowly, Samuel lifted a hand to her cheek, grazing the back of his fingers against her soft, flushed skin until he reached the back of her neck. Placing his forehead against hers, his breath hitched and his heart raced.

"I love you, Murielle Mac Cuill. I've loved you for so long."

"I love ye, Samuel," she whispered, still clearly unsure of what was happening. Slowly, he lowered his lips to hers and gently slid his tongue into her mouth. She sighed and tilted her head, allowing him to drag his lips along the salty column of her throat, tasting her soft skin. She groaned softly as he pulled away, dropping down onto one knee and taking her hand in his.

"Murielle, I cannot know our future. Will we live in my time or yours? Will we have children or just a pack of dogs? The only thing I know for certain is that I don't want to live another day without you by my side. Will you marry me?"

He held up the modest diamond solitaire ring that had once belonged to his mother, and her mother before her. He had only a few distant childhood memories of her, but she was kind, happy, and spoke well of her marriage with his father before he passed. This ring had secured two happy marriages, and he hoped it would ensure a third.

"Oh, Samuel!" Murielle nodded, and her hand shook as he placed the ring on her finger. She got down on her knees beside him and wrapped her arms around his neck. "I love ye so much! Ye ken, I will marry ye! This ring is beautiful. Oh, I never thought to own anything so wonderful. I want to live here with ye."

Samuel knew Murielle preferred to stay in his time, and he'd love for her to get the opportunity to stay, but there were details like the fact that she had no birth record here. "We will figure everything out."

With a squeal of happiness, she pulled him in for a searing kiss that stole his breath. After two years of secretly loving her from very, very afar, Murielle was now his fiancée. The thought warmed his blood and made him wish to carry her to the courthouse right now and make her his wife. They'd overcome more obstacles to be together than most, and Samuel wasn't going to allow anything, not even time, to get in their way.

Samuel pulled Murielle into his lap, where she happily settled and rested her head against his chest. "I'm so happy, Sam. This moment is worth every tear and every struggle."

"Well, our struggles aren't over. We'll need to go back and speak with your brother. We can't just run away. When Caitriona returns, we will head to the cave—tonight!—and try to pass through. Caitriona needs to get back to Brodyn and Lucas."

"We will figure it all out together," Murielle whispered. "Right now, we are alone."

"That thought hadn't crossed my mind at all," Samuel chuckled, leaning in to capture her lips with his, enjoying the feel of her resting in his lap, her breasts grazing his chest while their tongues mingled slowly, torturously. He'd already imagined a hundred different things he'd like to do with her, here and now. But, Caitriona would return soon, and a hasty coupling wasn't what Murielle deserved for her first time.

Murielle pulled away, heaving for breath as she looked into his eyes. "Make love to me."

He shook his head. "I cannot. Not now, as greatly as it pains me. You deserve better."

"Ye put a ring on my finger and are already telling me what I deserve? As if I cannae speak or think for myself?"

He felt the heat in her gaze, the frustration seeping through every pore. He shared that frustration. "No, but Cait will return eventually, and I will not dishonor you by mounting you on my floor like a beast in the byre. We can save that for other nights." He waggled his brows when she gasped and flushed.

"Is it odd that I quite look forward to it?" she asked, leaning in to kiss him as she giggled.

"It's not odd at all. It's natural. Still…" His hands slid upward from her hips to her breasts. He sighed and closed his eyes as he caressed her for the first time. Need surged and his erection pressed painfully against his jeans, but it was a torturous pleasure, one that heightened his anticipation to finally bury himself deep within her heat. But for now, they could enjoy a gentle exploration.

Murielle sucked in a breath and tilted her head back when his fingers grazed her nipple through her tunic. He felt it pebble and harden, and he grew desperate to lay her bare to his gaze. Murielle must have had similar desires, for she slowly slid the tunic down her shoulders, her blue gaze burning into his, demanding he touch her.

When the fabric dragged over her nipples just before falling to her waist, Samuel watched in a daze as her perfect, round breasts stood before him, only inches away. With a groan of both pleasure and restraint, Samuel looked his fill before cupping each of them in his warm palms, running his thumbs across her nipples. She released a soft moan and arched into his touch, and he wondered at her natural, shameless passion, how sensually she responded to his touch.

It had been so long since he'd laid with a woman. The temptation to toss her skirt up and bury himself inside her, to watch her writhe and cry out as he pumped into her, grew more imminent by the second. Still, he harnessed his need and focused it on giving Murielle her first taste of pleasure as he reveled in his initial taste of her flesh.

Leaning in, he dragged his tongue across one nipple before gently sucking it into his mouth. Murielle dug her nails into his arms as she clung to him, gasping and wriggling in his lap. She breathed his name on her sweet, parted lips, and he swore he'd lose control soon if he didn't slow down.

He felt something graze his erection and looked down to see Murielle running her fingers up and down the painful bulge in his jeans. Quickly, he removed her hand and shook his head. She frowned, but he stifled her sadness with a plundering kiss, slipping his tongue deep into her mouth as he held her hand.

"My love, I do not reject you or your touch, but I fear I will come undone if you touch me right now. I don't want your first experience to be me, spilling my seed in my blue jeans."

She nodded her understanding, looking disappointed but accepting his explanation. "But," he whispered, leaning in to trail his tongue down the long column of her throat before taking her pink nipple into his mouth again. "I can give *you* pleasure." Her glassy eyes widened with a curious innocence. Damned if this woman wasn't going to be his downfall.

With her straddling his lap, Samuel slipped his hand beneath her skirt and slowly glided his fingers up her silky thigh, feeling the heat of her core as he grew nearer. "When the time is right, and we can finally be together, I will bury myself inside you," he whispered into her ear, feeling her quiver with anticipation and need. "Right here." His finger softly stroked her woman's heat, and Murielle bucked her hips in response, her breasts rising and falling with her breathing as she arched, silently begging for more. She was ready for him, slick and warm, and he bit his lip to prevent releasing a frustrated growl.

He slipped one finger, then two, inside her wet heat until she gyrated and bore down, her body desperate for more, knowing instinctively how to draw her pleasure. Her beauty mesmerized Samuel. He was but a fool in love with a goddess who walked amongst mortals. His thumb circled her sensitive nub as she pressed herself against his hand, and within moments, Murielle tensed and released a cry so powerful a tear trickled down her cheek as she closed her eyes and parted her lips.

"Samuel!" she cried, clinging to his shoulders and panting for breath. He pulled her close, resting her head on his shoulder as she caught her breath. Samuel stroked her back, reveling in the feel of her smooth skin against his palm.

"I... I never knew a man's touch could be so powerful," she sighed before sitting up and looking at him. "I love ye, Samuel."

"Murielle, sweet love," Samuel whispered as he dragged his fingers up and down her back before pulling her tunic over her breasts. As much as it pained him to cover up her beauty, Caitriona could arrive any moment, and already they'd tempted exposure. He wouldn't ever wish to disrespect Murielle and have her found undressed. "You cannot know how many nights I laid awake dreaming of a life with you, pining for what I could not have, plotting any number of ways I could close the distance between your time and mine so we could be together."

"I do ken it because I have done the same. Why do ye think I turned down Aldfrith and traveled through time to find ye? Samuel, no force in this world can keep us apart, not even time. And, if that is not proof that our love is a part of time's plan, I dinnae ken what is."

Samuel helped Murielle to her feet as he stood, taking her hands in his. "I see it now. No longer will I deny my feelings or our love. I promise, Murielle." He kissed her long and slow for several more minutes before the front door creaked open.

Cait walked in with a wide grin; she stopped in the middle of the living room, crossing her arms. "I see you two have come to terms?"

"Cait!" Murielle ran to her sister with a bounce in her step, putting out her left hand. "We are getting married!"

Samuel nodded and smiled when Cait raised a brow at him. "This is fantastic! Now, we need to tell Brodyn. That's going to be less fantastic."

"Where is the almond milk?" Samuel asked, noticing her hands were empty.

She rolled her eyes. "I'm leaving tonight. Obviously, 'almond milk' was code for 'giving you two time to sort yourselves.' Guess it worked. Now, it's my turn to kiss my husband. Let's go back to the cave and await the low tide."

Nodding, Samuel grabbed his keys and phone, took Murielle's hand, and locked up the flat. He'd need to call a student TA to fill in for him tomorrow and maybe the day after. But soon, he'd have to return and either give his resignation or announce his marriage. He hoped to stay in this time, for he'd worked hard to create his career, but he wasn't sure how to establish Murielle's existence here. It was a small matter, he was sure. People created new identities for themselves all the time.

No matter what, he'd have Murielle, and nothing else mattered.

CHAPTER SIX

J OPLIN PUSHED THROUGH howling wind and slanting rain as they reached the shore. Murielle's stomach knotted and tightened as they drew closer to the cave. Brodyn's words ran through her mind, his anger, his demand that she marry Aldfrith despite lack of her consent. She understood the ways of her people, and perhaps she had been the one to pull away from tradition and chase her heart rather than marry a stranger, but it was her life, and she resented her brother having everything he ever wanted—the kingship, a beautiful wife, a healthy heir, yet disregarding everything that mattered to her.

When Samuel parked his Jeep at the top of the cliff, the headlights flooded the darkness but only revealed a vast ocean and slanting rains. He parked the vehicle, then hopped out of the Jeep and circled around to help her and Cait out, linking hands with Murielle as he held a flashlight in his free hand. Cait held another flashlight as they carefully descended the cliff, following a narrow, windy trail that appeared barely used. Despite the trail's near invisibility in the darkness and rain, Cait and Samuel navigated it with ease, clearly familiar with this track of land.

Despite the deluge, once their feet landed on the gravelly shore below the cliff, the tide had lowered just enough for them to slide along the cliff's base until reaching the cave's entrance.

Caitriona shook her hair out like a wet dog once they were within the cave's dry space, and Murielle twisted hers to wring out the heavy water weighing her down. If only she could do the same for her sodden tunic. Shivering, she wrapped her arms around herself, pleased when Samuel took her into his warm embrace.

"I'm sorry I didn't have an umbrella!" he shouted over the rhythmic patter of rain slamming against the cave walls.

"I dinnae ken what an umbrella is, but I assure ye, rain isnae a deterrent for me. I rather enjoy it." However, the chill in the cave threatened to freeze her to the bone if she didn't get warm soon.

Cait shined the flashlight toward the back of the cave as they entered the small alcove, where Taylor was once buried. The small space made Murielle's flesh crawl, knowing Caitriona's former betrothed had tried to kill Brodyn in this very spot. It was Samuel who saved Brodyn by shooting Taylor first with a weapon from his time. This space held millennia of bad energy, and she wanted out of there as quickly as possible.

"I dislike this space." She shivered and clung to Samuel. "How do we cross over if the thistle is gone?"

"It's not the thistle that helps us cross over," Samuel explained. "Just touch the wall, close your eyes, and envision where you need to go. It will take you there."

Nodding, Murielle did as Samuel explained, but her heart wasn't in it. She didn't want to go home, not yet. She knew she had to go home eventually to explain herself to Brodyn and once again refuse Aldfrith's proposal when he arrived, but she had only just gotten to 2023 and still had so much to see. She and Samuel hadn't yet had a chance to discuss their future, and Murielle wasn't ready to tell Brodyn.

Squeezing her eyes shut, she imagined Brodyn's angry face when she arrived on Samuel's arm, his shouting, his disappointment. Tears streamed down her cheeks as she felt her brother's rage. He'd spent his life protecting her, asking only one thing of her, and she had failed. Still, she would not, could not, do as he asked. The ground shook, and lights flashed, but when Murielle opened her eyes, Samuel and Caitriona were gone. Had they crossed over before her and already exited the cave?

"Sam? Cait?" she called out to them but was met with only the echo of her own voice. Rain and darkness consumed the world just outside the cave, much as it had when she entered. "Sam?" Murielle spun around but saw no sign of him. He'd never leave her, nor would Cait. She knew this.

Panic welled in her chest. Running out of the cave, she noticed the slight differences from her time—the lack of shoreline and the differing foliage atop the distant cliffs. Though it was dark, she knew the silhouette of towering trees hadn't been there in her time. She was still in 2023, and they'd passed through without her.

Running back into the cave, Murielle rounded the corner to the alcove and placed her hands on the wall. "Send me home. Send me to the year 686," she whispered. After a long moment of standing still, nothing happened. "Sam!"

Defeated, Murielle slid down the cave wall, pulling her knees up to her chest. She knew he'd come back for her, but she couldn't be certain how long that would take. He couldn't just leave Cait alone. He'd have to escort her back to the village on foot and then head back, which could take hours. She'd given Cait's credit card and ID back, so for now, Murielle was stranded in this cave with nowhere to go as the freezing cave walls clawed at her flesh. Wrapping her arms around her knees, Murielle lowered her head and shivered, praying Samuel made it back before she froze to death.

"MURIELLE!" SAM SHOUTED when he turned to find her gone. "She didn't pass through!"

"Go back to her! Now!" Cait shouted. "Here!" Cait reached inside the pockets she'd had sewn into her tunics and handed Samuel her ID and credit card. "Take these for her. I have a plan, but I need time. For now, she can use these to get by. Go!"

"I can't leave you, Cait! It's not safe!"

Cait wandered toward the cave's entrance and pointed at the sunlight streaming in. "It's daylight here with clear skies. It's only a mile, and I can make it alone. But she can't make it alone in the dark and rain! She will freeze to death with her wet clothing inside that cave. If you escort me back, she will be in far greater danger than I if you left me to walk home!"

"Queen Caitriona?"

Spinning on her heels, she gasped when she saw Ronan's familiar face peering into the cave from outside. "Ronan!" She ran toward him, never so relieved to see one of her husband's guards. "What are you doing here?"

"Brodyn has had me stationed here awaited yer return. He's been down here often, as well, but had business to tend to. I'm to escort ye and Murielle back… from the future," he said with uncertainty.

"She isn't with me. Something happened, and she didn't cross through!"

"Did she choose to stay? The king will be verra angry. I have never seen him in such a rage. These past three days have been miserable for us all."

Cait shook her head. "No, I think she tried to cross through. I'm not sure, but Sam is going to cross back. Take me to Brodyn, and I'll explain everything." She spun back to look at Samuel. "Murielle must try to cross through again, eventually. She has to be present when King Aldfrith comes back from his pilgrimage. If we stand any chance of continued peace with the Britons, we cannot disrespect him."

Samuel nodded, hoping his actions hadn't caused a rift between the clans that could have untold effects on the timeline. He wasn't sure what had happened to Murielle, but he had to get back and find out.

"Cait… if she cannot pass through… if she is stuck, you know I shall take good care of her."

"I know, Sam." She smiled and took his hand, giving it an

affectionate squeeze.

"I cannot leave her alone, so if she can't pass through, this may be my last time."

Cait swallowed her emotion and nodded again. "I know that, too, Sam. You're a good man. You'll be my brother once you marry Murielle. No matter how many years separate us, we are family."

She embraced Samuel, and he did his best to choke back the emotions. He'd lived his entire life for the sole purpose of bringing Cait through the veil of time so she could fulfill the destiny of marrying Brodyn and uniting the clans, but now his life was his own to live, even if it meant never seeing her or Emilie again.

"Give Lucas and wee Anya a hug for me, and tell Emilie I will miss her."

"I will." Cait wiped a tear away before it left the corner of her eye. "Now, go. Murielle will be alone and scared."

Without another word, Samuel rushed toward the back of the cave to reach the alcove. Placing his hand on the stone, he focused on the year 2023 and Murielle. Immediately, he felt the hairs on his body rise as energy charged through his every nerve and lights flashed behind his eyelids. The ground shook, and a burst of light flooded the small space. When he opened his eyes, he saw Murielle huddled on the cave floor, shaking from the cold. His flashlight had fallen on the ground when he passed through, and it lay there now, offering a small amount of light.

"Murielle!" He sat down beside her and placed a hand on her knee. "Are you all right?"

She nodded, frowning. "Aye, I am fine. I tried to pass through and couldnae. What if I cannot go back? I'll never see my family again."

"Oh, my love. Let's get out of here and get you somewhere warm." Helping Murielle to her feet, Samuel grabbed his flashlight and escorted her out of the frigid cave and into the rainy night. The storm had weakened, and now only a light mist floated from the sky.

"Have you been waiting long?"

"Nay, verra little time at all."

"Ronan was on the other side. He's been posted by the cave for three days awaiting you and Caitriona. She is on her way back to Brodyn and will tell him everything."

"Three days? But I've only been here one day."

"It's hard to calculate the shift in time. It seems there is no one answer; all I know is time passes much faster on their side than ours."

Slowly, they walked up the trail using Samuel's flashlight. Soon, his Jeep came into view, and Samuel rushed Murielle into the passenger seat before getting in himself.

"Here." He gave Murielle Cait's ID and credit card. "Caitriona said she plans to help you stay here with me. She just needed some time. What were you thinking about when you tried to pass over?"

"I… I was thinking about Brodyn and how angry he will be with me. About how much I've disappointed him." She lowered her head and fidgeted with her fingers. "Now, I may never see him again."

"Murielle, if you came through once, I believe you should be able to cross through again. The veil is a fickle thing. I don't exactly know how it works, but if you were afraid to go to that time, perhaps it didn't think you were truly ready. Let's go home. We will sort everything out, love."

"I dinnae have a home here."

Samuel placed a finger beneath her chin and forced her to look up at him. "Your home is my home. I thought you understood that. I'm going to take the rest of this week—this sennight—off, so we can get you used to this place. We can find you new clothing, and when I return to work, you can stay in the classroom and listen, stay in my office, or stay here. Whatever you choose."

"I want a purpose, Samuel. I need to contribute something, or else I will go mad."

Samuel started Joplin and turned on the headlights. "You will find your purpose, Love. One day at a time. One moment at a time. We are together in this, and we will build a life together."

Her smile warmed his heart and raised his spirits. There was no guide for this, no book filled with magic antidotes for time travelers to settle into their new time. But Samuel had learned to navigate the harsh and often dangerous world of the Picts, where merely looking at someone wrong could mean a sword through the heart. The modern world wasn't perfect, but tolerance for different people was expected, and the chance of someone running Murielle through with a sword was minimal. They'd survive this—together.

AS THEY DROVE back to Samuel's flat, Murielle's excitement turned to trepidation. Was she stuck here? Was she ever going to learn all the oddities of this time? As she pondered this, headlights blinded her from all sides, and a loud, sudden sound startled her out of her skin, making her shriek and cling to Samuel's arm.

"It's just a car's horn. It's all right." Samuel placed a hand on her lap to calm her, but her muscles tensed as the cold fabric of her tunic froze her to the bone despite the heat Samuel blasted from the vents. She was learning a hundred new things per minute, and her head throbbed from the overwhelming sights and sounds of this time.

"Are you all right, Murielle?" Samuel asked as they pulled into his parking spot and turned off the Jeep. "You can be honest with me. If you are having second thoughts about us, or about being in this time, you can tell me."

She looked at him and shook her head. "I have no second thoughts about anything. I want to be here with ye. But, aye, 'tis overwhelming. Everything here is so bright, fast, and loud. We traveled here in twenty minutes. It would have taken hours in my time. It's amazing yet scary. I dinnae ken why cars require so many horses."

Samuel bit his lower lip in an attempt not to laugh, but she caught it and swatted at his arm, laughing. "Dinnae laugh at me!"

"I would never!" he said with feigned indignance. "I just find you absolutely, perfectly wonderful. That's all."

She looked down at herself and cringed. "I look like a drowned rat."

"Not true. I'm very much attracted to you right now, and I assure you, I've never been attracted to a drowned rat." Before she could give him a rebuttal, Samuel leaned in to silence her with a brief kiss before exiting the car and coming around to open the door.

"Why do ye open the door for me every time? I ken how to do it."

"It's called being a gentleman. I suppose it's a habit men form as they grow up. We are told to open the doors for ladies."

"I see. Sort of how a man is to drape his cloak over a puddle if a lady must step through it."

"Precisely."

They walked up the stairs, and Samuel's keys jingled as he opened the door, allowing Murielle to enter. Even the simple act of him flipping a switch and creating light from glass orbs had Murielle on edge. Hearing about the future from Sam, Emilie, and Cait was much different than experiencing it. Suddenly, she was glad Ronan couldn't pass through. He'd have lost his mind in this odd world.

"First things first. We need to get you out of those soaking wet clothes before you get sick."

"I havenae spare clothing yet."

"Follow me." Samuel moved down his short hallway to the only bedchamber in his flat, and she followed. "Here, you can wear one of my shirts. And, I have a spare, clean toothbrush in the bathroom. I keep them on hand in case I ever have overnight guests."

Murielle knew what a toothbrush was, at least. Samuel brought them to Pinnata Castra for those who knew his time-traveling secrets, and Murielle had been given one. It surely was better than scrubbing her teeth clean with a wet cloth.

"Do ye have guests sleep over often?" Suddenly, Murielle was self-conscious. Sam was an incredibly handsome, intelligent, and worldly man. He must have had many women share his bed. As she stood in his bedchamber at the foot of his bed, she wondered when the last time was that he'd shared it with a beautiful modern woman.

He seemed to sense her darkening thoughts as he stepped up behind her and wrapped his arms around her waist, scooping her damp, frizzy hair aside as he nuzzled into her neck. "I have not had anyone in this flat since I moved in two years ago."

"Nobody?" she asked, feeling her core tighten as his hands slid down her belly.

"Nobody," he murmured against her ear, sending pleasurable shivers through her body as her nape tingled. "I haven't bedded a woman in almost two years, if that's what you're asking."

She turned in his arms and raised a brow. "That is a long time for a man, or so I've been told."

Samuel chuckled. "It hasn't been easy, but since the moment I met you, I haven't had an interest in any other woman. I only want to be with you."

Murielle turned in his arms, incapable of hiding her smile. "And now ye are."

"My betrothed," Samuel said with a wide grin before kissing her on the forehead and stepping away. "You've had a long day. I will order food while you change. Feel free to use the shower. You know how to, right?"

She nodded, disappointed that he'd pulled away, but she was desperate to be rid of this wet tunic, clean herself up, and slip into his small white tunic, or *shirt* as he called it. She didn't understand what he meant about ordering food, but she decided not to waste time with questions. She'd learn more as the days wore on.

Once Murielle had taken a long, steamy shower, she dried herself off with the fluffiest towel she'd ever felt before slipping into his shirt, which fit her like a tunic that only went to her mid-thigh. She hesitated to walk into Samuel's living area wearing it, for it was much too short and thin. But, some wonderful scent wafted toward her from the kitchen area, and her stomach grumbled in protest.

Hesitantly, Murielle left his bedchamber and followed the smell of food, stopping short when she found Samuel pulling green platters out of a cabinet. Samuel's eyes widened when he spotted her. She fidgeted self-consciously when his gaze slid down her body, his dark eyes shining with approval.

"Feeling better?" he asked, clearing his throat. Murielle nodded, and rivulets of water dripped from the ends of her long hair, soaking into the already sheer fabric, making it transparent in some areas.

"What smells so delicious? I have never seen or smelled anything quite like it." Murielle stepped closer to Samuel, who used an odd wheel-like tool to cut into the circular, flat food item.

"It's pizza. A favorite in America, where I am from, but it originated in Italy, where my family still lives. You will love it." He handed her the plate, and her stomach growled again. Together, they sat on his comfortable blue couch and watched what Sam called *National Geographic* on a strange object called a *television*. It was a magical box with people inside it. Murielle understood that the people were acting, for Caitriona had told her all about her years as an actress before becoming an archaeologist. Sam told her the people inside the box could not see or hear them. There was much to learn in this new time, which felt more like a new world with switches and buttons and running water and delicious foods. But, she had the rest of her life to learn about the wonders of this time, and Sam indulged her questions with a handsome smile, which only encouraged her to continue asking them.

Murielle watched the magical box with delight as she ate the most delicious meal of her life. Now that she was clean and fed, she began to perk up. This place was wonderful, and she was here with the man she'd been in love with for years. It felt almost too good to be true, and she still had to deal with Brodyn and Aldfrith. Still, she had some time until then and vowed to make the most of the situation.

As the night wore on, Samuel talked about his work as a professor and promised to take her to work with him when he returned. Tomorrow, he said, would be devoted to taking her out to buy modern clothing and other items.

In return, she longed to teach modern people all about the Picts. There was so much these people didn't know about her culture. Somehow, she would find a way to share her knowledge, but she knew—as Cait had told her—she'd need evidence. That was the issue.

"Are you excited about getting new clothing tomorrow?" Samuel asked, placing his arm around her shoulder as she nuzzled into his side.

"Are ye saying ye dinnae want me walking around in yer old shirts?" she asked with a grin.

"Oh, no. This is for my eyes only. I like it much more than I should." Samuel placed his other hand on her thigh, and her entire body immediately responded to his touch.

"I'd begun to think mayhap ye didnae like it. Ye havenae touched me all night," Murielle said, unable to hide her trepidation. All night, she'd hoped Samuel would kiss and touch her like he had earlier. She wanted to be his in all ways, yet now that they were alone and betrothed, he barely touched her. Meanwhile, it took all her strength and power not to rip off his clothing.

Samuel turned toward her and took both her hands. "I want you so badly that I literally ache. I didn't want you to feel rushed or pressured. It's been a long two days for you."

Though she knew he was being considerate, she wanted to see passion from Samuel. She wanted him to tear her shirt off and ravish her body. Maiden or not, Murielle was well past the average age a woman in her time got married. She knew what happened between a man and a woman, and she wanted that with Samuel. The only pressure she felt was the kind building between her legs.

Standing from the couch, Murielle balled her fists and put them on her hips. "Ye ken, I fled my life to be here with ye. I turned down my only decent match for a husband, ruined a potential marriage alliance, angered my brother, and snuck away… traveling over 1,300 years into the future so that I can be with ye. And yet, ye barely looked at me since this afternoon. Have ye already lost yer interest? Was I a complete fool?"

Samuel jumped up from the couch with a look in his eyes she'd never seen before, anger mixed with sadness laced his every feature. "I spent the past two years traveling between your time and mine just to be closer to you! I have sacrificed much of my career… hell, I haven't been on a dig since Caitriona passed through the cave. I haven't slept with another woman because I wanted to spend every moment with you. I asked you to marry me! I gave you my mother's ring! Damn it, Murielle! Don't mistake my manners as a lack of desire for you. All I want—all I've wanted for so long—is to have you in my bed, to feel your naked body pressed against mine, and to bury yourself deep inside you. Above all, I want to love you, marry you, and make you happy!"

Murielle swallowed as she stood in front of Samuel. She wanted to regret upsetting him, but his temper bespoke the passion the man kept just below his cool exterior. She wanted to see the side of Samuel nobody else saw. Not the polite professor. She wanted the savage beast within, waiting to stake his claim… and mayhap she just found him. "Well then," she whispered, stepping closer to him. "What are ye waiting for?" Biting her lower lip, Murielle dared to grab the bottom hem of her shirt and tear it over her head, throwing it onto his carpeted floor and she stood naked before Samuel for the first time, a mixture of nervousness and arousal making her knees grow weak.

For a split second, Samuel didn't move, and she thought perhaps he was angry with her. But then he grabbed her arm, pulling her against him. His mouth slashed across hers, his tongue slipping between her shocked, parted lips as his hands cupped her backside almost painfully. She felt the bulge in his pants against her abdomen as he held her there against him.

Frantically, Murielle pulled Samuel's blue cotton shirt over his head, running her hands over his sleek, defined muscles. He wasn't bulky like the warriors in her village, but he owned an elegant strength that suited him perfectly. Smatterings of coarse, black hair trailed down his chest, and she reveled in the friction created when her sensitive nipples pressed against him.

Samuel wrapped his strong arms around her waist, lifting her off the ground. Murielle squealed and wrapped her legs around his waist for support as he walked into his bedchamber and dropped her onto his bed. It was the softest bed she'd ever laid on, but sleep was the last thing on her mind. His bed was larger than the one from the motel, with blue and green plaid sheets neatly covering the mattress. A faint light atop one small table illuminated the room in a soft glow.

"God, you're breathtaking, Murielle," Samuel sighed as he undid the fastenings of his jeans and shucked them off, kicking them away with single-minded determination.

His proud erection pulsed with need, and Murielle gaped at its size. She had never seen a man's anatomy before, but she imagined Samuel was much better built and much more endowed than the typical man.

Murielle lay on the bed, propped up on her elbows as she watched the man she loved with awe. Her heart pounded like a drum against her ribs, and her breathing grew labored as he stared at her naked body like a starved wolf ready to feast. "You're... you're perfect," she croaked. And he was, in every single way. And soon, he'd be her husband. No matter what anyone else said or what stood in their way, she'd be his wife.

With the swiftness of a feral cat, Samuel wrapped his hands around her ankles and pulled her closer to the edge of the bed. She yelped at the sudden move but loved the way he commanded her body. "I've been dreaming of this moment for so long," he whispered, getting down on his knees in front of her. "Now that it's here, I can't decide where to start."

Samuel placed his warm palms on her knees and spread them, exposing her most intimate area to his gaze. She ached, throbbed, and yearned for him to do what he did earlier again, but she also wanted to bring him equal pleasure. "I'm not sure what to do," she whispered, suddenly feeling uncertain of herself. For all of her bluster, Murielle was as virginal as could be.

Samuel climbed atop her on the bed, hovering over her with his arms on either side of her head. She stared into the depths of his dark eyes, feeling his breath fan across her face as he leaned in to capture her lips with his. Lingeringly, Samuel worshipped her mouth with his, sliding his tongue into her mouth with equal measures of painful slowness and beautiful delicacy. How she had longed for this moment, and here Samuel was, his naked body lying atop hers. One hand wandered down her body as he trailed kisses across her throat, still slightly hovering above her. His manhood pressed against her as he shifted to capture a nipple in his mouth. Murielle gasped and quivered as new sensations enveloped her in a blissful euphoria. She loved the slow sensuality he offered but was desperate to finally feel him inside her.

"Samuel," she whispered his name as she squirmed beneath him, the need in her core overwhelming her senses. "Please."

He looked at her with lust-glazed eyes, a hint of pink in his cheeks. "I've wanted you... wanted this for so long. I'm torn between taking my time to savor it or letting myself go completely."

"We have the rest of our lives, aye? I cannae wait any longer, Sam!"

His muscles bunched and tensed as he lay above her, slightly propped up by his arms as he closed his eyes and took a deep breath. When he moved one hand and shifted, she felt his hardness between her legs just before he pressed against her mound. "I love you, Murielle." Before she could respond, Samuel released a guttural groan as he thrust into her. She cried out and held her breath as the slight stinging sensation of breaking her maidenhood slowly disappeared. She'd expected it, but the pain was there and gone in an instant. Now, she was no longer a maiden. Instead, she had the best man in the world lying atop her, pushing himself deeper inside her, becoming one with her. She moved against him, clinging to his backside as he rhythmically thrust his hips.

"Are you all right?" he asked breathlessly, looking down at her. She nodded and slid her hands up to his back, preferring to show him rather than use words, for she couldn't begin to find any that expressed how truly all right she was.

Arching against him, Murielle urged him to go deeper and faster. Samuel cupped one of her breasts with one hand as he straightened his back and plunged deeper into her, using his other hand to stroke that magical spot between her legs. Murielle couldn't decide whether to close her eyes and savor every moment or keep them open and watch him move against her.

She decided to watch him, for he was the most beautiful man she'd ever known, and watching him flex and move as his hips thrust rhythmically only heightened her experience. This seemed like a fantasy, but it was so much better than she'd ever imagined in her dreams. The real Samuel was sensual, passionate, and perhaps even more experienced than she expected.

Shocks of ecstasy surged through her body, and she cried out, digging her nails into his back as he quickened his pace. His body tensed, and his hands slipped to her hips. His fingers dug into her flesh as he thrust, groaned, and threw his head back just before shuddering against her.

Stars exploded behind her eyelids, and she gave herself to the pure love and pleasure flooding her veins. Samuel panted for breath when he released a final groan and collapsed beside her, pulling her into his arms. His sweat-slicked limbs encased her, and she found it wholly enthralling to know she'd affected him as powerfully as he had her.

"Sam," she whispered as her head rested on his heaving chest, his heart pounding beneath his ribs hard enough for her to feel. "That was... everything I ever thought it would be, and so much more."

"You're everything I thought you'd be and so much more," he whispered, kissing her forehead.

With her lust temporarily sated and her energy thoroughly spent, Murielle felt the weariness she'd been fighting finally consume her. Placing her arm across Samuel's bared chest, Murielle couldn't stop herself from smiling as she allowed her eyes to close as sleep swept her away.

CHAPTER SEVEN

T EARS OF LAUGHTER slid down Murielle's face as she sat on Samuel's couch, watching reruns of some show he'd put on for her. Even though she didn't understand much of their conversation, watching six friends sit on an orange couch inside a place where coffee was sold was somehow the most fantastic thing she'd ever seen. He'd told her this show might help her understand modern life a bit more, even if it was over twenty years old.

Last night had been the most wonderful night of her life, and the soreness between her legs and aching in her muscles every time she moved was a sweet reminder of the two times they'd made love last the night before. After the first, more urgent coupling, they'd fallen asleep in one another's arms. But at some time in the night, Samuel awoke and began placing soft, sweet kisses on the nape of her neck, and soon, she felt him slipping inside her from behind as they lay in bed, slowly making love while he reached between her legs, touching that one magical spot again. At that moment, Murielle discovered that there were many ways to make love, and she looked forward to learning them all.

Sitting in Samuel's blue and red plaid shirt with buttons lining the front, Murielle waited for him to return. After sleeping in and making her a delicious breakfast of bacon, scrambled eggs, and pancakes, he'd cranked up the heater and left to get her a few basic supplies like a change of clothes and personal care items. He promised to take her out again when he came home, but she couldn't very well leave the house in her old tunic, which was now torn and stained from her adventure through time.

When someone on the show put a whole uncooked turkey on her head, Murielle burst into laughter again, yet she was confused as to why anyone would want to do such a thing. She hoped she'd never be expected to do that. Was it some sort of modern tradition?

A knock on the door made Murielle stop laughing and sit straight up on the couch, unsure what to do. Maybe if she remained silent, they'd go away.

"Samuel?" She heard a woman's voice filtering in from the other side of the door. "Are you home? I hear the television." The woman knocked again, and Murielle sighed as she shuffled toward the door. She wasn't dressed well enough to meet Samuel's friends, but she didn't want to be rude. If she was going to be his wife, her job would be to welcome his friends into their home.

Slowly opening the door, Murielle peeked her head out from around the back of the door. Spotting a slim, tall woman with red hair, Murielle frowned. "May I help you?"

The woman also frowned and took a slight step back. "I'm looking for Sam."

"He is out right now," Murielle said. "He should be back soon. 'Tis been a few hours since he left."

"Might I come in and wait for him?" the woman asked. "I have something of his he may want back."

Again, Murielle frowned. All she wore was his old shirt and a pair of his boxers, which hung quite loosely around her waist. "I'm not properly dressed."

"Can you get properly dressed?" the woman asked hesitating-ly, tilting her head. Murielle felt her cheeks warm with embarrassment at the reasonable question, feeling childish and uncomfortable.

"Nay, I cannae. I... I just arrived and my only clothing got ruined in the storm. Samuel ran out to buy me clothing. Ye can call him if ye wish to locate him."

The woman crinkled her brow as she observed Murielle. She wore a tightly fitted black skirt that clung to her body and ended at her knees. Her shoes were bright red and had what looked like sticks attached to their soles. Their color matched the woman's painted lips and blouse.

"You are not from around here, are you?" The woman asked.

Murielle shook her head, growing more uncomfortable by the moment. If this woman began asking questions that Murielle couldn't answer, she'd not have Samuel's help. The woman's eyes narrowed as she scrutinized Murielle's features and forced a smile. "So, you're the woman Samuel was talking about the other night."

Having no idea what the woman spoke about, Murielle remained silent.

"My name is Eva. I work at the university with Samuel. Has he mentioned me?" Again, Murielle shook her head.

"What is your name?"

"M-Murielle," she stuttered, wishing Samuel would return and save her from this awkward interaction.

"May I come in, Murielle? I promise I won't judge your clothing… or lack thereof… I wouldn't normally insist, but I do have something of Samuel's that is quite important."

Nodding, Murielle stepped back to open the door, beginning to panic and running out of options.

"Eva?" Both Murielle and the woman followed the familiar voice. Samuel climbed the last step to the second floor and walked toward them carrying several black bags.

"Samuel!" Eva said, her face lighting up.

He cast Murielle an apologetic look and came to stand beside her, blocking her from Eva's view. "I'm surprised to see you here. How do you know where I live?"

"That's why I came all this way. Here." She handed Samuel what looked like his ID card. "You left this at the pub this weekend. I was going to give it to you at work today, but you had a TA filling in. I figured I'd take the time to bring it to you and see if everything is all right. I had thought only injury or illness would keep you away from your job, but…" She raised a sculpted brow and smiled knowingly at Murielle. "I see you've played hooky."

"Thank you," Sam said with irritation lacing his voice. "Come on inside." He stepped aside so Eva could enter his flat, and Murielle cowered behind him, embarrassed by the entire situation. She felt as if she had been caught in bed with him by his wife. This woman appeared to know Samuel quite well. Had Samuel lied to her about not being with other women?

"Give me a moment," Sam said to Eva before taking Murielle by the hand and dragging her into his bedchamber. "I'm so sorry," he said hastily, tossing the bags on the bed. "I went out for drinks with some other professors this weekend. I must have left my ID at the bar. It has my address on it."

Murielle understood enough of what he said in context, though weekends and addresses were still new to her. Murielle suddenly wondered if she's ever fit into this world. There was a beautiful, intelligent woman in Sam's flat who knew this world, *his* world. Eva obviously knew Sam well enough to have ended up with his ID and felt comfortable enough to show up at his doorstep and invite herself inside.

"Look in those bags. I didn't buy too much—just enough to get you started. Then we can go out and get more. I guessed your sizes, but I think I did ok. Here… put these on…" He pulled out a pair of soft, black pants that felt smooth and stretchy in her hands, then a fuzzy, purple tunic with long sleeves. "Yoga pants, a sweater, and… a scarf," he said as he pulled out a long strip of woven wool. At least, it appeared to be wool. Who knew what materials any of this was?

"Thank ye… is this really what women wear? This isn't any-thing like what Eva is wearing."

"Oh, yes. Yoga pants, sweaters, and scarves are timeless, especially here in Scotland during October. Also, I got you a bra. I hope it fits." Samuel pulled out an odd piece of fabric that appeared to have two bowls on the front. It was white and sheer with hooks at the end.

Scrunching her face, she held it up. "What is this?"

"It's for… uh… your breasts."

Murielle looked down at her breasts and frowned. "I do not understand."

"May I show you?" Hesitantly, she nodded and handed him the bra. Nimbly, his fingers unbuttoned her shirt, and it slid off her shoulders and onto the floor, leaving her naked aside from Samuel's boxers. Samuel cupped her breasts and groaned. "If we were alone right now…"

"Well, we arnae." She tried not to sound irritated, but despite Eva's kind smile and innocent reason for appearing on Samuel's doorstep, Murielle felt uneasy at the situation. How many other women would be showing up at his door? Though, she decided not to ask him, afraid she was being jealous or irrational.

Samuel frowned as he placed the bra over her breasts and reached around to clasp the back. "Perfect fit," he said with pride before pulling off some odd, rectangular parchment dangling from the back. "There. I removed the tag. Turn around." She did as he said, looking at the odd contraption cradling her breasts.

"I dinnae understand what this is for."

"It's what modern women wear to support their breasts," he said with a shrug.

She slipped the yoga pants and sweater on, looking at herself in his wardrobe mirror. "I am dressed like a man."

Samuel laughed and leaned in to kiss the top of her head. "You are dressed like many modern women."

"But Eva is wearing something different."

"There are many styles of clothing in this time. She's dressed for her profession. I'm sure she wears similar clothes to these on her days off… not that I know," he said, putting up his hands in defense when Murielle scrunched her brows and narrowed her eyes. She didn't like that this beautiful woman clearly was interested in Samuel, but as long as he didn't share those feelings, there was nothing to do.

Samuel guided Murielle out to the living area, where Eva stood, looking bored. When she saw Samuel enter the room with Murielle at his side, the woman lit up like a flower in the sun, walking over and placing a hand on Samuel's arm. "Will you be back in the office tomorrow?"

"I took the week off. I had to take today off to help Murielle go shopping." Eva cocked her head in confusion. "It's a long story."

Eva looked Murielle up and down, pursing her lips as she nodded. "Perhaps I can help."

"What?" Both Murielle and Samuel asked in tandem.

Eva crinkled her nose and looked at Sam. "I can see you tried your best, but this needs a woman's touch. Murielle said she isn't from around here. I know the area well and have a little time before I need to head home. I came all this way—I may as well be of use."

Murielle clutched onto Samuel's arm, silently willing him to reject the offer. She didn't know this woman at all, and it wouldn't take more than a few moments alone before Eva realized Murielle was very different. She hadn't even existed in 2023 for more than two days, and most of that time had been spent inside his flat. She understood nothing about the world outside these walls.

"Oh, I couldn't put you out like that," Samuel said to Murielle's relief. "You've been plenty helpful bringing my ID back. I couldn't put this on you."

"Nonsense," Eva responded, waving off his concern and widening her smile. "I can see she is... in need of help." Eva scrolled Murielle's length with her discerning eyes again. "She is a beautiful woman with a fantastic figure. But this outfit doesn't do her justice. It won't take long, I promise. Let me help you guys out. It's the least I can do for a good friend and his... girlfriend?"

"Fiancée, actually," Samuel said, looking at Murielle with a smile that made her heart flutter and her insides melt.

Eva's gaze snapped to Samuel, and her smile wavered. *"Fiancée.* I see. I suppose congratulations are in order. No wonder you took some time off work to celebrate. But Samuel, we really do need you back at the department soon to prepare for lab clinicals. All hands on deck."

"Thank you, Eva. That means a lot coming from you. And, of course, I shall return to work by next Monday." Smiling, Samuel put a hand around Murielle's waist and pulled her into his side, looking her in the eyes. "Murielle, before you head out with Eva, there are new boots for you in our bedroom."

"Will you come with me for a moment?" Murielle walked down the small corridor leading to his bedchamber, turning on her heels when she heard Sam enter behind her.

"This is a terrible Idea. She will notice that I am different. Already, she took one look at me and kenned I was not from here. I dinnae think she likes me."

"Oh, come on. She just met you. She's going to love you."

"It's verra nice of her to drive so far to bring yer ID to ye. It's a three-hour drive there and back. But I cannae help but think she had other intentions. Women arenae so different here than in my time."

"She likes me, yes. But I love you. I've told her as much, and she accepts that. She seems like she means well, and it would be great for you to spend time in the company of a modern woman. I genuinely do believe she is trying to be kind, Murielle. Why else would she offer?"

Murielle hesitated for a moment before letting out a breath of resignation. "All right."

"Great. I'm sure everything will be fine. She'll know what you need." He gave her a soft kiss, which helped to ease her tension, but only slightly. She had a bad feeling about this woman.

Leaving the room, Samuel held Murielle's hand as they walked toward Eva, and Murielle didn't miss when the woman's gaze landed on their linked fingers, focusing on her ring.

"Ready?" Eva asked. Murielle nodded. She wasn't at all ready, but if she wanted to live in this time with Samuel, she had to get used to the people here. What better way to learn than immersing herself? She only hoped she didn't embarrass herself.

Samuel handed Murielle his credit card and kissed her before she headed out of the house. Awkwardly, Murielle followed Eva to her car, which was shiny, red, and smaller than Samuel's Jeep.

When they got into the car, Eva pushed a button that started the car, and Murielle did her best not to appear impressed. This was likely a normal thing, even if Samuel's used a key. The car peeled out with a screech, and Murielle clung to the door's side handle to brace herself.

Just act as if nothing around you is unfamiliar or strange, Murielle silently reminded herself as they passed different colored lights and different types of cars.

Eva eyed Murielle wearily when they stopped at a red light. "You know. When I was with Samuel the other night, he said he'd lost you. So, how did you end up back at his place?"

Murielle wasn't sure if the woman actually cared or was just being nosy like the gossiping hens in her village. She decided to try to be as honest as possible. "Well, I come from a small, more traditional village. My brother tried to arrange my marriage with a local laird, but I ran away to be with Samuel."

"A laird?" Eva said with a snort. "You turned down a laird of a castle to live with Sam in his 600 square foot flat?" Eva gave her the side eye again, and Murielle nodded.

"How did you meet Sam in the first place?"

Murielle bit her lip as they flew down the road again, passing huge buildings with dozens of windows. The iron birds Cait had told her all about flew overhead, undoubtedly carrying many passengers. What a bizarre world this was. Close to Samhain, the festival called Halloween in this time, Murielle saw stores decorated with spider webs, skeletons, and carved gourds, and she stared in awe to see how her people's sacred fire festivals had changed and survived in the year 2023.

Murielle decided on a way to explain everything to Eva without offering too many details.

"Well, Samuel was in charge of a dig inside a cave near my village, and he came there for supplies a few times. We became friends and eventually fell in love."

"Ah, yes. I recall. One of his team members went missing during that dig and then later showed up pregnant with some man's baby. It was all over the news, like a movie."

"Aye, she hit her head and was taken in to be cared for at my village. She married my brother, actually."

"I heard she went off the grid after she was found. Though, Sam says he still sees her. Burghead is only eight miles from here. Is that why Samuel got this flat? So, he could be closer to you?"

Murielle nodded, afraid to say more than necessary.

Eva continued, "I had wondered where Samuel disappeared to so often and why. You do not speak with a typical Scottish burr, do you? I obviously have an American accent, myself. I'm from Chicago. Moved to Aberdeen to teach at university but will likely be relocating to Edinburgh. Does your village still speak the older language… Gaelic?"

Murielle began to panic. Even Gaelic wasn't as old as her language. It became popular in Scotland perhaps a hundred years before her time and had somehow survived to this day, but her language was completely forgotten. Murielle simply nodded again.

"If your village is so close, why do you have no clothing? Surely, you could have packed a bag."

"I…" Murielle hesitated to answer that question. She knew Eva was looking for information, but she wasn't certain why. "I ran away from home before my brother could make me marry someone else."

"How old are you, Murielle?"

"Twenty-three."

"You know Samuel is thirty-six, right? Isn't he a little old for you?"

Murielle was done with Eva's investigation and her condescending tone. Her demeanor had changed from kind to inquisitive, and now she was borderline hostile. "No, I do not think he's too old for me." Already, she was overwhelmed by this woman and her questions. Murielle suspected that Eva had no intention of actually helping her.

Eva glared at Murielle before looking back at the road and crinkling her nose as if she smelled something unpleasant. "I'm just curious how a simple girl like you was able to capture the heart of a man like Samuel. He had two PhDs before he was 30 years old. He's been active in the field since he was twenty. He zoomed through his courses faster than anyone else. Not only that, we both know Samuel is a solid ten."

Murielle had no idea what that even meant, but she grew more aggravated hearing this woman tell her about Samuel as if she didn't already know.

"You do realize I am aware of all of that? I'm his betrothed. I know everything about Samuel."

"Betrothed?" Eva shot Murielle an odd look before turning off on a side road and pulling over. "Who says 'betrothed' anymore? Look, Murielle… *sweetie*." Eva put the car in park and turned to look at her. "You're a beautiful young woman with your whole life ahead of you. There are many things you do not understand about life. *I'm* Samuel's age. I also have a PhD. Have you even graduated from college?"

Murielle was done with this woman's rudeness. Honesty wasn't working, so now it was time for a lie. "Yes. I did. I also studied anthropology."

"Where at?" Eva raised a brow. She was a professor at the best anthropology school in Scotland. There was no way Murielle could lie and say she went there.

"Yer questions wear on my patience, Eva. 'Tis none of yer business, nor is my relationship with Samuel."

"You're right. You aren't my business, but Samuel is. I've

known him for many years, and I know you are not what he needs. Some young, silly girl from a small village who has to run away from home to marry him?" Eva shook her head. "I don't know what sort of spell you wove on him, but I feel obligated to end this insanity before Sam spends the rest of his life catering to an infant."

Eva started the car again and continued to drive down a long road toward the coast. "You know what *is* your business, Murielle?" She asked, raising a brow as she turned down another street. "I slept with Samuel. Did he tell you that?"

Murielle gasped, then pursed her lips to prevent any further reaction from giving away the sudden onslaught of pain slashing through her heart. She reminded herself that whatever Samuel did before her wasn't her business. Still, if this was true, why was he going out for drinks with this woman and allowing her to take Murielle shopping?

A sudden and terrifying thought struck her. Men in her time kept both wives and mistresses. Was Samuel planning to keep Eva as a mistress, hoping Murielle would approve? No... surely, she was overthinking this.

"Oh, so he didn't tell you?" Eva chuckled. "It was two years ago, just before that cave dig, actually. We were still teaching in California back then, but we were both recruited to stay as professors here. He accepted the job first, and I accepted, as well. It was a step up, but it also allowed me to stay closer to Samuel. Naturally, after our affair, I thought more would happen between us. But then... well, I suppose he met *you*." Eva scowled with disgust. "The man is a legend in the bedroom, isn't he? Hung like a horse, too." She turned to look at Murielle and winked before turning back to the road.

Swallowing her humiliation and pain, Murielle feigned disinterest and shrugged. "What he did before me isnae my business. Samuel is in love with me now, and that's what matters."

"Oh, you poor sweet, innocent child. Love and sex are two entirely different things. Samuel is regarded as the most available bachelor in the archaeology community. Students and staff alike pine for his attention. Do you really think he won't stray after much time passes? How certain are you that you will keep his interest?"

"You don't know what you're talking about," Murielle snapped, though she found herself struggling to breathe. Her stomach tightened as images of Samuel lying atop this woman assaulted her imagination.

But, that was his past, Murielle reminded herself. His attraction and romantic feelings for Eva disappeared two years ago—because he fell in love with Murielle, and that's what mattered.

"I'm afraid I do know what I'm talking about. Like you, I was young and in love with a handsome professor. Oh, I thought I was special. You need to understand that Sam has girls your age throwing themselves at his feet every day, visiting his office, wearing their low-cut tops with pushed-up cleavage, and batting their long, fake lashes. They are dying to become a notch on his bedpost. He has several notches, I might add. Perhaps he stopped sleeping with other women for you, but how long do you expect his interest to last? One year? Two? What happens when he travels to another country with eager, young women at his side, desperate to prove themselves worthy of both his team and his bed?"

"Stop!" Murielle shouted, covering her ears as tears began to slide down her cheeks. "Why are you being cruel to me?"

"I am trying to help you. A man as worldly as Samuel has too much experience and too many admirers to be pinned down to one woman forever. He may think he will be faithful, but they never are." Eva glanced at Murielle and sighed. "I need to tell you something."

Murielle creased her brow and bit her lower lip, desperate to fight back any more tears. This woman could be telling Murielle nothing but lies, after all. Women really hadn't changed. Just as Sarah, from her own time had lied to Emilie about sleeping with Goodwin, Eva could be lying about Sam. Although, he was very well endowed, as she mentioned. Perhaps Eva merely guessed accurately.

The area they drove through seemed vaguely familiar, though entirely different at the same time. A sign on the side of the road said "Burghead," and Murielle panicked. Worse, the symbol on the sign was the Pictish bull, her brother's sign. "Pictish fort one mile ahead" was printed on the sign. Where was Eva taking her?

"Why are we here?" she asked, trying to open the car door, panicking more when it wouldn't open.

"You do not recognize your own hometown?" Eva asked as she parked in front of a small building.

"I do," Murielle lied. "But why are we here?"

"Murielle, you are a runaway. I realize you're an adult, but something is off about all of this. Is your brother or family abusive?"

Murielle shook her head.

"Good. Then, I intend to help you get back to them."

"I'm not getting out."

Eva narrowed her gaze on Murielle, pursing her red-painted lips. "You prefer to stay in the car with the woman Samuel kissed just two nights ago?"

"Wh-what?" Murielle asked, stunned by Eva's words, feeling nauseous and suddenly weak as her limbs shook. "That's not true."

Eva gave her a dramatic pout, and Murielle recognized it as insincere and condescending. "Believe whatever you want. Ask Samuel. If he's an honest man, he will tell you that we kissed two nights ago after leaving the pub. I wanted more, I admit. I always want more from that man," Eva sighed. "Now, get out and go home. I don't have time for anymore of this nonsense. It's a long way home for me."

When Murielle froze and looked out the window, wiping away her tears as she wrung her hands together, Eva sighed with frustration. "It's not a huge deal, Murielle. I'm sure you can just pack a bag this time and call Samuel to come pick you up. Better yet, drive yourself back. You *can* drive, right?"

Murielle shook her head and swallowed her panic. "Nay, I cannae. Ye had no intention of helping me, did ye?"

"Oh, I did. I admit I wanted to learn more about you in the process. But after all you've told me, my gut says something is off about you. Besides, I said I'd help you get clothes. You have clothes at home, I presume. Now, go home—let your brother know you are safe."

"I… I cannae. I have nothing." She suddenly felt irrelevant, pathetic, and helpless. Perhaps all of this had been nothing more than a foolish dream. Murielle obviously didn't belong here, and if Eva was an example of a typical modern woman, Murielle wanted nothing more to do with this place.

"Your family is here, no?" Eva asked irritably.

How could Murielle explain that her family hadn't been here in over 1,300 years? She'd left Cait's ID and credit card at Samuel's flat and had no phone. That had been on their list of things to acquire today before Samuel allowed this horrible woman to take her out.

Disgust for both herself and Samuel roiled in her gut. First, he'd pushed her away, telling her to marry another man. Next, he confessed his love, kissed her for the first time, walked away, then kissed this woman right after—on the same night. Had Samuel meant anything he'd said? Had he truly meant to return to her once he knew she wasn't Aldfrith's wife, or had all of it been an excuse to return to his own time and rekindle a relationship with Eva? Murielle couldn't believe that. Not her Samuel.

Panic set in, and Murielle reached out to touch Eva's arm in a plea. "I cannae be here. Ye dinnae understand. I have nobody and nothing here. I have nowhere to go!"

"So, your family is not from here?"

"Aye, they are, but they arenae here anymore."

Eva pulled a mirror out of her bag and re-applied her red lipstick. "That's too bad. I suggest you get out and start walking through town to find a ride back. Maybe you'll find some clothing stores on the way. Better yet, maybe you'll find a man more your age and more your… intellectual equal."

"But… I—"

"Get. Out!" Eva snapped. "I didn't come all this way to babysit Samuel's infantile fiancée. I'm sure you'll find your way back to him. And, when you do, tell Samuel he can't just kiss me one day and get engaged the next. If he wants to play games with me, I'll play them right back."

The door beside Murielle clicked, and Eva raised her brow again. "That's your cue to leave."

Murielle realized there was no reasoning with Eva, nor was she willing to further humiliate herself and beg. She opened the car door and stepped out. The second she shut the door behind her, Eva sped off, leaving Murielle in a cloud of dust.

Standing in the town that had once been her home, Murielle wrapped her arms around herself and looked about, unsure where to go or what to do. It was late afternoon, and the autumn sky was heavy with dark clouds. Colorful leaves littered the street as the wind blew to the south. The familiar scent of brine wafted in the air, and Murielle forced her feet to move toward the coast, following the main road leading through town. She passed several buildings and onlookers, perhaps not used to seeing newer faces in their small village. Murielle understood that all too well. Were any of these people her descendants? That thought stopped her in her tracks as she tried not to panic.

Cars sped past her with their many horses for power, iron birds flew overhead, and unfamiliar music played through some invisible source she couldn't see. She was stranded in this strange place. She had Samuel's credit card but nothing else. No phone, no knowledge of his phone number or how this modern world really worked. She was, for the first time in her life, utterly alone.

Passing what appeared to be a kirk, Murielle looked around for anyone who could help her. She saw a small business to her right, but it appeared to be closed.

The town's welcome sign had mentioned a visitor center, and though Murielle hadn't any idea what that was, she was a visitor and hoped they could help.

A couple passed by, their laughter floating on the wind and their breath coming out as visible wisps as they held white paper cups in their gloved hands. The scarves wrapped around their necks and woolen coats enveloping their bodies protected them from the biting wind, but Murielle's sweater and scarf did little to stave off the increasing chill as she grew closer to the coast and the sky darkened.

Homes lined the street, many with small cars parked out front. Children's laughter rang out from somewhere unseen, but it helped to lighten her mood to know this place still lived on with happiness and laughter, even if her own village no longer existed.

As she continued down the wide street, she stopped when she saw a sign for the Pictish well. Had their well actually survived the hands of time? Murielle wandered in that direction, only to find she couldn't access it. An old man with graying hair and wearing a beige plaid coat smiled as he walked past Murielle, and she sucked in a breath to gather her courage. This would be the first modern person she spoke to without being introduced to them by Caitriona or Samuel.

"Excuse me… Sir?" The old man turned and smiled.

"Good evenin' young lady. What would ye want from an auld man like me?" There was kindness and humor in his tone, and she felt safe enough with him.

"I'm lost. I… I need to find a ride out of here. Where is the visitor center?"

With a shaky hand, he pointed up the road. "Follow that road all the way. 'Tis a large, round, white building that stands atop the hill where the fort once was. They have telephones. Ye can make some calls. May as well enjoy the scenery while ye are here. Ye ken, we have the remains of a Pictish fort at the furthest end of the village. Are ye from around here, lass?"

She nodded. "I am, but 'tis been a verra long time since I've been in the area."

He nodded and smiled. "Deep roots here. My pa liked to say we were descendants of the Picts, but I dinnae ken how he came to believe such things. They disappeared and were never heard from again. How could he be certain?" The old man chuckled. "I think we all like to believe we are connected to the past. Gives us a sense of purpose, ye ken?"

Murielle felt cold waves of panic wash over her. The Picts vanished from history? Why? Why did nobody know what happened to her people or what their symbols meant? Their monks did record it all within the walls of the wee kirk in their village. Had everything been destroyed? Suddenly, flashes of violent wars destroying Pictish homes, lives, and villages antagonized her imagination, and she wondered if it was all her fault for leaving. Perhaps war was waged between Brodyn and Aldfrith after she left, which caused a weakening in the Pict's defenses, which led to their ultimate downfall.

Shivers ran up her spine, and she wrapped her arms around her body to hide her trembling.

"Are ye all right?"

"Aye. Thank ye verra much for the help." She forced a smile and turned down the street the man pointed to, walking toward the town's northernmost point. She saw the white-washed building in the distance, and her heart raced to know it stood just where her village once had. Despite the change in buildings and roads, the sealine was the same she used to stare at when she climbed the ramparts and looked over the parapet. People have changed what they can in this world, but the ancient sea remained untouched despite its rising tides.

When she reached the visitor center and saw the pictures and signs hanging that depicted her people and their way of life, she felt like the world had opened up and swallowed her whole. The layout of their village was primarily accurate, but some of the clothing was not, though it was close.

The bull symbol was depicted on many stones inside the

small museum, reminding Murielle of her brother and the pain she had caused by running away. He was nothing but dust beneath her feet now. He was gone, and she was all alone. Had he died before seeing her again? Had they ever repaired their relationship after she left?

Relics she'd seen in person only two days ago now littered display tables as reminders of a forgotten past, making Murielle dizzy and nauseous with grief. Tears slid down her cheeks as she read the plaques, looked at the reconstruction of her home, and remembered Eva's cruelty. Panic tightened in her chest. Never had Murielle felt so bereft.

"Excuse me, miss. I dinnae mean to interrupt. Are ye all right?"

Sniffling, Murielle sucked in a deep breath and turned, preparing to put on a brave face. But when a familiar face stared back at her, all bravado fled. Ronan stared back at her, only this man wore a name tag that said "Callum." He had the same hair color, eyes, cheekbones, and proud nose as her beloved friend and guard. This man had to be Ronan's descendant, but how could he look so similar after so many generations?

Seeing the concern in his blue gaze, Murielle immediately felt a connection with this man. "I am lost. I dinnae have a phone or a car. I have my fiancé's credit card, but no way to get home."

The young man nodded and smiled. "I will help ye, miss. What is yer fiancé's name, and where does he live?"

"Samuel Sullivan. He lives in Elgin."

"Verra well, miss. I will look him up. I see ye are verra interested in the Picts. Have ye any questions for me before I look for your fiancé?"

She shook her head, then paused. One question plagued her. "What happened to the Picts? Why did they disappear?"

He shrugged. "Nobody kens for certain. The last king of the Picts, Kenneth mac Alpin, became the first king of Scotland when the tribes united. Many historians believe the Picts assimilated with the other tribes. But we've yet to find any texts left behind by the Picts. 'Tis odd since they were early Christians and did have monks and scholars who recorded everything. But those texts are gone… likely forever." He shrugged. "I will be right back while I try to locate a Samuel Sullivan in Elgin."

"Thank ye," she whispered, looking back down at the model of her village. The three walls guarding their hillfort were clearly marked, as was the hill her home once resided on. Looking at another plaque, she gasped and held onto the wall when she read that this visitor center resided within the same upper bailey where her house once stood. Could she and Brodyn be standing in the same space, just 1,300 years separated?

It felt like a fist had slammed into her lungs as she struggled to breathe through her rising torment. She gasped for air and slid down the wall, no longer able to see through the blur of unshed tears or the dizziness making the room spin.

"Miss!" The man ran back after several minutes and kneeled beside her. "I have located him! He's on his way! Ye dinnae seem well… do ye wish to find a bench or have some water?"

"I am not well, Ronan… I mean Callum…" She hiccupped and wrung her hands. "Nothing is right!"

He furrowed his dark brows. "How did ye ken the name Ronan?" he whispered. "'Tis a verra common name in my family. I am one of the first males born in my line not to have the name. It's said to have been in the family since the time of the Picts. Ye see, my family have lived here at Burghead or in the neighboring area for as long as we can recall."

Murielle swiped a tear away, trying to explain her clumsy words. "I used to live here, remember? I believe my family kenned yers. Ye look like yer pa." She lied and prayed he didn't question her.

He nodded and smiled. "Makes sense, then. I do look like him, rest his soul. I cannae shake the feeling that ye suffer greatly for reasons unknown. Do ye wish to speak of it?"

She shook her head. "Thank ye, Callum, but nay. I am simply overwhelmed. Perhaps realizing how much history we stand on, the lives lost, the people forgotten. 'Tis quite depressing if ye think about it."

"Aye, I do think of it often. When I stand on the remains of my ancestors… well, it often makes me queasy, Miss. Ma used to tell tales of those who could travel through the stones. She said they live among us and ken that which we cannae. I always wanted to be one of them, between ye and me. I tried. Ye ken that cave just a mile east of here, along the coast?"

Murielle popped her head up and looked at him, frowning and nodding. "Two years ago, an archaeologist went missing there. People searched for weeks. She showed up out of the blue, pregnant! Can ye believe it? I think she passed through the veil. I've tried myself, but alas, I cannae. Perhaps 'tis all a local legend, but I cannae shake the feeling that this land is connected to the past."

Looking up into Callum's innocent eyes, Murielle bit her lower lip, wondering if she could confide in him. "What would ye do if ye came across one of these travelers?" she asked carefully.

His eyes widened at the question. "I dinnae ken—never thought about it. I think I'd believe it. Aye, for certain, I would. And I'd ask a million questions until they tired of me," Callum said with a laugh.

Swallowing, Murielle took a deep breath and touched his hand. "Callum, may I confide in ye, even if ye believe I'm insane?"

"Ye are a traveler, Miss, arnae ye?"

Murielle's stomach tightened and she hesitated. Dare she tell him the truth? Deciding the worst that could happen was he believed her to be a madwoman, she sucked in a deep breath, closed her eyes, and nodded. "How did ye ken?"

"I had a feeling. Usually, visitors have phones, ID, or cars, yet ye dinnae have any. Ye appear lost, and not in the usual way. Also, ye gaze at these artifacts as if ye ken more about them than we do."

"That's because I do, Callum. I called ye Ronan because ye

are the identical image of my guard. I believe he is yer ancestor. I see it in yer eyes and feel it in yer being."

"Ye dinnae mean…"

"I am the sister of King Brodyn, the man whose bull symbol ye have all over this town." She held a finger to his lips when he began to speak. "Please… dinnae say a word. I cannae explain it all right now, but ye must listen. I have nothing in this time, and I am scared. My home was once on this spot. Being here is the greatest torture!" Murielle covered her face as fresh tears slid down her cheeks. "I just want to go home!"

Callum patted her on the shoulder. "I believe ye, Miss… what is yer name?"

"Murielle. Murielle Mac Cuill."

"That was King Brodyn's surname… of course," he said warmly. "I believe ye. My father died twenty years ago, just after I was born. By the looks of ye, ye are too young to have kenned him. Do I look so much like my ancestor, Ronan?"

Murielle nodded and sniffled. "Just like him. 'Tis quite baffling that 1,300 years can pass, yet his very likeness remains. He was… nay, *is* a good man. And, if ye are anything like him, Callum, I believe ye are trustworthy. I just need someone to understand!" Murielle cried.

Callum sat beside her in silence for a few moments. "I may not be able to truly understand, but I believe ye. Does that help?"

She nodded and sat silently on the visitor center floor beside Ronan's ancestor as she awaited Samuel. Callum's presence eased her mind, but only slightly. Murielle was at a crossroads, stuck between two worlds, and she belonged to neither. And, after learning what would befall her people and all that Eva had shared, Murielle knew that she couldn't stay here any longer.

And one thought plagued her beyond all the rest: What if her leaving Pinnata Castra had led to the eventual end of her people? Was she responsible for the downfall of the Picts?

CHAPTER EIGHT

"WHAT DID YOU do?" Samuel shouted at Eva through the phone as he hit the gas and swerved through cars, determined to make it to Burghead in record time.

"Something you should have done yourself. I told her the truth about us."

Samuel growled into his phone as he switched lanes. "There is no *us*! I made that clear to you."

"Before or after you kissed me?" she snapped. "How dare you set me aside for that… that… girl! She doesn't have the slightest idea how this world works. What are you even doing with a girl who has to run away from home to be with you? You put me in a bad position, Sam. But I did what was best for her. I brought her home."

"You have no idea what you've done!" he retorted. "You know nothing about her, and it's none of your business."

Eva scoffed. "I asked her if her family abused her. She said no. Therefore, I saw no reason she shouldn't return home. They must have been worried sick!"

"She is a grown woman, not a child, Eva! I never want to speak with you again."

"You may not have to if I get that job in Edinburgh."

"Good—I hope you do. I'm on my way to get her now. A man called me from the Burghead Visitor Center and told me she's scared to death!"

"That's just it, Sam! Why? Why is she scared to return home

if she is safe there? Something is wrong with her. I did you both a favor. Just three days ago, you said you broke up. Then you kissed me. Now, you're engaged? Make up your mind!"

"I did, and I chose Murielle!"

"Well, have fun with that hot mess." The phone went dead on the other end of the line, and Samuel roared his frustration, tossing his phone onto the vacant passenger seat. Bile rose in his throat as he mentally cursed himself for trusting Eva would have good intentions with Murielle. Was he really so blind to her true nature? He had wanted Murielle to have a woman friend. But he'd certainly underestimated Eva's feelings for him—that was his fault, and now he'd have to beg Murielle to forgive his poor decisions, including kissing Eva and not trusting Murielle's instincts about her. He'd have many words for Eva when next he saw her, but for now, he had to find Murielle.

Samuel followed the road leading into Burghead until it turned into a dead end. Parking Joplin, he ran the rest of the way to the visitor center, throwing the door open as he looked around.

Immediately, he saw a young man who eerily resembled Ronan huddled on the floor beside a crying blonde woman.

"Murielle!" A sickening feeling knotted his stomach as he rushed toward her and kneeled. "Are you all right?"

"Are ye her fiancé?" the man asked warily. When Sam nodded, the man, who wore a nametag with "Callum" on it, stood and awkwardly shuffled his feet. "I will leave ye two alone. Murielle..." He turned to her before he left. "Ye will be all right, no matter what ye choose. Tell my ancestor that I said hello from the future if ever ye see him again."

Samuel frowned as the man walked away. "He knows?"

Murielle sniffled and shrugged. "He is Ronan. I ken it. 'Tis why Ronan couldn't pass through. His soul is in that man's body, and I kenned I could trust him."

Swallowing, Samuel stared in Callum's direction even though he was already out of sight. Somehow, the news that he'd just met Ronan's descendant didn't shock him as much as he'd have expected. After all, this *was* Pinnata Castra, and many families had remained in the area over the centuries. Still, there was something surreal and comforting to see a familiar face here and to know the bloodlines of his ancient Pict friends still lived on.

Looking at Murielle, he put out a hand and prayed she'd still trust his idiotic decision to send her out with Eva. "Come, let's get you home."

Murielle swatted his hand away and stood on her own. "I dinnae want yer help."

"Murielle, Eva means nothing to me. You must believe me."

"Oh, aye? So ye just sleep with women ye dinnae care about? Where does that leave me? And ye kissed her the same night ye left me?" The pain he saw in her watery eyes was somehow worse than the pain he heard in her trembling voice. Never had he wanted Murielle to feel this way. Samuel had intentionally shielded her from his past because none of it mattered. He'd been a lonely man who slept with women and walked away, never looking back. It had been a temporary way to relieve his perpetual misery. But he'd changed when he met Murielle. Now, he wanted her and nobody else.

"Murielle, I was devastated when I returned home," he whispered. "I had intended to ask Brodyn for your hand in marriage only to find out he was set on marrying you to Aldfrith. I told you that I couldn't risk destroying the timeline. Walking away from you that day was the hardest thing I ever did."

"So hard that ye went home and kissed another woman immediately?" Murielle scoffed, wiping tears away. "I ran away from home to be with ye! I left everything I kenned, everyone I loved! I risked my life to cross through the veil and enter an unknown world just to find ye and be with ye! I poured my heart out to ye, told ye I wanted ye and no other man! And ye deny me, run home, and immediately turn yer affections on another woman."

When Murielle folded her arms around herself and shivered, Samuel removed his black hoodie and draped it over her shoulders. She tossed it onto the floor. "I dinnae want yer cloak or anything else from ye. I just want to go home."

"Fine, let's go home, and we will discuss this more and work it all out. I love you, Murielle." He reached out to touch her, but she turned her shoulder on him.

"Nay. I mean my home in 686. I'm going home."

"Murielle…" Samuel felt his world start to spin, worried it would crumble around him if he didn't find a way to fix this. Panic made his hands tremble and his knees weak, but he sucked in a deep breath and put out his hand again, desperate for her to give him another chance. "I was… no, I *am* an absolute fool, but we can work this out."

"Work what out? I am the fool! I went the distance to be with ye after ye rejected me. I understood yer reasoning, so I decided to take matters into my own hands. I can forgive ye for not wanting to disturb the timeline, but I cannae forgive ye for leaving me behind, brokenhearted and all alone while ye found solace in another woman! I would never have done that to ye!"

Indignation roiled in his gut. He wanted to shout his innocence, to proclaim his faithfulness to her, to make her understand the depth of his pain. Before he could defend himself, Murielle scrambled to her feet and pushed past him, leaving him to follow her out of the visitor center and into the frigid wind. Puddles littered the uneven ground around them, and Samuel reached out to support her, but once again, she pushed his hands away.

"Murielle. Yes, you went through the veil to be with me. How many times did I do the same for you? Once Cait married Brodyn, my job was done. I could have gone home and focused on my life here. Instead, I continued to come to you."

"Ye were visiting Caitriona and Emilie," she shot back, balling her fists and placing them on her hips.

"I was visiting you!" he shouted louder than he'd intended. "I couldn't stand to be away from you. I couldn't stand to create a life that didn't have you in it!"

"And then ye left when I finally confessed my love. Why stay so long just to leave me in the end?"

"Because all the other kings who called on you were idiots and unworthy of you. But when Aldfrith arrived, I knew who he was. He's a good man. He'd make a good husband and a great alliance for Fortriu. He is well-recorded as one of the best kings your time will ever see. If he could make you happy and create peace, I couldn't interfere with that. I had to walk away for you and the greater good. Now that you are here, don't you see the impact we could make on this timeline if we make a mistake? Look at Callum in there!" Samuel exclaimed and pointed to the visitor center. "He is very clearly Ronan's decedent. Ronan is yet to marry or have children. Can you imagine if Ronan had crossed the veil and become stuck here? Countless generations of his descendants would immediately be erased from the timeline. This isn't a game! I had to be careful. But, that same night I came home, I looked up Aldfrith and learned that he had married another woman. That's when I planned to go back and get you."

"After you stuck yer tongue down Eva's throat! That was the day of our first kiss, then you left me and kissed her!" she yelled. He'd never seen Murielle so angry or hurt. Knowing he caused it was the greatest pain and remorse he'd ever felt in his entire life.

"Murielle." Samuel took her hand in an attempt to appease her, but she pulled away and looked down. "I shouldn't have done it. The second I did, I regretted it immediately and told her I loved someone else. Then, I went back to my motel room… alone. I was devastated… destroyed. God, Murielle!" he shouted in frustration, mostly at himself. "I've never been so down in all of my life. I went into my office to work. She came in and invited me to have drinks with some other professors. I drank more than usual because I was trying to drown out the pain I felt from losing you. Leave it to Eva to kiss me while I'm intoxicated and then hold it against me."

"Dinnae blame her for yer actions. Ye let her take me shopping, kenning that she is in love with ye. What were ye thinking? Why would she help me?"

Samuel shook his head and frowned. "I wasn't thinking about anything but a modern woman taking you out for a nice time. I had no idea she would do such a thing to you. I'm so sorry. Please, please forgive me and come home with me," he plead, feeling as if he'd be sick. Never had he felt such anguish.

Murielle closed her eyes and stiffened, and Samuel watched in horror as he lost the woman he loved in the blink of an eye.

Slowly, she slid his mother's ring off her finger. "It's more than that, Sam. Being here… seeing the ruins of my people? I left them. They're all dead! Dust beneath my feet, and I left them! I just walked away to be with ye without considering the sacrifice or damage."

"I don't want this ring back." He shoved it back at her, feeling his heartbreak shifting into anger. "Keep it—it's shit to me now!" he yelled. An old man walked past and frowned at him but continued on his way. Water droplets fell on Sam's cheek, and he wasn't sure if it was rain or his own tears. Perhaps it was both. The dark clouds hovering overhead reflected the dark storm of angst brewing in his heart.

"I love you, Murielle. I don't want to lose you. But, if you've made up your mind, I will escort you back. You aren't going back alone."

"I need to go back. Perhaps not forever, but I need time to think. I have a plan, but I must return home to make it work. I betrayed my brother to be with ye… and ye kissed a woman right after kissing me." She shook her head. "I ken ye drank a lot, and I ken ye were upset. But ye didnae waste any time moving on, and I dinnae ken if I can trust ye right now. If ye hadnae bedded her in the past, perhaps I could let it go, but ye obviously are attracted to her if ye keep going back to her."

"Moving on? Damn it all, Murielle! You truly have no idea how much I love you! I kissed a woman while I was four drinks deep. I was lonely and destroyed inside! But, I cannot keep explaining myself. I sure as hell did not move on!" It took all of his strength not to fall at her feet and beg her to stay. She'd spent her entire life being told what to do and made to feel like she couldn't control her life. He wouldn't make her choose between him and her life at Pinnata Castra.

"Does your plan include me?"

"What?" she asked, tilting her head as her brow dropped.

"You said you have a plan. Does your plan include me?"

"I want it to, Samuel. I just need time to make matters right at home and come to terms with what happened today with Eva. I cannae do that here with ye. I have nobody else here and nowhere else to go, and the last thing I want right now is to be stuck in a small space with ye, unable to think clearly."

Samuel ran a hand through his hair and scoffed. "Stuck. That's not a word I thought you'd ever use to describe how you felt about me."

"Samuel—"

He put up a hand. "You've said your piece. I will not force you to stay here and be stuck with me. Once I safely escort you home, I will leave you to do as you wish."

Before Murielle could say anything more to destroy his heart or thrash his soul, Samuel walked back to his Jeep, opened Murielle's door before she was anywhere near it, and climbed into the driver's seat. Starting the engine, he watched as the rain began to pelt the earth in earnest. He wasn't a self-absorbed man, nor did he often believe in signs, but at that moment, as Murielle entered his Jeep and awkward silence befell them, Samuel wondered if the earth cried for him.

After a lifetime of serving the universe and sacrificing everything for everyone else, he had nearly found his happiness, but just as quickly, it slipped through his fingers like the sands of time—and he had nobody to blame but himself.

RAIN PELTED THE windshield as Samuel drove along the coast

toward the cave. The sound was soothing but not enough to tame to storm brewing inside Murielle's gut. Keeping her head down, Murielle fiddled with her fingers, not knowing if she should talk to Samuel or leave him alone. She desperately needed to return home and sort things out, but she hadn't expected any of this to happen. If Eva hadn't taken her back to Burghead, she'd never have felt the impact of leaving her people. Maybe it all happened for a reason. Perhaps Eva's intentional cruelty was a blessing in disguise, leading Murielle back home to save her people.

Inside, her heart was shredded to pieces, and she fought off waves of nausea. This wasn't what she wanted at all. She wanted to stay here, marry Samuel, and teach the modern world about her people. In time, she supposed, she could overcome the hurt of knowing Samuel kissed another woman just before she arrived. The very thought made her stomach churn, but Murielle understood that Samuel rejected her because he felt he had to. He had returned home just as heartbroken as she was now. So for that, she could understand a man deep in his cups seeking solace in another. But beyond the kiss, he rejected Eva even though he could have gone home with her. That had to mean something.

Plus, he'd also told Eva about her.

"I'm sorry, Sam." She whispered, keeping her head down.

"As am I, Murielle," he whispered back.

It took no time at all to reach the cliff where the trail to the cave began. The rain had subsided, but the pain in her heart only worsened as Samuel stopped his Jeep and looked at her. "Ready?"

"Nay, but I dinnae believe I have a choice."

Silently, he nodded and exited the Jeep, rounding the front before opening her door. When he put out a hand to help her down, she looked at her clothing and frowned. "Oh, nay. I cannae return wearing this!"

"Well, when I rushed out of the house to find you, I didn't think to pack you a bag," Samuel said gruffly.

"I ken I gave ye back the ring, but I still want to marry ye," she said, looking up at Samuel. "I just need more time." Regret slashed through her when she saw the pain in his dark eyes.

"It will be hard to marry me while you're there and I'm here. I have a spare tunic in my bag." Samuel left her side to grab a bag from his backseat. His terse answer felt like rejection all over again, and Murielle pursed her lips and sucked in a breath, determined not to cry. She'd made this decision and stood by it, but she hadn't expected it to be permanent. Her situation was uniquely complex, and she needed a place to heal, think, and regather herself. But his response left her little hope of a future with him. He'd already closed the door, and it was her fault.

Sam returned with a dark blue tunic and a simple rope belt. "It'll be big on you, and it's not fit for a princess, but it's better than what you have."

Nodding, Murielle slipped the tunic over her head and tied the rope around her waist before stepping out of the Jeep. "Thank ye."

He nodded, then he also changed into a tunic, pulled a flashlight out of the bag, and took her hand, helping her walk around mud puddles.

"If it's high tide, we will not be able to access the cave," he reminded her. As much as she wanted to return to her home, she desperately hoped for a high tide if it meant more time in his company. This felt like a final farewell, and the knots tightening in her stomach only added to her misery.

She was a woman trapped between worlds, and now she understood exactly how Caitriona and Emilie had felt when they were pulled into her time, forced to leave everything they knew. She wanted more than anything to stay here, but if Aldfrith became angry when she rejected him again, it could mean war.

"Samuel. I'm worried the Picts disappeared because of me."

"What?" He stopped and turned to look at her with his furrowed brow. She already missed him even though he stood right beside her. He was distant and cold, and she wished to feel his comforting arms embrace her just once more.

"What if my rejection of Aldfrith causes friction between our people? What if this weakens the Picts and eventually leads to their downfall? The loss of one ally could mean losing an entire war."

Samuel's eyes widened in understanding. "I understand that you feel guilty for leaving your people, but I didn't realize this was weighing on you."

"When I learned that my people completely disappeared, I wondered if my refusal to marry him eventually led them to that fate."

The wind howled atop the cliff, and she shivered, wrapping her arms around herself despite the long-sleeved tunic and sweater she wore beneath it.

Slowly, hesitantly, Samuel reached out and placed his large, comforting hands on her folded arms, pulling her into his warmth. "Do you think I'd let something like that happen? I walked away from you because I was worried about affecting the timeline and doing irreparable damage. Nothing else in the world would have kept me from you. So, when I proposed to you, Murielle, I did so knowing our marriage wouldn't affect the timeline."

"But, how can ye ken that so certainly?" Hope for a future with him once again blossomed in her chest. She should have trusted that Samuel, who was knowledgeable about such things and who'd spent his life trying to correct the timeline, wouldn't do anything to jeopardize it. But, learning that her people go extinct directly after learning that Samuel kissed Eva created an emotional storm whose dark clouds blocked out any amount of rational thought. All she knew was that she had to return home and make certain that Aldfrith wouldn't wage war if she rejected him. She'd rather live a lifetime in misery as another man's wife than sentence her people to a lifetime of war and destruction.

"Nobody knows what happened to your people, but it wasn't a genocide. Aldfrith marries a woman who is later declared a saint. She's as pious as he is, and according to many records, they are very happy. He brings peace to his people and is always considered a close Pictish ally. All of that is clearly documented. That's how I knew we were safe to marry. Your people don't die off, Murielle. Times change, leaders change, politics change. One man will rule all of your land one day and become king of what is now Scotland. He had Pictish blood in his veins. I think he simply brings unity to all the tribes, and they all begin to regard themselves as one people, one culture, and assimilate peaceably. The Picts simply become part of a greater whole. This is my honest belief."

"Oh," she murmured as she felt comfort in the warmth of his embrace. She felt foolish, impulsive, and childish. She still needed to return and make things right with Brodyn, but more than anything, she wanted to come back and be Samuel's wife. "I'm sorry," she said, swallowing her pride.

He pulled away, but only slightly. "Do not apologize for worrying about your people, Murielle. Your situation is wholly different than Caitriona's or Emilie's. They knew their people were yet to be born and that their society would still flourish. Caitriona was able to find love with our brother and save the future of Scotland. You sped forward 1,300 years, where everyone and everything you ever loved or knew was gone. You had to face the ruins of your people. I cannot even imagine that pain. I will help you get back to them."

"But… will I ever see you again?"

Samuel scoffed. "You gave me back my mother's ring, demanded to go home, and are angry at me because of Eva. I'd have gladly started a life with you in 686 and left this all behind, but now that you broke off our engagement?" he shook his head. "I wanted you to be a part of my life, but I won't force you. I understand your concern, your need to be with your people. I'm only sorry that my drunken mistake has added to your pain. I regret it more than I can ever say. I was just so lonely and so broken inside."

"You didn't really answer my question," she persisted.

"After I deliver you home, I will not be returning to your time. It hurts too much. But, there will always be a place in my heart for you. And while I have no interest in being with anyone else, I cannot spend the rest of my life in misery, pining for a woman who died 1,300 years ago. You know, the way you felt when you saw the ruins? That's how I feel every time, too. Knowing you, Cait, Emilie, and everyone else I love in your village is nothing more than dust? I live with this notion every day of my life. Having an opportunity to marry you was a balm to my soul. But I see now I was asking too much of you; you don't expect me to go back into your time—I shouldn't expect you to stay in mine."

"I see," she murmured, her heart breaking into impossibly smaller pieces. So embroiled in her own feelings, she'd not stopped to consider his. She wanted to cling to him and beg him to take her back. Could he possibly forgive her after she gave him back his ring and asked to leave? Could he forgive her jealousy?

"Come, let's walk down the path and check out the tide."

Hesitantly, she took his hand and followed his lead as they navigated the slippery, muddy trail in the dark with only his flashlight to guide them. The shoreline was visible, and the cave's entrance was accessible. Her heart plummeted.

With heavy feet and a heavier heart, she followed Samuel into the cave, using all her willpower not to beg him to stay in her time with him. It wasn't fair to ask, especially since he'd been so selfless allowing her to return. To ask him to come with her and stay? *No.* He'd given up enough of himself already, not only for her but for Cait and Emilie and all of her people. And, all of Scotland.

How could she have accused him of anything with Eva? He wasn't selfish, he was the most selfless man she knew.

Entering the small alcove, Murielle placed her hand on the stone wall, closed her eyes, and imagined her village as it was in her time. Her heart wasn't truly in it, so when bright lights accosted the back of her eyelids, and pulsing energy threw her backward, she was shocked that it let her through the veil.

But when she got up and looked around the small alcove, Samuel wasn't there.

CHAPTER NINE

"MURIELLE!"

Samuel spun in a full circle, but there was no sign of Murielle. She'd crossed over, and he hadn't. In all these years, not once had the veil rejected his entrance. Why now?

Panic welled in his throat as he banged his fist against the cave wall. "Let me through!" he shouted, hearing his voice echo off the walls. "You jerked me around for years, and now you won't let me through to make sure she gets home safely?" He yelled with all his strength, cursing the forces at work against him. Despite years of time travel, he still had little understanding of how it worked or how it decided who passed through, when, or why. But he'd always come and gone as he pleased without issue.

He didn't get to say goodbye or safely deliver her to Pinnata Castra.

No, he wasn't going to roll over and give up. He'd been pliable and obedient his entire life. He followed every rule his parents gave him, even though he remembered his past lives and could function independently. He was just a boy in appearance, but his mind was that of a grown man with all his memories. And still, he obeyed. He zoomed though school, skipped grades, and aced every course because he remembered the information from past lives. He juggled his teaching career, overseeing archaeological digs, and literally saving the entirety of Scotland by helping to deliver Caitriona to Brodyn, where she replaced the woman he was to marry and sealed an alliance. He'd done all of that and never asked for anything in return.

And, in every memory, there was Murielle. He'd loved her in every life. If he ever married Murielle and had a family, he couldn't remember. And, after a lifetime of predictable outcomes, having some mystery in his life was a welcome change. But right now, he'd love some guidance from the universe. Instead, it played games with him.

Even now, he'd given in and let Murielle call off their engagement without a fight. Inside, he seethed with anger at himself and burned with a passion to win her back. He yearned to call her wife, to have a family, to share her bed, and to make love to her every night. He wanted her laughter, sadness, joy, anger, frustration… he wanted all of her, and he'd let her walk away without a fight because that's what obedient Samuel did. He never rocked the boat or showed his full range of emotion, even when he suffered greatly.

Well, the hell with that. He was done being passive, compliant, and settling for less than true happiness.

Letting out a guttural roar that reverberated off the walls, Samuel clenched his fists and jaw, freeing his anger for the first time in his life. He suddenly regretted his complacency. Where had it gotten him? The woman he loved just walked away, and he could not follow her because the veil of time had turned against him.

"What do you want from me?" he shouted with all his strength. "What did I ever do to you? Nothing! I've done nothing but help everyone else but myself! It's my turn!" He hollered until spittle flew from his mouth, and heat coursed through his body as rage boiled in his veins.

Touching the wall, he tried again. And again. Nothing. The unyieldingly cold, lifeless walls of that cave had turned their backs on him, standing sentry over a crack in the veil of time that they apparently deemed him no longer worthy of passing through.

Samuel began to worry that the veil separated them for a

reason. Perhaps they were about to make a grave mistake that would affect the timeline forever, destroying future generations. He tried not to think of himself as a powerful man, but knowing his every move could change time's course had been a burden he'd carried on his shoulders at all times. Perhaps his love for Murielle had blinded him, and the cave corrected his lapse of judgment.

Immediately, he shook off such notions. The veil had allowed Murielle to pass through and find him. So, why close itself to him now?

Cursed cave! Leaving the alcove, Samuel noticed the rising tide and cursed again. He was out of time for the night. If he didn't leave immediately, he'd be stuck in this frigid, wet place until morning.

"I'm not done with you," he shouted at the cave. He may be barred from entry now, but he would come back every day to keep trying.

Picking up his satchel, Samuel left the cave and slogged up the muddy trail to his Jeep, where he jumped in and sped away, angrier than he'd ever been in his entire life. This was all his fault, and he wasn't even given a chance to fix it. Now, he may never have that chance. He prayed Murielle made it back to her village safely and that Brodyn, diligent as ever, had guards posted in the area who'd find her, much like they found Caitriona and Emilie.

YAWNING, SAMUEL DRAGGED himself into his already-full classroom as students stared at his disheveled, tired appearance. It wasn't like him to be late or unkept, but he's slept very little the night before, and what little sleep he'd had was riddled with images of Murielle reaching for him through the veil. He'd spent all his remaining energy trying to reach her, but she'd dissolved into millions of grains of sand at his feet as soon as he did.

"Are you all right, Dr. Sullivan?" One of his female students in the front row asked. "I thought you were going to be out all week?"

"Oh, yes. I'm sorry to be late. I have a long commute, and there was an accident. I had a change in my circumstances."

"You still managed to nab a cappuccino," his TA said with a laugh, knowing Samuel couldn't function well without it.

"How shrewd of you to notice. I figured it was best to stop at the coffee machine in the staff room for two minutes rather than waste all of your time while I sleep at my desk."

The class chuckled as Samuel dropped his bag on the dark blue carpet beneath his desk and quietly thanked his TA, Alex, for covering for him.

"Anytime, Dr. S. It was my pleasure. Here are the reports you asked me to collect."

Samuel smiled and took the stack, placing them inside his bag before he started his lecture. Absorbing himself in his work helped make time pass faster while he forced himself to remain professional. These kids, or their parents, paid a small fortune for these classes, and he wouldn't allow their money to be wasted because he was tired or heartbroken.

After teaching four classes in a row, noon arrived rather swiftly, and as his last student left the room, Samuel sighed and plopped into his chair, loosening his tie and unbuttoning the top of his dress shirt. He wanted to pull his phone out and look at the low tide schedule, but he still had a stack of papers to read, so he stood back up and walked through the halls and down the stairs to his private office, frowning when he saw his door ajar. He hadn't made any appointments for the day, but perhaps his TA had scheduled one while he was out.

Pushing the door open, Samuel grimaced when he found Eva sitting behind his desk. Wearing crisp black slacks and another pair of heels with those fancy red bottoms, Eva sat with her feet propped up on his desk as if she thought she belonged there.

"What do you want?" he barked. "I told you I didn't want to

see you again."

Eva frowned and put her feet down, sitting straight up in his chair before pushing to her feet and adjusting her royal blue silk blouse. "I know. I came to apologize. I was completely out of line."

"Yes. You were." Samuel crossed his arms and narrowed his eyes, biting back all the insults he wanted to shout at her for what she'd done to Murielle. Eva had traumatized her in a way she'd never understand, nor could he accurately explain the situation. It wasn't her business anyway.

"I know. Look…" Sighing, Eva walked over to him but stopped a respectable distance away. "When we kissed after the pub, I had high hopes we could give it another go. I know—" she held up a hand when he opened his mouth to retort—"you told me you weren't interested. That was my mistake. But, when I showed up at your flat to return your ID, I guess I wasn't expecting to meet your fresh-faced fiancée, especially because two days prior, you were single. But it wasn't my business. I offered to take her shopping because I was curious about her. I wanted to understand what she could offer you that I couldn't. Honestly, I still don't see it, but again—it's not my business. I swear to you that I had no plan to tell her about us or to bring her back home. But when we were out, she told me she had run away from home. We were so close to her town, and…" She paused and swallowed before looking back at him with nervousness glazing her eyes. "My sister was a runaway. We never saw her again. To this day, we don't know if she's dead or alive. My dad still puts a plate out for her every day. I couldn't allow her family to go through that. She's an adult, yes, but she's young, and her family would be devastated. She said they never hurt her, so I dropped her off. Was it the right thing to do? Maybe not. Did I get involved where I shouldn't have? Yes. Was jealousy a factor? It was."

Samuel listened, trying to resist the pity brewing in his heart. Eva was catty at times, and he knew this. He should not have trusted her with Murielle. It was a ridiculous decision and one he now paid a very heavy price for. "I'm sorry that happened to you and your family," Samuel murmured.

"I don't tell you that story for pity, Sam. I just wanted to explain the motive behind my actions. It wasn't my finest moment, and it was laced with malice, but it was mostly done with good intentions, and I do hope you will forgive me. Also, I didn't get the position in Edinburgh."

"So, you're only apologizing because you're stuck here and have to face me?"

"No!" Genuine hurt flashed in her eyes as she flung her red hair over her shoulder with an air of indignance. "I may be many things, Samuel, but I always accept responsibility for myself. I was going to apologize to you either way. In fact, I came straight here thirty minutes ago when my last class finished up early from testing. I only received the call from Edinburgh twenty minutes ago. I was already here."

"Okay, fine." Samuel sighed and shook his head. "I can understand to a point, Eva, but the damage is done. Murielle called off the engagement after you told her we kissed."

"Yes, that was the malice part," she whispered and shifted uncomfortably. "I can fix this for you… I promise. She's young—a little too young if you ask me. You're worldly, educated, and seldom home. It's not my business, but it's hard to imagine you with someone with so little life experience."

"You're right. It's not your business. And there is nothing to fix. Please leave it alone. I appreciate your apology. I'm sorry you lost your sister and that Murielle triggered emotions about that loss for you. But I'm not ready to forgive. You tore my life apart, and you did it on purpose. Regrets for your actions can only go so far, but they can't fix the damage you caused to both Murielle's and my life."

She chewed her lower lip as she processed his words and eventually nodded. "I know. I don't expect your forgiveness. I don't even forgive myself. I only wanted you to know that I am very sorry. I do regret it. I can see the pain in your eyes. You love her, and I'm to blame for you losing her."

"No, no, Eva." Samuel sighed and ran his fingers through his hair. "I play a part in this. I kissed you only a day after we broke up. I realize I was free to do so, but that act comes off as moving on, as far as she is concerned. And I can't blame her. I'd be beside myself if I found out she kissed another man right after we broke up. It's petty but isn't that love?" he scoffed. "We don't think straight when we're in love."

"She still loves you, Sam. She didn't just fall out of love with you overnight."

"It doesn't matter anymore, Eva. It's over. She gave me back my ring, and I told her if she walked away, it was over. And she did. I cannot follow." Saying those words out loud felt like a fist squeezing his heart. The finality of it made it hard to breath through the relentless ache inside. "I'm... I'm sorry, Eva. I just can't talk about this anymore. It hurts too much."

"Very well then. I will give you a wide berth. Just know that I carry this mistake very heavily in my heart. I'm not a bad person, just a human with issues to work on. I really care about you. I wanted to be with you. I suppose I got carried away."

Samuel nodded. "I appreciate it. Don't avoid me. We can be civil." He didn't want to see her, but the gentleman in him always won out. However, he'd never go to drinks with her or trust her again. A professional relationship was all they'd share, and only if they were forced to be in the same room for staff meetings.

"I'd like that. I know I'm the last person you'll call on if you need anything, but I'm here." She walked past him and out of his office, leaving him alone with his brooding thoughts.

Throwing his bag onto his desk, Samuel plopped in his chair, pulled out the sheaf of papers his TA had collected, forced his pain deep down into his gut, and began correcting his students' work.

CLIMBING INTO HER BMW, Eva typed in a Burghead address and sped out of the parking lot, a woman on a mission. Samuel may have not wanted her help, but the guilt had been eating away at her, and she was determined to make things right.

Her phone's GPS said it was an hour and forty-five minutes to Burghead due to traffic. She groaned at the long drive time but understood now how much Murielle must mean to Sam if he chose to drive this commute twice a day just to be closer to her.

She cranked up her favorite rock station to pass the time as she navigated traffic, and after enduring stop-and-go conditions for nearly two hours, the Burghead's welcome sign appeared on her right. She wasn't a woman inclined to anxiety, but damn if butterflies and knots didn't build up in her gut as she slowly rolled through this small, quaint town. Now that she was here, she had no idea where to begin.

An internet search proved useless in finding a woman named Murielle associated with Burghead, except for one article she quickly dismissed about an ancient princess who was sister to a Pictish king on this site well over a millennia ago. Perhaps Murielle's family named her after this princess, or perhaps there was no connection at all. Either way, there was no number or address listed for Murielle, and Eva didn't know her surname.

Slowly, she pulled into a small deli's parking lot and got out of her car, looking around. People casually milled about, some drinking coffee across the way, others simply enjoying the sunshine pushing through the crowd of clouds in the sky. The ground still showed signs of wetness, potentially from late-night rain or morning sprinkles, but for now, the weather appeared tame on this fall afternoon. Multi-colored leaves lined the curbs and skittered down the streets as small gusts of wind propelled them southward.

Eva stepped around a puddle, protecting her designer pumps

from any damage. Curious glances in her direction told her that this small town didn't get too many posh visitors. Either that or they knew her as the wicked witch of the southeast, who'd dumped Murielle here the night before.

"Excuse me," she said to a kindly looking old man who walked beside his wife on the sidewalk. His bowler hat spoke to a time long ago, and she wondered if this man simply enjoyed the classics or if this town had never changed with the times. That may explain why Murielle had appeared doe-eyed and confused by much of Eva's conversation. Eva couldn't tell if the girl was ill-educated, skittish, soft in the head, or the epitome of pure innocence. Based on what she observed in this town, perhaps Murielle grew up isolated and didn't understand much of the ways of the world outside Burghead. Either way, Eva was here to make it right and move on with her life.

"Yes, dear?" the older woman said with a warm smile.

Eva smiled back. "I'm looking for a friend who lives here, but I cannot remember her last name. But her first name is Murielle. She's young and slim with blonde hair and blue eyes. She mentioned living with her brother. Do you happen to know her?"

The old couple looked at one another and shook their heads in tandem. "We've lived here our entire lives and ken most everyone here," the woman said.

"Aye, but people come and go," the husband kindly reminded his wife, who nodded.

"True. Has the lass recently arrived here?"

"I believe she grew up here. She's around mid-twenties in age."

"If she was here as a wee lass, she'd likely have gone to primary school with our grandson, Callum. We have but one primary school here. Ye should head up the road to the visitor center. He works there. Perhaps he kens the lass."

"Thank you very much… what are your names?" Eva asked, wanting to be polite to these two generous souls. The way they looked at one another was unlike anything she'd ever seen. So tranquil and comfortable, and she got the sense they had spent an entire lifetime together, given their tangible connection.

"Och, our names are Anya and Edwin," the man said, tipping his bowler hat and displaying a balding head beneath. "'Tis mighty fine to meet ye, Eva."

"Thank you for your help," she said, smiling at the couple and watching as they continued to amble in the same direction as before. As Eva walked back to her car, she crinkled her brow and looked over her shoulder, but the couple must have already rounded the corner. Had she told them her name? She truly could not recall, but she did often start conversations with her name habitually since she met new students and colleagues often enough.

Climbing into her car, she headed up the main road that seemed to cut through the center of the town until she saw a large, white building at the very end. A small sign at the very top of the building marked it as her destination, but there was no direct road leading toward it, so Eva parked and leaned over her seat to reach into the back, where she kept a spare pair of ballet flats for such occasions. She really didn't want to climb up that hill in her heels, even if it wasn't very far or steep.

Reaching the top, she walked in and looked around for anyone who could be Murielle's age.

"May I help ye?"

Turning around, she saw a young man who was quite attractive, with dark hair, green eyes, and a strong jaw. Too bad he was far too young for her. She preferred men her age of thirty-three or slightly older.

"Hello," she looked down at his name tag. "Oh, Callum. You are just who I'm looking for."

"Oh?" he cocked his head and raised a brow. "How can I help ye? Did ye wish to look around the Pictish fort remains or read any brochures? We have a reconstruction of the hillfort we are standing atop just through those doors."

"Perhaps I will, but first, I wanted to ask if you knew a young lady named Murielle. Your grandparents sent me here to speak with you. They said you might know her from school. I just wish to speak with her."

Callum's face contorted in confusion. "Murielle? My grand-parents?"

"Ah, yes. Their names are Anya and Edwin, and they said their grandson, Callum, worked here and may know Murielle."

Eva frowned as she watched the young man's face blanch before her eyes. "Are you all right?"

"Aye. Uh, those arenae my grandparents, Miss. They are related to me, aye, but they've been dead nearly 150 years now."

"E-excuse me?" she stuttered, wondering if the young man was insane. "I saw them as clear as day."

"Aye, 'tis been told that they are seen now and then, wander-ing up Grant Street or popping up when one of our family members needs help. They are like our guardian angels. Mum said they've wandered these lands in many different bodies and times. Soulmates in every lifetime. I honestly didnae believe it."

"Well, I am not family, so how could I see them, and why would they help me?"

Callum shrugged, still as white as a ghost... or perhaps not, for the ghosts she'd apparently seen looked like warm flesh and blood. Though, she still didn't believe any of what he said. She was a woman of science. Ghosts didn't exist, and small towns like this tended to cling to local lore like a baby clings to long hair in their sticky-fisted vise. "I dinnae ken. But, they werenae wrong. I do ken Murielle, only she didnae go to school with me. I just met her here yesterday. I dinnae ken what else I should say about that encounter. Only that she was verra upset."

Regret tugged at her belly, and Eva diverted her shameful gaze toward a drawing on the wall behind his head of ancient men sowing a field. It occurred to her that though she was finally at a place where she could admit her faults and wrongdoings, she still had difficulty looking people in the eye when she did. Staring at the ancient farmer, Eva sighed. "That would be my doing, I'm afraid. I upset her, but I've come to apologize."

When she dared to look at Callum and face his judgment, she couldn't understand why she cared what he thought. Something about this young man made her uneasy. Perhaps it was the feeling of *deja vu* she felt the moment she saw him, like he was a younger version of someone she once knew, though she couldn't place it.

"I promise ye, whatever it was ye said or did to upset her wasnae the reason she left this place. She was upset about something much more profound."

"She left? Did she say where she was going?" Now worry overtook her. If Murielle hadn't gone back to Sam and she wasn't here, where had she gone?

"Aye, I ken where she went, but ye cannae follow, I'm afraid."

"Now you have me worried. I'm sorry, Callum, but I will have to call the police and report her missing if I don't know where she is. From what I know of her, she has no job, no car, no money, and now no home."

Callum licked his lips nervously and looked over his shoulder, nodding toward a small, private room. Eva followed him into the back, wondering what he had had to say that made him so nervous.

When he shut the door behind him, he took a deep breath. "My family has lived on this land for as long as anyone can remember. Murielle said I looked like her old guard, Ronan, and he lived 1,300 years ago. So, I dinnae believe we've ever lived anywhere else, and those in the area ken that something strange happens here."

Eva scrunched her nose as she listened to Callum, wondering what on earth he was talking about. "Murielle had a guard named Ronan, who lived 1,300 years ago and looked like you?" Was everyone in this town bat-shit crazy?

He nodded. "She is a Pictish princess, Miss. Her brother is the Pictish king, Brodyn, from the year 686. She traveled here through the cave just along this shore." He pointed toward the water that they couldn't see through the walls.

"Did she tell you that?" Eva asked, taken aback by how absurd this story was and more so by this young man's belief in it.

"Ye think I'm insane, but I amnae. Ye saw ghosts just now. I assure ye, Edwin and Anya are dead. If ye can believe that this isnae so different. There are parts of the world where more is possible. This is one of those places. An archaeologist disappeared on a nearby dig two years ago. When she returned, she was pregnant. Murielle said that was Caitriona, who is... or was... depends on yer perspective, her brother's wife."

"That was the name of Samuel's student who went missing," Eva murmured as she chewed nervously on her manicured nail. The idea was insane, though she'd often wondered where Caitriona had gone—as if she'd fallen off the face of the earth—and suddenly reappeared, only to disappear again. Samuel, too, also seemed to come and go from an unspecified location.

But was she crazy for listening to this nonsense? Somehow, despite its insanity, the story addressed some of her questions, like how Samuel met Murielle, why she seemed so out of place in this world, where Samuel disappeared to so often, and why he insisted on living so close to this place.

There was one thing she could do, and that was research. Eva pulled out her phone and started pushing buttons. "What are ye doing?" Callum asked.

"An internet search for King Brodyn," she said, waiting for the page to load. When a site about Pictish kings pulled up, Eva clicked it and scanned the article, gasping, and nearly dropping her phone when she saw the name of his queen. "Caitriona..." she whispered. No. It wasn't possible. But... "Murielle said this archaeologist traveled to the year 685 and married her brother, King Brodyn?"

Callum nodded. "Aye, that's what she said." He tilted his head. "I called a man named Samuel Sullivan for her, and he picked her up. She was verra upset and demanded to be taken back to her time. I believe he must have taken her back, but I ken nothing more than that, and that is more than I should have said. But I dinnae want the police to search Burghead for a missing woman who doesnae exist. I know that they willnae find a record of her."

Could it be true? She itched to call Samuel and ask him point blank if Murielle was from the past. And, she wanted to know if he'd met her in her time while searching for Caitriona. Samuel had been gone for much of that time, apparently searching for her. But he'd been out of touch, out of sight—no one had known where he'd gone. It is possible that he crossed through some wormhole?

The pieces of the puzzle fit neatly together, which was crazy, considering time travel made no sense whatsoever.

Eva knew she was insane for even considering it, but she was compelled to explore this option on her own. In fact, she was sure that with some in depth research, she'd learn soon enough that this was all local folklore. She might even prove that Murielle was either insane or a con artist—which she dearly hoped, for Sam's sake, was not true.

Or, Murielle might have been telling the truth.

No matter what, Eva had come this far and would find answers without alerting Samuel to her whereabouts. Then, once she'd found a logical explanation, she'd move on and never have to admit to anyone that she'd entertained this fantasy for even a moment.

"Where is this… 'portal' that delivers people through time? How do I access the cave?"

"Och, 'tis quite dangerous. Ye can only access it at low tide. I've visited the cave myself. Nothing ever happens." He shrugged. "Perhaps I amnae meant to travel."

"Perhaps it's all crap," Eva said, cringing once the words escaped her mouth. "I'm sorry. I don't mean to insult you or the locals here."

"I understand. 'Tis far-fetched at best. All I can say is we've had enough inexplicable things happen, such as reports of people walking the shores in ancient clothing before they disappear. It's either ghosts, time travel, or both. All I can tell you for sure is—Murielle was verra distraught over seeing the hillfort remains on this site. She wasnae faking her emotions."

Eva wanted to point out that Murielle was likely unstable and needed medical attention. Worse, she was the one responsible for putting the young woman in this position. The least she could do was find her. That made much more sense.

"Will you help me find her?"

"I believe 'tis my destiny to do so. Why else would my ancestors have appeared to ye and directed ye toward me? They must have kenned I saw her. My mum said great-great-great-grandma Anya only appears to family members when something verra important is about to happen."

Eva wasn't family, but she decided not to point that out. "When do you get off work?"

Callum looked at his watch. "I still have three hours, but I havenae taken my lunch break. I have a motorized scooter. It will get us down to the cave in 15 minutes."

Eva frowned. How had she ended up in this position? She should have minded her own business. This newfound conscience of hers was suddenly more trouble than it was worth.

Within moments, she found herself sitting astride a beat-up, chipped, blue scooter, wearing a bright orange helmet, and clinging to Callum's waist as they sped down the hill, out of town, and down a steep trail that led to a pebbly shore.

They bounced atop the scooter whenever the tire hit a rock or bump in the dirt trail, but she was surprised at how easily the scooter maneuvered. She was also surprised at the smile on her face as wind slapped her cheeks and tangled her hair. Thank goodness she'd worn slacks and changed into flats.

When a series of caves appeared on their right, Callum slowed to a stop and dismounted, holding out a hand for Eva. She let him help her down. He took off his helmet and looked at her strangely. "Is it me, or does it feel like we've kenned each other for a lifetime? I cannae place it."

"As odd as it sounds, I do feel like we've met before. I can almost picture when and where, but it's hazy. Have you ever attended Aberdeen University or taken anthropology courses elsewhere?"

"No, Miss. I havenae attended any university. Odd thing, isnae it? Anyway, it appears we have a low tide. Ye are verra lucky, but it willnae last. This is the spot. See that cave?"

Eva held a hand in front of her eyes and squinted through the beams of sunlight reflecting off the glittering water's surface. She saw the cave he pointed to and noticed the entrance was accessible.

"This is the one. I cannae promise ye anything beyond here. If the cave accepts ye, ye will disappear. I had a mate once disappear and come back. He never spoke about it. But I cannae go through. Here, I'll walk ye in."

To think one could simply travel through time inside a cave was absurd. Eva couldn't believe she was even here. All she'd wanted to do was find Murielle, and though she had enjoyed the adventure down to the cave on a motorized scooter with a strange lad, Eva didn't know how she'd come to stand here now.

Despite her proper appearance and professional mannerisms, a love for adventure ran through her veins. It was what had led her to become an archaeologist. With her love for history, traveling, and solving puzzles, her profession came naturally—as did finding herself in odd predicaments. Yet, nothing in her life had ever led her to follow a lead that wasn't based on science.

Perhaps that was why she felt no anxiety as she stood just outside the cave. There was no way anything was coming of this. She'd pop in, look around, leave the way she came, and continue to search for Murielle.

Stepping inside, Eva felt excitement rush through her as she noted the old Pictish engravings. The local government had done well to keep this cave free of modern tagging and debris. Locals were likely very respectful of the cave's history, which helped. Coupled with it only being accessible at random hours of the day, Eva imagined few people visited, less so if they knew its lore.

"Now what?" Eva asked, looking over her shoulder at Callum.

"Follow me." Callum approached then, stepped around a large puddle on the cave's floor from the last high tide and rounded a corner into a small alcove. "This is it. If the veil of time allows ye through, this is the spot."

Eva looked around the small space, spinning in a slow circle as she looked for anything suspicious. But, aside from gray stone walls and a gravelly floor that appeared to have been recently disturbed, likely from Samuel's excavation, nothing appeared unusual in the darkness. Taking out her phone, Eva switched on the flashlight app and shone it around the small space, looking for anything out of place. When her light caught something bright purple, Eva looked down and saw a thistle growing out of the ground. How in the world was a lone thistle growing out of rocky soil in a pitch-black corner of the cave? No natural light could ever reach this alcove.

Leaning over, Eva touched the thistle to make certain it was real and not some plastic plant a tourist had placed there for effect. When one of its thorns pricked her, she winced and pulled away, sucking at the drop of blood on her finger.

"Be careful, Miss," Callum said warily.

Eva spun around once more. "Well, nothing is happening. Either I'm not meant to pass through, or this is all local lore on steroids."

With a sigh, she placed one hand on her hip and the other against the cold stone walls as she thought about what to do next. Sparks flew from her fingertips, and she yelped as energy zapped her flesh, as if she had just slid down one of those old plastic slides that used to make her hair stand on end.

"Callum!" she shouted as a light burst from her hands, and a force lifted her off her feet, propelling her backward. Ears ringing, skin tingling, and vision blurry, Eva realized she was engulfed in pitch black again. Had her phone broken when she dropped it?

Feeling around the cave floor, she felt sharp pebbles dig into her palms but couldn't find her phone. "Callum? Callum!" The young man didn't respond, and Eva froze on her hands and knees, blinking into the dark.

"Hello?"

"Ah, shite. Another one." A deep voice spoke an odd language, but Eva was surprised to understand it. Perhaps her years of studying ancient dialects helped her piece the words together even if she'd never heard this exact language.

"Hello?" Slowly, she pushed to her feet and felt around in the dark until her palms met the smooth stone walls once again. Sliding along it, Eva rounded the corner, bumping into something that felt much more like a person rather than stone.

"Och, when will it ever stop?" Another voice spoke just before a hand reached out and grabbed her arm. Eva yelped and pulled back, but the hand tightened around her wrist.

"Ye are safe, lass," the man said warily. "Do ye ken why ye are here?"

"I…" Eva saw sunlight streaming through the entrance and two large silhouettes blocking her way. They appeared to wear rudimentary clothing with—based on the shape—something akin to swords strapped at their sides.

"It worked, didn't it?" she asked the men. She was weak and disoriented, but she recognized the tone of their voice. They weren't surprised to see someone randomly appear from the cave.

"If ye mean, ye are in the year 686, and that is where ye meant to be, then aye, it worked."

As Eva caught her bearings and walked out of the cave, she saw the ocean a much farther distance from the shore than it had been when she left, and the foliage appeared thicker, lusher, and more varied than the spattering of wildflowers she'd seen before. Two horses grazed nearby, the sea wind ruffling their manes and tails. It was peaceful, and so different from the shoreline she'd left behind. When she turned to regard the men standing behind her, Eva gasped and narrowed her eyes on one man in particular. "Callum?"

The man frowned and raised a brow. "Ronan. Murielle told me about Callum. Apparently, I will sow my seeds, after all." He held his hands wide, rather like a magician after performing some kind of magic act.

"Oh…" She wrinkled her brow at the man's odd statement. Callum hadn't made any of it up. Indeed, his ancestor looked exactly like him but taller, older, and built like a tank but covered in flesh and dark hair. "You are Murielle's guard. Is she nearby?"

Ronan's eyes darkened as he glanced at the man beside him. "Goodwin, she fits Murielle's description." Ronan then looked at her again, this time with disgust. "Ye are Eva, the one who left her atop our hillforts ruins after ye kissed Samuel."

"It's not that simple…"

"Why are ye here?" the man named Goodwin asked warily. "If ye've come to cause Murielle more trouble, ye arnae getting past this cave."

"No, I came to apologize."

"Ye came 1,300 years into the past to apologize to our princess?" Ronan asked, narrowing in on her with blazing blue eyes that made her heart skitter in her chest. Lord, he was a fine-looking man.

"Well, I came to Burghead to apologize, yes. I wasn't exactly planning on time traveling today. It just happened."

"Aye, tends to be the way," Goodwin said. "My wife came through looking for her best friend, our queen, but she couldn't pass through when she tried. She only fell through when she wasn't expecting it."

"Is your wife Emilie?" Eva asked.

Goodwin nodded. "Ye ken my wife?"

"She was in two of my classes, and she was best friends with Caitriona, one of Samuel's favorites. I've come to understand

Caitriona married Murielle's brother."

"Aye, she is our queen."

"Nice gig," Eva murmured, and Ronan crossed his large arms over his expansive chest.

"We were sent to guard the cave by King Brodyn. He didnae want Samuel following Murielle. He is no longer welcome."

Eva frowned, more regret and guilt eating away at her insides. Now Samuel wasn't allowed back, and it was her fault. She really had to make this right. "Why is that?"

"He sent Murielle back alone. We have orders to deliver him to Brodyn if he dares to come through."

"I can assure you that Samuel is devastated about Murielle returning. I wasn't there the night he brought her back, but I know he would have followed her if he could. He's a mess right now."

"Ye defend his love for Murielle, though ye want him for yerself. Why?" Ronan asked, stepping so close that he hovered above her, looking more like a sculpted marble statue than flesh and blood. Good lord, the man was solidly built.

"Murielle really told you everything, didn't she?"

"Aye. I am her guard. She tells me all. Ye arenae trusted here."

Eva straightened her back and lifted her chin. "I didn't come all this way to cause trouble. I wanted to apologize to Murielle and reassure her that Samuel loves her. He's devastated. I only wish to repair the damage I've caused, and then I will leave forever."

"Ye dinnae seem overwrought about finding yerself in another time," Goodwin said with a raised brow.

"I think I'm still in shock," she explained. "I was slightly prepared for this to be real, thanks to Callum. But I admit, I'm still not convinced I'm not dreaming." She chuckled nervously, wringing her hands as Ronan glared at her with an intensity that made her lady parts quiver.

"I will take ye to the village. First, ye shall have yer audience with the princess, and then ye will be escorted home." Ronan grabbed her arm and dragged her toward the large black horse grazing nearby, before grabbing her waist and tossing her onto the saddle as if she was a bag of feathers.

At the same time, Goodwin jumped atop his speckled white and gray horse. Ronan mounted behind her, his muscular thighs pressing against hers as one arm slid around her waist to keep her in place.

He urged his horse forward, and before Eva knew it, she was riding toward a Pictish hillfort with a Pictish warrior enveloping her in his entirely overwhelming presence.

CHAPTER TEN

"YE ONLY JUST arrived back, Murielle," Brodyn grunted as he watched her flutter around the village making arrangements to leave once more.

Turning, she huffed. Her heart ached so badly, and her stomach churned so violently that anger was the only emotion she'd allow to infiltrate her exterior. If any sadness seeped through, she'd crumble to the ground immediately and lose all control of her barely harnessed thoughts.

"I ken that, and I cannae go back just now, not until everything is in place. But I will go back, once I've spoken to Aldfrith."

"Come with me, sister. We must speak." Brodyn walked away, leaving her no chance to argue. Of course, he did. He knew how she worked by now. She decided to follow, for she owed him that much.

When she'd returned yesterday, Brodyn wasn't angry or arrogant. Instead, he was sympathetic and remorseful for trying to force her to marry Aldfrith. Apparently, Cait had done a wonderful job speaking on Murielle and Samuel's behalf when she'd returned home. She told Brodyn that Murielle was not recorded as the queen of the Britons or as Aldfrith's wife. She'd also told Brodyn that Samuel and Murielle were betrothed. Brodyn was so relieved that Murielle had come home at all, he'd remained calm with her. But obviously, he'd finally decided it was time to talk.

Entering the nearly empty longhouse, Brodyn grabbed a loaf

of fresh bread off the table, tore off a huge chunk, and shoved it into his mouth. "Want some?" he asked through his full mouth. Murielle flashed him a look of disgust and shook her head. He shrugged and continued toward the front of the longhouse, where his large, engraved, wooden seat dominated the area. "Have a seat," he said, patting Cait's seat beside him. Reluctantly, Murielle did as he commanded, praying he didn't intend to convince her to stay.

She needed closure with Samuel. He hadn't been able to pass through the veil again, though she couldn't understand why. That meant she had to sort everything out here and find him. If he wouldn't forgive her for calling off the wedding, she'd be devastated, but still, there was more to her plan than simply winning Samuel back.

"I'm sorry, Murielle. I'm sorry I tried to force ye to marry Aldfrith. And I'm sorry ye felt the need to run away, not only from Pinnata Castra but from this time."

"It wasn't ye or anything else, Brodyn. I would have gone anywhere Samuel was. I love ye, and I love our people. That's why I came back. When I saw the ruins..." She took a deep breath and shook her head. "It made me wonder if our people suffered because I refused to marry Aldfrith or if I'd caused our people to disappear. But Samuel explained to me just before bringing me back that he wouldnae have proposed to me if it would cause any issues. By then, I'd already demanded to go home and had given him back the ring. I've made a mess of everything."

"No, ye didnae. We can fix this. It starts tonight, for I received a message that King Aldfrith has cut his journey short and is marching our way. He should arrive in time for supper, and we will put all of this to rest. I want ye to be happy, Murielle. When ye think about yerself happy, what do ye see?"

Murielle closed her eyes and imagined her perfect future. It didn't take long for images of Samuel to materialize in her mind. Samuel meeting her at the altar, sharing her bed, and rubbing her swollen belly as several children surrounded them. But something else manifested—a vision that made her heart palpitate with excitement. She was teaching a group of tourists about her people and explaining their language and symbols. It was the part of her plan she'd been scrambling to resolve, but now that she imagined it with such clarity, she knew she had to make it her future in truth. "I'm married to Samuel with lots of bairns and teaching people about our people. Oh, dinnae ye see, Brodyn? All of our records are lost. Nobody kens our language. Nobody understands our symbols. It's all lost to time. But I can teach them! Only, Samuel says that without archaeological evidence, nobody will believe me. I cannae make this true unless I find a way to preserve our records. And I must find a way to make Samuel forgive me," she said with sadness as her visions of a perfect future dissolved into a puff of smoke. None of what she hoped for was even close to becoming a reality, but she was determined to make it so.

"Then I will do all I can to help ye achieve that future. Ye are my dear sister. I ken that Aldfrith and I will have a peaceful relationship even if no marriage binds our people. I only hope he isnae arriving today with hopes of a union."

"I will speak to him. I hope ye ken that I will always put our people first. If he demands a marriage to solidify peace, I shall do what is needed."

"We will find a way, Murielle. And I shall call off the guards at the cave. If Samuel attempts to pass through, he is welcome back. I believe ye when ye say he didnae intentionally send ye here alone." Brodyn patted her hand and shifted in his seat conspiratorially. "As for finding documentation about our people, I have spoken with Caitriona, and we have a plan. It requires obtaining records from the monk at the kirk."

"I considered that. The monk, Ivan of Iona, has spent much time documenting our lives, language, and symbols, but those records are wasted, for they have yet to be found."

"Caitriona says they willnae be found unless we find a way to make it so. The tome's pages are too fragile and likely suffered ruination from a fire, flood, or another natural disaster."

"What does she suggest?" Murielle asked, cocking her head to the side in curiosity.

"Leave that to me," Caitriona said as she snuck up behind Murielle, making her jump out of her skin. "I need to get the tome of records from Ivan's death grip. He's not going to allow his precious records to be removed from the kirk, and while I understand his purpose, he doesn't understand that his hard work will never be found, and nobody will remember our people. Let's just say I will need to get my hands dirty and pray for forgiveness later. Let me handle that. You have enough going on."

"I cannae forgive myself for how I reacted to Samuel kissing another woman. I ken why it happened now that I've had time to think about everything. It still hurts, but it wasnae his fault. And now, he is stuck on the other side of the veil. I need to get to him as soon as possible. Aldfrith's early arrival is a blessing, for I can leave here verra soon." She looked at Cait and Brodyn, feeling like an ingrate for saying such things. "Please, dinnae think I wish to leave ye all. I just want to move forward with my life."

"We understand, Murielle. Once I fell in love with Brodyn, I only wanted to be where he was. It's time you lived for yourself. The success of our people is not tied to this marriage. Both Samuel and I are sure of that."

"Thank ye." Murielle squeezed Cait's hand with gratitude. Thank God her brother had a wonderful wife. If he'd married a shrew, Murielle would be in misery. "I only hope Sam and I are able to visit, but now that the veil closed on him, I dinnae ken if we can. What if I'm not allowed through again, and we are separated forever?"

That thought only just now hit Murielle over the head like an avalanche of snow weighing her down with icy tendrils of dread, freezing her from the inside out.

"If you and he are meant to be, it will be," Cait said reassuringly. "Don't worry about Eva. She always wanted Samuel but never stood a chance. She isn't his type."

"Ye ken he bedded her two years ago, aye?" Murielle asked with a raised brow.

Cait scrunched up her nose in response. "I did not know that and preferred not knowing. She was my professor. *Blech!* But my statement remains true. He never wanted anything romantic with her. I saw him push her away many times. She must have gotten to him at his weakest. Two years ago, he met you. I think he completely changed after that."

Commotion just outside the longhouse caught their attention, and Murielle, Caitriona, and Brodyn walked outside. Murielle's heart flipped in her chest. Was Aldfrith already here? She had not realized how much she dreaded seeing him again until this moment as her stomach clenched.

"My king, queen. Princess," Ronan said as he dismounted his horse, locking eyes with her nervously. "I was guarding the cave as ye requested in case Samuel crossed through, but instead, this woman appeared. She was asking for Princess Murielle."

All Murielle saw was a figure astride Ronan's horse, wearing his cloak across slight shoulders. When the woman looked over her shoulder and locked eyes with Murielle, nausea roiled in her stomach as bile rose up her throat.

"What is she doing here?" Murielle barked.

Caitriona frowned and stood by Murielle's side just as Emilie pushed through the crowd to greet Goodwin, who sat astride his horse in silence.

"Professor Johansson?" Emilie asked, running forward. "What are *you* doing here?" Emilie turned to look at her best friend. "Cait, what the hell is going on?"

"We haven't gotten that far," Cait said, stepping forward to greet Eva. "Professor Eva Johansson. Welcome to Pinnata Castra. I assure you that you are safe."

"She isnae safe from me," Murielle scoffed, crossing her arms. "What are ye doing here? Have ye come to make my life more miserable than ye already have?"

"She came to apologize, Murielle," Ronan offered.

Murielle shot a warning glance at Ronan. How dare he defend this vile woman! He understood nothing and only saw a bonnie face.

Carefully, Ronan helped Eva down from the horse, making certain his cloak adequately covered most of her odd clothing. Villagers pretended not to pay attention as they walked past and continued their chores, but Murielle noticed several heads craning toward them, not the wood they cut or the cow they milked.

Murielle stared Eva down. Why was she here? She had been nothing but cruel to Murielle, and there was little doubt anything she could say would change Murielle's opinion of her.

"Tell her what ye told me," Ronan whispered to Eva. Already, Ronan seemed to connect with Eva in a way Murielle had never seen him do with any woman. It was true that he'd had a strong attraction to Emilie and tried to win her heart away from Goodwin once, but that was a physical desire. Never had she seen Ronan show tenderness to a woman the way he was with Eva, and Murielle wasn't pleased that Eva managed to attract every man around her despite her malicious nature.

Eva focused her attention on Murielle. "Murielle, I realize finding me here is unexpected. It is quite unexpected to me, as well. I didn't even believe this was possible. I'd be scared out of my mind right now if not for—" she turned and lifted her eyes to the man standing beside her—"Ronan."

Murielle resisted the urge to roll her eyes. Did this woman regard herself as some siren, using her red hair, dark eyes, and lithe body to control men?

Ronan stood straighter than ever if that was even possible for her rigid guard.

Ridiculous man. "Now ye ken why I was scared when ye left me stranded in yer time. Mayhap we should do the same with ye and see how well *ye* fair." Murielle knew she was being unusually unkind, but this woman had caused her much distress in 2023, and now she was here continuing the job in 686.

To her credit, Eva didn't back down or deny Murielle's accusations. "I deserve that. After everything that's happened, Samuel was furious with me. You'll be happy to know he said he never wanted to see me again. I did see him again, of course, because we work together. But he was a mess, Murielle. I was out of line and apologized to Samuel for my behavior." She lowered her gaze. "I'm trying to be a better person, but I allowed my jealousy to guide me, and I regretted it immediately. I wanted to apologize, but when I went to find you at Burghead the next day, you were gone. Some old couple named Edwin and Anya told me to ask their grandson, Callum, to help me find you. And he did. I didn't believe his story about the cave, but he took me to it, and here I am." She paused. "It was odd—is odd—how he looks almost exactly like Ronan, but younger and less... well... appealing." She blinked at Ronan, flirtatiously.

Ronan puffed out his chest and bit back a grin. Murielle really did roll her eyes this time. Goodwin grinned ear to ear, likely glad Ronan had finally found another woman to focus on aside from his wife, even if Eva was just passing through.

"Wait." Cait held up a hand and stepped closer. "Did you say you met an old couple named Anya and Edwin?" She looked at Brodyn and Murielle curiously before locking eyes with Eva.

"Uh, yeah. When I showed up at Burghead, they were walking down the street. They almost appeared out of place, like they were from another time. I just figured they were old-fashioned," Eva said with a shrug. "But when I went to meet Callum, he told me they are his three–times-great-grandparents who died long ago and randomly show up when someone in the family needs help. I don't believe in ghosts. Although, I don't believe in time travel, and yet, here I am." She made a face that would have been comical if Murielle's insides weren't twisted into knots and tightening with every utterance.

Still, the others were looking at her for confirmation. "Callum did look nearly identical to Ronan," Murielle agreed. "Only, as

Eva said, younger and… not a warrior." She couldn't bring herself to call Ronan appealing. He was handsome, but she'd grown up with him like a brother. "It occurred to me that he was one of Ronan's descendants because they looked nearly identical. It also occurred to me they may share a soul."

"Which would explain why Ronan couldn't pass through the veil," Goodwin added.

Emilie patted him on the shoulder with a grin. "Aww, you're learning." Goodwin scowled at her but couldn't keep the expression long before smiling widely at his wife, as he so often did.

"Exactly," Murielle added.

"Eva, Anya and Edwin existed in many timelines," Cait explained.

Brodyn nodded. "Anya crossed the veil during a war in her time, 1941. She was hiding from a sky attack… something about bombs and airplanes."

"Brodyn has a harder time imagining the future," Cait said with a chuckle. "But yes. Anya crossed through in 1941 and stayed because she fell in love with a druid here named Edwin. She'd lost everything in the war and had nothing to return to, either way. But she and Edwin have long been soulmates, finding one another in every lifetime."

Eva blinked at them all, silently staring as she processed everything she learned. Murielle understood that feeling of being overwhelmed all too well. Despite her desire to remain angry at Eva, she was too empathic not to feel the woman's distress as she learned everything she never believed in was true.

"But why would Anya and Edwin show themselves to Eva? She isnae their family," Brodyn asked.

"I assumed they meant to help Murielle?" Emilie added with a shrug.

"She isnae related to Edwin or Anya in any way," Brodyn said, shaking his head.

Murielle watched Ronan as he fussed over Eva, and she grew

uneasy. Was it possible they appeared to Eva because she *was* family? If Eva fell in love with Ronan and decided to stay here and have a family, that would make her their descendent. Or would she be their ancestor? A shiver rolled up Murielle's back. There was a lot to ponder in that one thought, and it was nothing she had the energy for.

"Murielle, can you ever forgive me for what I put you and Samuel through? I have literally traveled 1300 years into the past to seek you out and repair the damage. Samuel is madly in love with you. And it's obvious you feel the same way." Eva went on to explain that her sister ran away from home once and never returned, which motivated her to return Murielle to Burghead.

Murielle tapped her foot against the ground as she thought about what to say. The pain was too fresh and the trauma too raw to fully forgive her, but the woman *had* gone very far out of her way to make amends, and if true, her past had compelled her to act accordingly. Finally, she said, "Though it's still very painful, sending me back to Burghead helped me realize my calling, and I've returned here to make it happen. So, because of that alone, I can forgive ye. I do intend on returning to Samuel, but I dinnae ken if he will accept me after I called off our engagement."

"He will, trust me," Eva said with absolute confidence. "By the way, what is this calling you've discovered?" She raised a brow.

Clearing her throat and straightening her back, Murielle sucked in a deep breath. "I wish to teach your people about my people. I wish to teach them the language, the culture, and the symbols. But I ken I need evidence of these things for anyone to believe it. Without any surviving records, that's impossible. My greatest hope is to find a way to preserve some of our records so they may be found. Then I hope to make myself credible to the people I teach it to."

"So, you wish to be a professor?" Eva asked.

"Perhaps. Or even just a historian who speaks at universities or museums. I also have to establish an identity."

"You can be me."

Murielle turned toward Caitriona. "What did ye say?"

Cait shrugged and smiled as she held on to Brodyn's arm. "I spent several years of my life studying your people and earning my education as an archaeologist and anthropologist. I can't use it here, and I'm too busy being the Queen of the Picts and raising Lucas. I'd quite like my education to go to good use. Besides, you know more about the Picts than anyone in 2023. So, I don't feel bad fibbing that you are me. You have a lot of knowledge to offer, Murielle."

"Are… are ye certain about that?"

"Of course. I'm never going back. My life is here now. You already have my ID, passport, and bank card. I will give you all the information you need to take over my identity. Samuel can help you." Caitriona let go of Brodyn's arm and stepped closer to Murielle, taking her hand. "The only thing I want in return is for you and Samuel to be happy. You both mean the world to me. Go be with him. Go teach the world. Heck, you'll be me, so in an odd way, I get the credit, right? Besides, I was already regarded as one of the top Pict historians of my time. You can pass for me. We look quite similar."

"Ye do not!" Brodyn protested, making everyone around them laugh.

"They kinda do," Emilie said with a chuckle. "Sorry, Brodyn. Your wife looks like your sister."

"Nay, she doesnae!" he insisted, crossing his arms in protest. "But I do like this plan. Caitriona's education goes to good use, and you get to live yer life as ye choose."

"Ye support this insane plan, Brother?" Murielle looked up at Brodyn, biting her lip as she choked back tears. Her family was far too good to her.

Brodyn shrugged. "I've been accused of overindulging ye by many people, including every king who came calling on ye. The one time I tried to control ye, ye vanished through the veil. If this last indulgence secures yer happiness and future, I support it."

Emilie cocked her head and stepped closer to Caitriona. "But, what about your parents? I know you hardly saw or spoke to them since they travel nearly year-round at this point, but eventually, they will try to find you, and if they do… well, our old colleagues may not be able to tell she isn't you after a few years pass, but your parents will."

"Just leave that to me. I have a whole plan. Just let me work it all out."

"Thank ye." Murielle threw herself into her sister's arms, overcome by emotion as reality hit her. She was preparing to leave this time and place, possibly for good this time. She wasn't sure if she'd ever be able to come back. Samuel couldn't pass through after years of freely coming and going. Would that mean the cave or the veil—or whatever it was—would close her out? What if she couldn't go back to Samuel? A slight shock of panic shot through her, but it only motivated her to get to the cave as soon as possible and find out. There was no sense worrying about it until that time came.

Brodyn wrapped his large arms around her and Cait, pulling them in for a suffocating embrace.

"Already, I have learned much about your people," Eva said as she smiled. "King Brodyn, I never would have expected a Pictish king to be so doting on his women."

"Most kings in this time are not this way," Caitriona struggled to say as Brodyn enveloped her small body against his large frame. Murielle laughed and wiped away a tear.

"'Tis true. I am a verra fortunate woman to have a brother who accepts my whims, my stubbornness, my independence."

"She is a pain in my arse," Brodyn grumbled. "But aye, I have been a fool for my wee sister since the day she was born." Brodyn released Murielle and Cait from his death grip and looked at Eva. "We have a king joining us for our evening meal, so I have much to prepare."

"Ronan, you may escort Eva back to our home, where she can change into period-appropriate garments and prepare for the feast. That is…" Cait shifted her gaze at Eva. "If you are interested in experiencing a true Pictish feast, Professor Johansson."

Eva's eyes lit up, and she smiled at Ronan before looking at Caitriona. "Oh, my gosh, yes! I cannot believe this!"

"We know the feeling," Emilie said with a laugh. "We were in the exact same place as you not that long ago. And, we met our husbands here and never looked back."

"Oh…" Eva turned red when she looked at Ronan before looking away immediately. Murielle watched with amusement to see Eva, the successful professor and businesswoman, blushing beside Ronan like a fresh-faced lass. Perhaps her instinct about Eva being related to Edwin and Anya was accurate. After all, she spoke and understood their language immediately, as had Caitriona and Emilie when they first arrived.

Anya had once told Murielle that Cait understood their ancient language because she'd spent time here in a previous life. It was a repressed memory triggered by returning. If Cait's use of the Pictish language was proof that she'd returned here in every lifetime, was the same true for Eva? Murielle liked to believe she understood English because it was her destiny to always stay with Samuel in his time, but Caitriona had painstakingly taught her much of what she knew over the past two years.

The group headed deeper into the village toward the royal lodgings atop the hill. Murielle wondered what exactly Caitriona had planned in her mischievous mind, but she would do as her sister-by-marriage asked and leave the planning to her. Besides, Murielle had a king to reject and farewells to say before she went back to find Samuel.

She only hoped he would be as open to her plans as everyone else.

THROWING HIS SATCHEL onto the bed, Samuel shoved a pair of

clean trousers and a tunic into it, along with his toothbrush and some toothpaste he'd disguised in an old glass container. He didn't want to be caught in 686 with a tube of toothpaste that would raise questions.

Right now, time seemed to pass slower than a snail crossing the street. He kept checking the time on his watch, expecting hours to pass when only minutes seemed to drag by.

Low tide was at two in the morning, and Samuel's class didn't reconvene until the day after tomorrow, so he had time to attempt the journey back to Murielle without finding a sub for his class.

Since his conversation with Eva, Samuel had been considering her apology, wondering if he didn't owe Murielle the same. Worry for her safety consumed him. She was likely fine at Pinnata Castra, but Samuel couldn't concentrate on much else until he saw her and knew for certain and he was determined to return to the cave every day until the veil allowed him through again. While he couldn't give up his career and stay in her time, he'd do everything he could to convince Murielle to come back with him, to find a way to support her goals here as a historian.

The rectangular alarm clock on his nightstand flashed one in the morning, and Samuel decided it was time to go. He would arrive early, but he'd rather wait and watch the waves than stay cooped up in his flat for another minute.

No matter what he looked at or did, everything reminded him of Murielle, and the knots in his stomach wouldn't ease until he found her again, and the looming fear that he'd never be able to cross the veil again ate away at his soul. It still rankled that, in spite of all he'd done for the timeline—spending life after life stuck in the loop to save lives—the veil had had the nerve to cut him out just before he could achieve his own happiness. He'd rage and yell, but he had nobody to rage and yell at. If the universe conspired to keep him from Murielle, then he'd be faced with the realization that they weren't meant to be. Except, he knew the truth in his heart, and there was no way he would give up easily. Murielle was his soulmate. He'd seen Cait fall for Brodyn and Emilie fall for Goodwin. He knew about Anya and Edwin. If time travelers found their mates through the veil, then his was Murielle.

Grabbing his satchel, Sam walked into his dining room for his phone and keys before locking the door and heading down to his Jeep. The icy fingers of a mid-autumn night wrapped around his flesh, biting at his nose, and crawling up his spine. Wisps of frozen breath drifted from his parted lips as he shut Joplin's door and cranked up the heat before speeding toward the coast.

His headlights reflected off the signs he passed as he sped toward the cliff. Soon, the familiar nothingness engulfed him as he approached and parked at the top of the cliff. Grabbing his belongings, Samuel locked his car and turned on his flashlight. He'd likely be able to traverse this trail with his eyes closed for as many times as he'd traveled it, but he preferred to use his resources and not leave anything to chance as he shined the light downward, hoping to ward away any wildlife lurking on the trail.

When Samuel reached the bottom of the trail, he looked at his watch as the waves lapped at his boots. Already the tide was pulling away from shore, but he still had thirty minutes to wait. More than once, he'd considered investing in a small rowboat or canoe to reach the cave during high tide, but he always thought the better of it once he saw the violence with which the waves crashed against the side of the cliff. He'd be capsized and drowned before ever reaching the cave.

His nerves pricked with annoyance as he awaited time's passage, but looking out at the sky, he saw the full moon glowing overhead and the sparkle of distant stars peeking through smatterings of clouds. Deciding he needed to take a breath and calm his emotions, Samuel dropped his bag on the ground and sat at the world's edge, where the ocean ended, and the earth began.

Much like the ocean and the earth, he and Murielle were the merging of two worlds, and if the elements could create harmony, so too, could they. The water pulled away, then rushed forward while it churned and foamed. Alone out here, below the vast sky and flowing waves, Samuel felt peace wash over him with every swish of water across his boots. Nothing had ever been in his control. Every lifetime, he'd been born knowing he had a role to play, and he'd obeyed.

He thought being with Murielle was the one part of his life he could control, but the earth laughed at him when it shut its veil, refusing to let him pass, proving itself in control once again.

"I get it. I'm a pawn. You control my fate," Samuel sighed as he watched another wave crash onto shore before retreating. Every retreat of the waves exposed a tiny bit more land, reminding him that the world would continue to turn, time would continue to pass, and the tides would continue to change; he was a mere mortal who must succumb to its whims. All he hoped for was a life with Murielle as his wife. A life of peace and happiness. A life of exploration as he showed her the wonders of his modern world. He hoped to fill that world with laughter, children, and a grumble of pugs.

Rather than counting the seconds until his next pass through the veil, Samuel closed his eyes and focused on being present for the first time in his life. He smelled the brine of the sea and heard the peaceful, repetitive and rhythmic swish and hiss of the waves. A gust of wind washed over his face and through his hair, reminding him that while he might be a keeper of time, he was just a man, a speck of dust upon these shores. Someday, he'd join his ancestors and become part of the earth once more. But while he lived, right now, he'd enjoy every moment and every sensation.

Opening his eyes, Samuel stared up at the sky with newfound purpose, knowing precisely what he had to do. Energy zinged through his body, and awareness thrummed through his veins as the hairs on his arms stood on end like static from a balloon. The veil was opening to him. Never had he felt its call so strongly.

Looking at the water, Samuel realized that the low tide had arrived during his time of contemplation, and the shore was now limited but accessible. The cave's entrance was only yards away, and already he felt it calling to him, admitting him.

He couldn't understand the strength with which it called, but perhaps the earth had needed him to ground himself and reflect on his true purpose and desires to deem him worthy of passage once more. He'd never understand the complexity or vulnerability of the veil, but he'd never felt it so strongly as he did at that moment. He stood and strode toward the beckoning cave with more conviction than ever before. There was no doubt he was meant to be with Murielle. He was going to cross through and do whatever it took to win her back.

CHAPTER ELEVEN

OPENING THE LARGE chest at the foot of her bed, Murielle rummaged through a lifetime of belongings, carefully packing what could potentially help her in 2023. Picking up the beautiful compact mirror Emilie gifted her recently, Murielle opened it and sighed as she looked at her reflection. Red, tired eyes stared back at her, and a frown marred her usually upturned lips.

Thoughts of Samuel plagued her. Every time she closed her eyes, Murielle lived those depressing moments all over again. Handing him back his ring. Turning her back on him because he had kissed another woman before they were together.

She was prepared to leave her time and seek him out, begging for his forgiveness. But what if he didn't trust her anymore? The fear that she'd never see Samuel again or that she'd ruined her chance at happiness ate away at her bit by bit. Still, she was determined to push forward and do everything to make things right with him.

Finding Eva here was the last thing Murielle had expected, but the woman indeed seemed contrite. She'd described Samuel as heartbroken, which only added to Murielle's misery. However, it also offered her hope that she'd be able to repair the damage. This time, she'd travel alone. Ronan couldn't cross the veil, and Caitriona needed to stay here with Brodyn and Lucas. She had a people to rule and keep safe. Murielle couldn't pull anyone else into her web. But she'd left Caitriona's bank card and ID with

Samuel, so she was uncertain how she'd get around once she crossed through. Still, she hoped, she wouldn't have any problems. Maybe she'd find Callum as she had before, and he could contact Sam for her. At least she'd be able to shelter in the visitor center.

The thought that Sam wouldn't come to her was unbearable, and she pushed it aside.

Removing all of her clothes and packing them into her satchel, Murielle focused on the small baubles and objects she'd collected through her lifetime. None of them were of more than sentimental value. She closed her eyes for a moment, remembering the days of her youth as she prepared for her future. When she opened them, her gaze fell onto the doll made of twigs that she'd once given to her mother before she'd passed away. Murielle gently picked it up, carefully running a thumb over its rough surface, remembering how she'd created it as she sat on the forest floor. She'd been about five years old then, and her mama loved the silly twig doll so much that she'd carried it in her own small satchel tied to her belt until the day she died, which was only months after receiving the doll.

Murielle wrapped it in one of her tunics to keep it safe, then picked up a silver ring given to her by her father. At one time, it contained a stone of some sort, but the stone had either fallen out or been removed before her father gave it to her. Murielle hadn't cared about the missing stone. She only cared that she'd received the lovely gift from her busy father, who spent so much time ruling his people that Murielle often became an afterthought. Except for the night he'd given her this ring. That night, he'd walked past his sons, Brodyn and Talorc, to give her this special gift.

Placing the ring aside, Murielle removed the remainder of her belongings, mostly consisting of torcs or other items one would expect a princess to own, even if she rarely wore them. Nay, Murielle always preferred to live a simple life and keep items of value buried and hidden. She never felt royal and never wanted to lord it over everyone else. But perhaps Caitriona would enjoy these.

Murielle placed them in a small clay basin by her bed so she could give them to Cait before she left. After all, her sister was giving up her identity and any chance of returning to her time just so Murielle could be with Samuel. She owed her far more than some old baubles, but it was a start.

Ronan knocked on the door before peeking into her chamber. "Ye are needed downstairs, Princess."

"Come in here for a second. I haven't had a chance to speak with ye alone since I arrived back. I want to apologize for trying to force ye through the veil with me. I was being verra selfish."

Ronan smiled and shook his head. "I am yer personal guard. Yer safety is my only concern. I go where ye go, even if it's the future, and I'm sorry I couldnae follow. I would have quite liked to see it. Ye are all talking about it, and now there's Eva." His eyes seemed to glow with emotion as he said her name, and Murielle couldn't help but be struck by it. She'd never seen him so open with his emotions. And yet, here he was, looking a little lovesick.

"Aye. What is it with Eva? Ye seem to have grown attached to her in a matter of hours."

He shrugged, but Murielle noticed the slight tinge of red spread across his tan cheeks. "She is a beautiful, interesting woman. Naught more than that. She isnae from here, so no sense hoping for anything to come from it."

"Ronan. Ye are a good man and deserve happiness. I ken ye will find it someday, for I met the evidence in Burghead, which is Pinnata Castra in the future. Yer line doesnae travel verra far from this land, and yer descendent looked exactly like ye. I vow he is a younger version of ye. He even said he felt as if he kenned me. I think yer soul is in him, and it recalled me."

"So, if I have descendants..."

"Ye will one day have a family, aye. And Anya and Edwin showed themselves to Eva. I cannae say what that means, but if they only show themselves to blood relatives when they need help, and Eva was desperately seeking me out... what does that make her?" Murielle cocked her head as she thought about it, but she didn't want to imply more than necessary, for it would break Ronan's heart if he grew attached to a woman who was soon to leave.

"It crossed my mind after ye mentioned that before. There is something about her. 'Tis like we ken one another already, but I dare not dream, for she is far too good for me and will be leaving soon. And, as I've discovered, I cannae follow her through the veil. It cannae be."

"Ye dinnae give yerself enough credit, Ronan. It pains me to say such things because I regard ye as a brother, but ye are an attractive man with a big heart and bigger muscles. Ye deserve a woman as good as Eva. I'm surprised I'm even saying that after she dumped me on the side of the road."

"She seems genuinely remorseful," Ronan gently added, clearly worried Murielle would be offended that he took Eva's side.

She smiled to reassure him. "I ken. Ye are correct. She wouldnae have come all this way if she wasnae sorry. I played a hand in all that happened with Samuel and must take the blame for it."

Ronan cleared his throat and stepped aside. "One thing at a time, Princess. Ye have a suitor below stairs awaiting ye."

All the blood left her face as she straightened her back and widened her eyes. Aldfrith had arrived, and now Murielle must gather all her courage to once and for all end this confusion. She sucked in a deep, steadying breath and closed her eyes, gathering her courage. She had to trust that Cait and Samuel were right that Aldfrith would marry another woman, one he loved deeply and with whom he shared a strong Christian faith. She also had to trust in Aldfrith's character and pray he would remain a close ally despite the lack of marriage alliance. After all, peace had been achieved in many tribes without exchanging brides.

Smoothing out the wrinkles on her worn and faded green tunic, Murielle wondered if she should change before heading down but thought against it. She wasn't attempting to seduce or impress the man. Being rejected by a woman in a disheveled tunic would probably lessen the blow.

Reaching the bottom step, Murielle looked up and stopped in her tracks, gasping as her breath hitched and her stomach flipped. The man who waited for her wasn't Aldfrith! "Sam?" she whispered, desperate to run into his arms but unable to move her feet. Shock and confusion made her head spin. "Why… how?"

Hesitantly, Samuel took one step closer, then stopped. "I had to see you, Murielle. I hope you will hear me out."

"Of course, I will," she said, trying to remain calm as she wrung her hands together.

Brodyn and Caitriona stood up from their seat at the table, readying themselves to leave before Samuel stopped them. "I would like you to remain if that is all right. I won't take much of your time." He turned back to Murielle and took yet another step. Her stomach fluttered with anticipation as she watched Samuel hesitantly approach her.

"I made many mistakes, Murielle. But the greatest mistake was giving up on us so easily. You were confused, scared, and hurt. I should have begged you to stay and talk everything through with me, but all I wanted was to make you happy after disappointing you so much. Then, the veil closed on me. I've been worried sick about your safety. I needed to know you were all right."

Murielle frowned and felt disappointment wash over her like a bucket of icy water from the loch pouring over her head. "Ye only came because ye were worried for me?"

"No, of course not. I was, yes, but I assumed Brodyn had guards watching the area."

"Ronan found me immediately."

He nodded. "I came here to…" Samuel cleared his throat and shifted his gaze away from her for only a second before settling his dark eyes on her with an intensity that melted her to her core.

Murielle closed her eyes to gather her strength. She wasn't certain what brought him here—her heart longed to hear that he still wanted to marry her, but her mind remembered his words before they parted all too well. He said he couldn't continue waiting and that they were over if she left. Yet, here he was… But why?

Opening her eyes, she found Samuel before her on one knee. Her heart pounded like a drum as she looked down at him. "Sam?"

"I love you, Murielle. Only you. In every lifetime. That's how I know for certain we are meant to be and that our union will only bring happiness and peace, not war or destruction. I know in my heart that this time loop I'm stuck in life after life is about more than just correcting history. It's about bringing me to you.

"I let you go without reassuring you that my love is infinite and transcendent. You can choose to stay in this time, but I will love you more with every beat of my heart even if I'm 1300 years in the future."

Murielle heard Caitriona sniffle, and she struggled to hold back her own welling tears. Already, unshed tears blurred her vision. "Oh, Samuel," she whispered. "I love you so much. I dinnae want to live without ye, either, and I'm so sorry I panicked and fled."

"You had to return here after what you saw at Burghead, and I understand that. The fault is mine. All of it. I do not deserve you, yet I feel compelled to ask this once more. If your answer is no, I shall leave you alone and accept my failures. Murielle…" Samuel held up the ring he'd once given her, his hand shaking as he gripped it between his thumb and forefinger. "Will you please marry me? Be my wife for the rest of my life?"

Swallowing, Murielle's breath hitched in her chest as she stared down at Samuel holding the ring. She'd known this was his question the moment he got down on one knee, but hearing those words again still knocked the wind from her.

"Aye, my dearest love, I want nothing more than to be yer wife!" Murielle let a sob escape from her stinging throat, no longer caring if she wept before everyone. She wouldn't allow anything else to come between her and Samuel ever again, not Aldfrith, or Eva, or her own insecurities.

Samuel slid the ring on her finger and stood, taking her into his strong, comforting embrace, enveloping her in his warmth. His lips came down on hers, and she gasped, not expecting him to be so brazen before her brother. But he was her betrothed now, and even her brother couldn't interfere.

"This is wonderful!" she heard Caitriona exclaim and clap. Murielle kissed Samuel back with all she had, feeling heat creep up her cheeks and desire shudder in her core.

When Samuel released her from his impassioned kiss, they looked up and saw their loved ones surrounding them with wide smiles.

Then Eva stepped out of the shadows, and Samuel's face dropped, and he turned white. "Eva?" Samuel looked between Murielle and his co-worker with bewilderment. "What the hell are you doing here?" He said with confusion and anger lacing his rough tone.

"It's all right, Sam," Murielle said, taking his hand in hers and squeezing it reassuringly. "It's a long story, but she came to apologize to me."

"Came here? When? H-how? I only saw her earlier today after she apologized."

"We will fill you in on everything," Cait said, stepping forward. "Everything is well in hand, and you and Murielle are finally back together. Nothing else matters."

"She spoke with Callum, Ronan's descendent, when she went to Burghead to find me and apologize. He told her how to find me, and she did. I will explain more later, love, I promise," Murielle said softly. "I amnae mad that she is here. On the contrary, I find much peace in how everything has happened. Now I must await Aldfrith. He arrives tonight, and I pray he takes the news of our betrothal well."

Samuel nodded, but she knew he had many questions. "Let's go for a walk in the village, and I'll explain everything," she said with a smile as she took his hand. "I'd rather explain everything now before Aldfrith arrives, which should be verra shortly."

Samuel willingly left the house with her, and a peaceful calm washed over them as they walked hand in hand, smiling at her people, who smiled and waved back, not at all surprised to see her and Sam together. Perhaps everyone knew all along that she loved him from the first moment he stepped foot through their gates. She only prayed that she hadn't let them down.

Despite her joy, a sense of dread still niggled at her belly. Dusk was upon them, and Murielle prayed that when Aldfrith arrived, he'd not be angry that she had decided to marry another man. For if he was, the consequences could be dire.

"MY KING. KING Aldfrith has arrived with his retinue. Would ye have him enter or meet ye in the longhouse for business?" Lawrence, their largest warrior, asked as he stepped into the doorway.

Brodyn sucked in a deep breath and swiped a large hand down his face as he often did when in distress. "Best to not leave the man waiting any longer than necessary. He has traveled far and deserves honesty and respect. I only hope he doesnae draw his sword."

Lawrence nodded and left to relay the message to Aldfrith.

"He willnae, or a battle will break loose," Goodwin said calmly. "He is a smarter man than that."

Murielle's knees began to shake, and she felt sweat forming on her brow. "Och, I am so nervous. My stomach hurts," Murielle whispered.

Samuel squeezed her hand before letting go. "It's going to be all right," he soothed. "I'm here with you." He stepped behind her and took his place by the wall, watching but not interfering. As usual, she realized. Samuel was a man who understood his duty and the role he was meant to play in their time, even though he was now her betrothed.

Murielle nodded and took courage from his quiet strength. More than anything, she disliked disappointing others, but there was nothing to be done. The truth must be spoken, and it was her duty to speak it.

When Aldfrith stepped through the doorway, he nodded his head respectfully and Murielle offered him a shaky smile before giving him a curtsey.

"Welcome back, King Aldfrith," Brodyn said as he stepped forward to clasp wrists with the man.

"Thank ye for having me back earlier than expected. My pilgrimage was cut short, and I must return home, but I wished to conclude our business before returning."

"I do hope everything is well back in Northumbria?" Brodyn asked with concern lacing his brow.

"Oh, aye. All is well. I'm afraid that what I have to say concerns Murielle, and I only hope there will be no hard feelings between our people after I say what I must."

Murielle sucked in a deep breath and held it as Aldfrith turned toward her and stepped closer. Samuel shifted behind her, and she appreciated that he wasn't some jealous man who'd try to claim her in from of Aldfrith and make everything worse. Her rejection would surely be hard enough on the king, and he didn't need Samuel rubbing salt into the wound.

Aldfrith took her hand in his and gave her a kind smile. "I hope ye ken what a lovely woman ye are, Murielle. Any man would be fortunate to call ye wife. But, that man cannae be me."

"Oh?" His words shocked her, and though she was pleased to hear it as the tension immediately left her body, she couldn't help cocking her head to the side and crinkling her brow. "I do hope our people havenae insulted ye in any way, King Aldfrith."

"Och, nay. Quite the contrary. I value our friendship and look forward to years of peace between our people, that is, if King Brodyn still wishes for such a relationship after what I must say. But, ye see, while on pilgrimage, I fell in love."

Aldfrith sighed and shook his head. "I am ashamed of myself, for I am truly an honorable man who always keeps his word. 'Tis not the norm for a king to follow his heart rather than his senses, but I have no defense. I fell in love and cannae imagine marrying another woman. It would be unfair to ye if we married while I loved another woman. She is a good Christian woman and was on her way to the same shrine. Ye see, we share a profound faith in our Lord, and her brother is the king of Wessex. She spoke of an alliance between us all that would benefit us all. Truly, I made certain my decision would also benefit yer people. I can only pray ye forgive me for considering my heart in this manner."

Aldfrith looked at Brodyn, who appeared slightly shocked, before setting his gaze back to Murielle. "I ken ye didnae wish for this marriage, so I do hope my news offers ye only comfort and not distress, and I pray our people may continue a peaceful union. But, if my decision will bring ye shame or cause war between our people, say the word, and I shall do my duty."

So struck by this turn of events, Murielle was at a complete loss for words, and she stared gape-mouthed at the king, who still gripped her hand.

Seeing her state of shock, Brodyn stepped forward to address Aldfrith. "I must admit, King Aldfrith, I do find this news surprising. However, I am certain I speak for everyone when I say that we are verra happy that ye have found true love. I, of all men, cannae blame ye, for I am a fool for my wife and only wish others to experience the same contentment. Ye may rest assured that our people still value our alliance with ye and will continue to support the Northumbrians. I shouldnae have tried to force the union. It was unfair to both of ye."

Tension visibly left Aldfrith as his posture relaxed, and a smile crept up his handsome face. "I cannae say how pleased I am to hear this. I had a feeling ye would understand, King Brodyn, but I dinnae wish to dishonor ye, Murielle, or our alliance. But, Murielle," he said, directly addressing her. "I wish to hear ye speak yer mind on the subject. Had yer mind changed about our marriage?"

Murielle looked over her shoulder at Samuel, who kept his gaze down and his lips sealed, allowing Murielle to speak her own mind without his influence. She loved everything about Samuel, but his respect for her opinions and her right to decide for herself only made her heart swell with more love than she ever thought possible.

Murielle turned back to Aldfrith and prepared to speak, sucking in another calming breath. "King Aldfrith, ye are the most respectful and honorable man who came calling, and ye would have made me a wonderful husband. I can only say that I am verra glad for ye that ye found true love, and I dinnae hold any ill will toward ye for following yer heart. For, ye see, I too am in love with another, as I believe ye kenned. And he is here now and just proposed marriage."

Murielle turned and put her hand out to Samuel, who looked at her with a proud grin, laced her fingers through his, and came to stand beside her. "King Aldfrith, please allow me to introduce ye to Samuel, the man I hope—nay, I *plan*—to marry."

The men clasped forearms and exchanged smiles and nods, making Murielle sigh with relief. As all the pent-up tension from the past several days left her body, she felt as if she might collapse. But, she steadied her knees and took another calming breath. She couldn't have imagined a better scenario than King Aldfrith calling off the betrothal.

Sam said, "It is my deepest honor to meet you, King Aldfrith. In truth, I have heard only great things about you and your nature. I want you to know that Murielle holds you in high regard, as do I."

Aldfrith grinned and let out a small chuckle. "I am pleased to hear that. I fear many believe I will behave poorly as my uncle before me. But I am not him. I do not play the role of a warlord. Nay, my dearest wish is to spread the Lord's word and grant my people the peaceful existence they all deserve after generations of war. There is a great world out there full of art, learning, and growth. I hope to bring that to my people, and war only destroys progress."

"I cannae agree more," Brodyn said, and Murielle smiled at her elder brother, proud of his personal growth as a man.

"I hope ye ken, much like yerself, that I was willing to marry ye if it meant keeping my people safe. We both ken what is at stake and care for our people above ourselves. I'm only glad we mutually agree that marriage doesnae suit us, nor does it determine the fate of our people."

"I'd never wage war on an entire people because one woman didnae wish to marry me. 'Tis a new era, and I believe we shall make it a peaceful one."

Brodyn stepped forward and smacked Aldfrith on the back with a grunt. "Let's drink to that. Tonight, we feast and celebrate our peaceful union with Northumbria, even if there is no marriage to join us."

Aldfrith nodded his agreement. "My men and I would be eternally grateful for yer hospitality. 'Tis been a grueling month of travel for us, and we have a sennight of traveling left to return home."

"Wait." Murielle stepped forward and looked at her brother, an idea brewing. Samuel would need to return to his time soon, and she'd leave with him. But she was here now, surrounded by everyone she loved. "We can still have a wedding," she said slowly, raising a brow as she pulled Samuel toward her. "Samuel and I can marry tonight before we leave. Nothing would mean more to me than to marry him surrounded by my people. That is, if it suits King Aldfrith."

"I'd be humbled and honored to witness yer marriage ceremony, Princess Murielle." He bowed and smiled at her.

Turning toward Sam, she looked into his dark eyes and felt

her stomach flutter as it always did when she gazed into his eyes, which were like mirrors into his soul. "Only if ye wish it, as well, Samuel." She didn't mean to make important decisions about their life without consulting him. The whim had simply struck her, and she spoke without thinking. She held her breath, hoping Sam would agree.

"It would be an honor to become your husband tonight, Murielle. It's been a long time coming, and I don't want to sleep another night without you by my side."

Emilie and Cait held hands beside one another and bobbed on the balls of their feet with excitement. "What do you say, Husband?" Cait asked Brodyn, looking up at him with excitement.

"I cannae think of a better time than tonight to marry my sister to Samuel. We shall tell the priest to prepare for the ceremony."

Cait squealed and danced her way over to Murielle, pulling her into a strong embrace. "Oh, my sister and my mentor will be married!"

Everyone in the room lit up with energy, and Murielle even noticed a wide smile on Eva's face as she stood shoulder-to-shoulder with Ronan. When they made eye contact, Eva winked at her, and Murielle smiled back. Never mind what had happened before; everything led to this moment—the fulfillment of her dreams. She was going to marry Samuel, live in 2023, and share the story of her people with the modern world. It almost felt too good to be true, especially because everyone around her supported her decisions, even King Aldfrith and her brother.

"We've got no time to lose!" Emilie shouted loud enough to make Murielle jump out of her skin. She took Murielle by the hand and pulled her toward the stairs, wee Anya on her hip. "We have a wedding to plan! Call all the maids up to Murielle's room! We shall have her looking like the most beautiful bride in no time!"

"That's impossible. Ye were the most beautiful bride,"

Goodwin said to Emilie, making her grin and blush.

"Oh, stop. You're biased," she said, shrugging off his compliment but glowing with happiness.

Murielle laughed and leaned in to kiss Samuel one last time before being dragged away by a mob of women, including Eva, before ascending the stairs.

This night, Murielle was a bride. But, more importantly, she had become an independent woman with her entire life ahead of her… just like a woman from the future. Her and Sam's future, in the year 2023.

CHAPTER TWELVE

S IPPING A MUG of ale as he awaited his wedding ceremony, Samuel listened to King Brodyn and King Aldfrith laugh and bond over shared trials as kings. He wasn't sure how his life had ever led to this moment as he awaited his Pictish princess bride while bonding over drinks with the king of the Picts and Britons.

King Aldfrith had always been one of Samuel's favorite historical characters, and little did the man know that he fulfilled one of Samuel's bucket list moments as he sat and had drinks with him. Life worked in mysterious ways, and Samuel wouldn't waste any time trying to figure out why or how everything had worked out. He was simply grateful that it had.

"Are ye ready to join this family, Samuel?" Brodyn asked, raising a brow.

"I've never been more ready for anything in my life, and I thank you both. King Brodyn, for offering us your blessing, and King Aldfrith, for not waging war on us all," Sam said with a cheeky grin as he raised his mug. The kings grunted with amusement, raised their mugs as well, and they all drank deeply until nothing was left.

"I would never stand in the way of true love," Aldfrith said. "I have found my true love and would stop at nothing to be with her."

"I have a feeling you will have a long, peaceful, and successful marriage," Sam said with a nod. He knew they would, but he couldn't say as much.

Goodwin walked into the longhouse and grabbed another full mug of ale from a nearby table as he walked over. "Ready to get married, old man?"

Samuel looked up at Goodwin with a look of mock indignation. "Old? I'm 35! Where I come from, I'm just a baby."

"Aye, well here, yer ancient." Goodwin scoffed. Aldfrith squinted at them with curiosity but shrugged off the banter.

"And, yes, I'm more than ready. The question is, is Murielle ready?"

"Why dinnae ye go ask her yerself? She is ready to meet ye in front of the chapel."

"Already?" Samuel went to check his watch and paused, realizing he didn't wear one and that the others wouldn't understand such a gesture. They used the positioning of the sun and stars to tell time, not analog watches. He pretended to scratch at his wrist to cover his action. "Yes, of course, I am ready."

He stood, ready to meet his bride, and a rush of excitement swept over him, making Samuel nearly giddy. It was really happening, and they had everyone here, even King Aldfrith and Eva. He was glad Murielle had taken time to explain how and why Eva had arrived at Pinnata Castra before Aldfrith arrived. Now, he could stop worrying about her and focus on Murielle.

"I have something for ye as a new member of the royal family." Brodyn cleared his throat and stood from his seat. It creaked and groaned as he stood, and Sam wondered how Brodyn's large muscular body fit into such a small wooden chair. He had a large throne-like chair at the front of the longhouse, but he preferred to sit here when he drank with others.

As Brodyn stepped up to Samuel, he removed the large pelt of fur draping his shoulders and slowly placed it around Samuel's.

Frowning, Samuel shook his head. "Oh, I could not possibly wear your furs. They are for royalty only."

"Which ye are about to become," Brodyn insisted as he adjusted the fur, closed it with a large silver brooch, and looked at Goodwin. "Do ye have it?"

Nodding, Goodwin handed Brodyn an object wrapped in a clean, white strip of linen. "Just finished. Took a lot of silver for the blacksmith to smelt and create this last minute, but it came out quite nicely."

Samuel raised a brow, curious about this mysterious object.

"No royal member of the family must go without one of these," Brodyn murmured as he unraveled the cloth to reveal a shiny, new, silver circlet for Samuel's head.

"Oh, no… no, no." Samuel waved his hand in dismissal, not because he didn't appreciate the gift, but it was all too grand for a simple man such as himself.

"If ye wish to marry my sister, ye must grow accustomed to some things. Ye dinnae need to wear this at all times, but for special occasions—such as yer marriage—wearing the fur and crown lend power and respect to yer position. Ye will be a Pictish prince. And now, ye look the part. Ye will become my brother, after all." Brodyn carefully placed the simple circlet atop Samuel's head, and Sam couldn't help but smile with gratitude that Brodyn was so gracious and welcoming.

Choking back emotion, Samuel lowered his head. "Thank you, King Brodyn."

"Thank ye for making my sister so happy. Now, get yer arse over to the chapel and go finish the deed. Ye must be there before the bride arrives, or she will be shunned. The groom must always be awaiting his bride with anticipation."

"Yes, it's the same in my ti—" he caught himself and cleared his throat. "Where I am from, I mean."

Brodyn winked at him and ushered him out of the longhouse, down one hill and slightly up another, until they stood before the chapel and a crotchety old priest who Samuel had never seen smile before… and likely never would.

"'Bout time ye showed," the priest groused as he stood in simple, unbleached robes with a rope belt around his waist and a tome in his hand.

"Is that the record of Pinnata Castra?" Samuel asked.

"The priest lowered his brow. "Aye, what's it to ye? I shall read from it during the ceremony and then record the date of yer marriage within its pages."

"Just curious," Samuel said casually, but in truth, he was lamenting that the very object that told the story of the Picts stood within arm's reach, yet it would go missing one day and never be found, leaving the Picts of Fortriu forever shrouded in mystery.

"Oy, here she comes," Lawrence said from the side of lined guards where Ronan and Goodwin also stood.

Samuel's gaze shifted from the warriors to the path leading through the center of town. Hundreds of men, women, and children lined the street with broad smiles and excited chatter as they awaited their beloved princess, who none expected to be married on this day.

As the voices faded into silence and the people formed a tidy line, Samuel's heart began to beat wildly against his ribcage. He knew his bride approached even if he could not see her.

And then, he did. And his breath caught in his chest.

Like an ethereal beauty in a soft, blue silk gown with her swaying hips, flowing blonde hair, and a smile that could light up any time in any place, Murielle floated toward him with Cait, Emilie, and Eva in tow. Even though it was late October and the sun hid behind masses of gray clouds as cold wind wrapped them in a familiar embrace, when she came up beside him, warmth rushed through him like that of a summer day…

"Samuel," she whispered as she put out a hand and her face flushed. She was always beautiful, of course, but right now, she stole his breath.

"Murielle," he whispered back, taking her hand and leading her toward the priest.

Time slowed and sped up at the same time. What was time, anyway? People came and went, and civilizations rose and fell, but he and Murielle would always withstand the hand of time. He knew he'd remember every word of the ceremony, even if he felt like he floated off the ground.

The priest recited vows in Latin before having them exchange rings. He slid his mother's ring onto her finger and promised to find her a matching band when they got home, and she slid a ring onto his finger that the poor blacksmith hastily created for the royal wedding. But it was perfect, and so was his bride.

"Well, lad. What ye waiting for? I told ye to kiss yer bride," the grouchy priest grumbled.

Snapping out of his daze, he smiled at Murielle, who tilted her head back and laughed just before taking one step closer. The tips of their shoes touched as she wrapped her arms around his shoulders.

"I see my brother endowed ye with the regality of royalty," she said, eyeing the furs and circlet upon his head.

"He did, though I do not deserve them—or you."

"Shut up and kiss me like Ross kissed Rachel in that show we watched."

"My modern woman." Dipping her back, Samuel lowered his lips to hers, feeling waves of euphoria wash over him as they finally, finally became husband and wife. The kiss was slow, passionate, and lingering as the crowd cheered them on.

Brodyn grumbled beside them, but Samuel paid no mind. He would kiss his wife thoroughly, and he would stop when he was damned ready.

When he pulled Murielle back upright, the crowd roared and whistled, lining their path as they walked away from the kirk, shouting support, waving arms, and making bawdy gestures. They sped through the crowd and found their way to the longhouse, which already looked much grander than it had when he'd left. Candles flickered and illuminated the room with a warm glow, and servants put out jugs of ale and mead as people began to filter inside. The scent of roasted deer and boar filled the room from the kitchens just behind the head table where the spits, ovens, and kilns were kept.

Brodyn and Caitriona entered directly behind Samuel and

Murielle, leading them toward the head table as the village and Aldfrith's men filtered in through the double wooden doors.

King Brodyn picked up a jug and filled his mug, which already sat in front of his seat in anticipation of his arrival. A serving woman rushed over to help him fill it, but he smiled and waved her away as he turned to address his people.

"Tonight, my wee sister becomes a woman!" The crowd whooped as they all found their seats. Soon, the longhouse was at capacity, and many people stood shoulder to shoulder, filling in the space. "Assuming she hasnae yet become one," Brodyn said wryly as he eyed Samuel knowingly. Sam simply looked away from Brodyn and smiled at Murielle, gripping her hand as she turned beet red.

"Brodyn!" Cait scolded, smacking her husband on the arm. He just chuckled and kept going with his toast.

"Tonight, I have gained a new brother in Samuel Sullivan, who I trust will take care of Murielle all the days of her life. He is now a member of your royal family and a prince of Fortriu. He shall receive your respect in all things with his new station. So, here is to Samuel and Murielle. May they live long, happy lives and find themselves surrounded by children, grandchildren, and perhaps even great-grandchildren."

He lifted his mug in salute, and everyone did the same. Following their king's lead, they guzzled down their beverages.

Murielle said nothing, but the glow on her cheeks and bright smile told Samuel all he needed to know, and he felt the same way. Two years of secret feelings bottled up inside, fear of never being good enough or ruining the timeline vanished like whisps of smoke floating from the candles and sconces around the room. He felt like he'd float away if not for Murielle's grip on his hand.

Samuel raised his glass and looked around the room. Never had he addressed these people. As far as they knew, he'd always been a traveler, a messenger from Dal Riata. To be here now as their prince was something akin to a fantasy. But it wasn't the status of royalty he ever coveted, only the beautiful woman by his side.

"I come to you all, a humble servant to King Brodyn and a friend of you all. Through my years of travel, I have never known a people as fierce and loyal as the Picts of Fortriu." The crowd cheered and raised their glasses, bolstering his courage. He'd lectured to thousands of students and colleagues yet speaking to this group of ancient men made Samuel slightly nervous. "I am proud to now be a member of the Pictish royal family, but I will never consider myself above anyone else. I am but a humble man who won the heart of the most beautiful woman who ever lived." Then, leaning close to Murielle's ear, he whispered, "I know this to be true. I have met women from multiple timelines."

She tilted her head and laughed before kissing him on the cheek and resting her head on his shoulder. He was pleased to see her nerves starting to calm. The crowd awed and celebrated as the royal family sat down at the head table. Goodwin, Lawrence, and Ronan sat with them at the table, ever at their king's side. Emilie sat beside Goodwin, holding wee Anya as she slept, and Eva—dressed now in Pict-appropriate attire—sat beside Ronan as a special guest of the king. King Aldfrith and his guard sat beside her, and Samuel knew by the look on her face that Eva was just as enthralled with being in Aldfrith's presence as he was.

Samuel leaned into Murielle's ear. "I don't wish to speak of this beyond this point, but will someone explain to me why Eva is still here?"

She nearly spit out her mead but managed to swallow it just in time. "She came to apologize to me. Why she is still here is best explained, perhaps, by Ronan."

Samuel looked over at Eva and Ronan with curiosity. They sat quite close together, their faces even closer as they chatted. Eva appeared flushed, which Samuel never thought her capable of. "Well, I'll be damned."

"There is more." Murielle briefly filled Samuel in about Edwin and Anya appearing to Eva in Burghead, guiding her to Callum at the visitor center. "He was the spitting image of Ronan,

Sam. And Anya and Edwin are said to show themselves only to family in distress."

"Was Callum in distress? You had just informed him that time travel was real."

"He already knew that. Burghead is full of such legends. When Cait went missing and returned from out of nowhere, Callum read it in the paper and kenned what had happened. I dinnae think he was the family member in distress."

"Then, who was?" The more Murielle told him, the more confused Samuel became. A lightbulb may well have comically lit up over his head as he finally understood what Murielle was insinuating. Looking at Eva and Ronan, Samuel shook his head. "You don't think…"

"That Eva was their distressed family member? Aye, I do. Callum is absolutely a descendant of Ronan. In fact, I dare say they share a soul."

"That is why Ronan couldn't pass through the veil."

"Aye, because his soul was already occupying a body in 2023. But this means Ronan will marry and have bairns someday."

"And you think he will do that with Eva…" Samuel paused to think over the situation. So far, every person he knew who passed through the veil found their soulmate on the other side. First, Anya met Edwin, then Caitriona married Brodyn, Emilie married Goodwin, and now he had married Murielle.

"I cannae say. But there is something between them. Ye should have seen their connection when she arrived. I've never seen Ronan so besotted, not even with Emilie."

"Perhaps the key to passing through the veil isn't just fixing the timeline or restricted to those whose soul isn't yet in a body. Perhaps the veil reunites lost soulmates."

"Ye think ye are my soulmate, then?" Murielle asked with humor glittering in her blue eyes.

"Oh, I'm certain of it. I remember nothing from my past lives beyond uniting Cait and Brodyn, but I remember you. Always you. Only you."

"Och, I love ye so much, Samuel Sullivan." Murielle leaned in, pulled his face toward her with both palms on his cheeks, and kissed him deeply. The bold move caught the attention of the entire village, and everyone roared with excitement.

Brodyn actually smiled and shook his head before returning to his conversation with Aldfrith. Samuel knew then that he was genuinely accepted and loved by the Pictish people. He'd miss them terribly when they left here, but he hoped the veil saw fit to continue letting them pass through. If only he had evidence of their wonderful ways to share with the modern world. He knew this was Murielle's dream, and he meant to speak to Caitriona and discover what her plans were to make that happen before they left.

Platters of food were brought to the table, and all the individual voices melded into one harmonious hum as the entire longhouse feasted and celebrated. Soon, the platters were cleared, and musicians began to play their flutes and harps, encouraging people to dance the night away.

Slowly, Samuel swayed with Murielle in his arms, the sweet smell of flowers drifting all around her glistening hair. Her silk dress clung to her every curve, enticing Samuel, and offering him a sweet reminder of what lay beneath it.

"Have I told you how beautiful you look tonight?" he murmured into her ear as they moved together on the dance floor. They were the only couple slow dancing as the music sped up, and this sort of dancing had yet to be invented, but he didn't care if everyone else thought they were insane.

"Only about a thousand times," she giggled, looking up at him with anticipation. His flesh warmed, and his groin tightened when he knew she was also thinking about the wedding night ahead of them.

"Well, it's true. You are so damned beautiful. Are you ready—"

"Aye," she said quickly, cutting him off mid-sentence. "I've been ready since yesterday." She laughed, but he knew how serious she was, for he felt the same way.

"Well, then, shall I escort you home?" Samuel asked. When she smiled and nodded, he surprised her by sweeping her off her feet and into his arms. She squealed and laughed, wrapping her arms around his neck.

"The bride and groom are coming through!" A man hollered at the crowd, which parted like the Red Sea, allowing them to pass.

"I do believe they are ready for the bedding ceremony!" a woman cackled.

"There willnae be a bedding ceremony for my sister!" Brodyn shouted. "Any man or woman… or child," he said, scowling down at a boy who appeared to be around twelve years old, "who tries to follow my sister and her husband into their chamber shall be chained and whipped!"

His voice brooked no argument, and Samuel wasn't certain if Brodyn meant the threat or not, but it certainly made everyone back off immediately. Murielle flushed and sent her brother a look of gratitude. Samuel would leave for 2023 immediately without any goodbyes if a single person attempted to follow them to bed. He'd never understood or agreed with the bedding ceremony, and he'd not stand for it. Fortunately, he didn't need to.

Samuel stepped out into the darkness with his bride cradled in his arms, his heart beating wildly with anticipation. "Are we going to your chamber?"

"Och, I almost forgot. Emilie, Goodwin, and wee Anya will stay with my brother tonight. They've left us their home for the night, so we may have privacy."

Samuel nodded and turned in the direction of Goodwin's modest lodgings, reminding himself to thank Goodwin in the morning for his thoughtfulness. Bedding his new wife under her brother's roof would have been slightly uncomfortable.

Reaching the front of the house, Samuel stopped and looked down into Murielle's beaming blue eyes. Her dress nearly matched them in color, and they seemed to glow. "By tomorrow, I shall be carrying you over our own threshold, my love. But for now, this will do."

She sighed and rested her head against his shoulder as he shifted her weight and opened the door to Goodwin's home. A fire already burned in the hearth with several logs piled up against the back wall to keep it alight. Candles flickered in sconces on the walls, and one smaller candle sat in a bronze holder near the bed.

Slowly, Samuel released Murielle and allowed her to slide down his body, enjoying every inch of her against him. Her hands remained locked around his neck as she stood on tiptoe and looked up at him. She was very petite, but she made up for what she lacked in size or stature with her powerful wit, charm, and humor. She was everything any man would ever wish for in a wife, but for Samuel, she was literally the woman of his dreams. One life to the next, he remembered her face and his love for her. He'd never know if he won her heart in every life, but this life was the one that mattered now, and she was his to love and cherish.

"'Tis odd how life works," she sighed before placing a feather-soft kiss on his lips. "How I've longed for ye since the day ye first arrived at Pinnata Castra. I never thought I'd ever be yer wife. I kenned I was supposed to marry a king, but I didnae want anyone but ye."

"You were never meant to marry a king or any other man. You and I are meant to be. I will never be a king, but I will always treat you like a queen."

She nodded and slowly dropped down onto her heels, releasing her grip around his neck, and taking a few steps back. The fire lit up her body, highlighting the sensual curve of her hips and the roundness of her breasts. His body ached and throbbed with awaiting passion, but he paused to soak up the moment, never wanting to appear overeager, even if the straining bulge in his trousers gave him away.

The knowing glint in her mischievous eyes and the slight

upturn of her pink lips told him that she knew precisely what she did to him. As he admired Murielle in her dress, readying himself to tear it off her body any second, she gathered the fabric in her palms and pulled the dress over her head. The blue silk fluttered to the floor, landing like a pool of water at his feet. But it wasn't the shimming silk that kept his gaze.

Goosebumps crept up his heated flesh as his wife stood before him, fully naked, as the firelight caressed her skin. He would be the one caressing every inch of her soon. How he longed to taste, suckle, and lick every sweet part of her delectable body.

Waves of golden hair hung loosely over her shoulders as she watched him with a mix of desire and apprehension. Despite her outward bravery, Samuel reminded himself that aside from their one night together, Murielle was still new to intimacy.

Stepping forward, Samuel placed a hand on her cheek and looked deep into her eyes, reassuring her without words. He wanted her to know he loved all of her, inside and out. Her body was enough to subdue any man, but it was her soul that kept him enraptured in every lifetime.

Gently, he tilted her chin upward and leaned in, pressing his lips against hers, a whisper of a kiss before gliding his tongue along her lower lip. She quivered before him, and he knew it was the pent-up need because he felt it, too. Every nerve in his body was heightened, desperate for her touch, but he wouldn't toss her onto the bed and roughly take her like a barbarian. No, he was going to take his time and offer her true sensual, almost agoniz-ing, pleasure.

Samuel dragged his fingertips down the smooth skin on her arms, entwining his fingers with hers and prompting her to come closer. Leaning close to her ear, he swept her hair aside with his other hand and whispered, "I am the luckiest man in the world," just before nipping on her earlobe. She shivered and pressed herself even closer to his body.

"I want ye, Samuel," she whispered back, wrapping her hand around his erection even through his trousers, making him groan with need. "I ken ye want me, too."

"More than you will ever know." Samuel captured her lips with his, slipping his tongue into her mouth, feeding the hunger that consumed him as she gripped him. Then he felt her nimble fingers untying the trouser strings just before they loosened, and she wrapped her fingers around his throbbing flesh.

He groaned again and deepened the kiss, his hands cupping her breasts before he even realized what he was doing. She made him lose all self-control. His desire for a slow, sensual experience was quickly being overruled by his body's need for release.

Taking a deep breath, Samuel closed his eyes and did something he never thought he'd do. He removed Murielle's hand from his manhood and shook his head. "You will have me undone in no time if this continues," he chuckled. "I want to make this moment last."

Murielle released her grip and nodded, and he was grateful she didn't take offense. He wanted her hands all over every inch of his body, but he needed to please her first. Samuel ran his thumbs over her nipples, watching them tighten into pebbles at his touch before leaning in to suck one, then the other, into his mouth. She arched and groaned, tilting her head back as he continued.

Sliding one hand down her abdomen and over her belly, he settled between her thighs and slid a finger through her wet heat. Murielle's fingers dug into his bicep as she clung to him for support when her knees began to quake.

Guiding her toward the bed, Samuel prompted her to lie down. Her flush cheeks and half-mast eyes were evidence of her building desire, but he wanted to make her cry out with pleasure before he made love to her.

"I want to see yer body, Sam." Her breathing hitched, and her chest rose and fell as she watched him slowly remove his tunic, trousers, and boots before straddling her on the bed. "Ye are a beautiful man, husband," she sighed just before he kissed her languidly. With one arm supporting his weight, he used his free hand to explore her body, running his fingers down her womanly hips and cupping her firm backside. His body shook from the restraint he had to exude to keep himself from plunging into her depths before he was ready. She lifted off the bed, needy, groaning as his tongue danced with hers and her nails slid down his back, resting on his backside, urging him to continue.

When his fingers once again grazed her sensitive woman's flesh and focused on the spot that he knew drove her crazy, she instinctively parted her legs for him and arched her hips, desperate for more. And more is what he wanted to give her, more than anything else in the entire world.

Adjusting himself so his shoulders rested between her thighs, Samuel met her bewildered gaze, determined to keep himself from losing all control when the beast inside wanted to ravish her, to bury himself deep within her and never leave.

"Samuel?" Her voice was soft and airy, hesitant, and curious.

"Do you trust me?"

"Of course. But ye arenae…"

"Just lay back, my heart. I vow you will understand in a moment."

She nodded and lay back, allowing Samuel to take charge of her body in a way that drove him mad. She was willing to make herself vulnerable to him, and that meant everything. When he leaned in and fanned his warm breath against her core, she shuddered and shifted but did not pull away. And when his tongue gently grazed her sweet flesh, she gasped and jolted her hips, but still, she did not stop him. Encouraged, he continued to taste her, to lick, and tease her as her breathing increased and small moans of pleasure grew into deep, guttural groans.

"Sam!" She called his name, grappling at the sheets, tugging on his hair, desperate to seek purchase in the storm of need that threatened to drown her in pleasure. His erection throbbed, desperate to slide into her as she panted and squirmed beneath him, writhing until her entire body tensed and she cried out his name. Tears ran down her temples as she came back down from the clouds, but Samuel had no more control left. He had to have her. Now.

Getting onto his knees, Samuel leaned forward and gripped her hips, pushing himself deep, deeper into her until he was fully sheathed inside her slick heat.

A grunt of relief escaped his parted lips as he looked down at his exquisite wife, awestruck by her beauty. "You are my everything," he groaned as he pushed in and pulled back, his hips meeting hers with every thrust as she met him with equal enthusiasm. His senses were on overdrive, and every touch felt like a thousand points of pleasure as her hands gripped his backside, urging him to move faster and push deeper. His head spun out of control, and spots flashed behind his eyes as his mind allowed his body's instincts to take control.

Waves of heat swathed his body and sweat ran down his chest as he neared the pinnacle of his pleasure. He kissed her and looked into her eyes. "I love you, Murielle. So damned much." And before she could whisper a response, his body shuddered, and every muscle contracted as he spilled his seed, waves of ecstasy washing over him as he closed his eyes and panted for breath.

Murielle cried out in pleasure and dug her nails into his back, tensing before going limp beneath him just as he felt the need to collapse. Rolling over, he took her with him and held her close, feeling her heart beating in tandem with his as their sweat-slicked skin touched.

Samuel didn't know if seconds, minutes, or hours passed as he held Murielle to him, running his hands through her tangled hair as they exchanged soft, seductive kisses. All he knew was that his heart was full to bursting with a painful, crippling love for his wife, and he would die a happy man so long as she was always his. But he planned to live a very long, healthy life. Nothing on this earth would ever pull them apart again. He made that vow to himself as he watched Murielle's blue eyes slide shut seconds before sleep carried her away.

Kissing her on the forehead, Samuel followed her lead and allowed his tired body and heavy eyelids to rest, for it had been a wonderous but tiring day, and on the morrow, they headed back to his time.

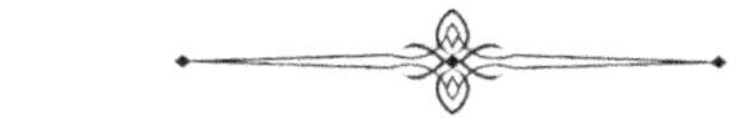

CHAPTER THIRTEEN

M IXING COOKED APPLES into her bowl of streaming porridge, Murielle sat at Brodyn's table, mindlessly humming to herself as she replayed the previous night in her mind. Her cheeks warmed, and she wasn't certain if it was from the memory of Samuel's head between her legs or from the heat rising from her bowl. The soreness throughout her body in her woman's flesh was singularly the sweetest discomfort she'd ever felt, for it served as a constant reminder that she was now Murielle Sullivan. She was Samuel's wife.

"I think the apples will turn into mush if you keep stirring them." A female voice shocked Murielle out of her thoughts, and she jolted upright, looking over her shoulder. Cait stood behind her with Lucas in her arms, and the sudden realization that she was leaving her family today made Murielle's heart drop.

"Is that a frown?" Cait asked, tilting her head. "No blushing bride should be frowning so soon after her wedding day."

Murielle shook her head and forced a smile. "Sorry. Seeing you here with Lucas made me realize that time passes quicker here. Next time I see Lucas, he will be much grown. It just gave me pause."

"Yes, I understand that. I wish we could all be in the same time together, but you and Sam have a wonderful life awaiting you. I have no doubts." Caitriona sat beside Murielle on the wooden bench, and Lucas reached out for Murielle. Porridge forgotten, Murielle took her dark-haired, green-eyed nephew into her arms, and held her nose to his head, inhaling the scent of innocence. She prayed that Brodyn's efforts to keep his people safe would result in Lucas having a long, peaceful reign of his own someday. It would be the hardest thing she ever did not to research his fate when she returned to 2023. She couldn't bear knowing if something awful befell the precious lad.

"I wish ye would tell me what ye have planned for our future," Murielle said to Cait, diverting her mind away from the darkness of knowing that her loved ones would be long dead once she left this time. It was better to focus on other things.

"That's why I'm here, actually," Caitriona said with a smile. "I assume you are here looking for Sam?"

"Aye, I awoke to him already gone from the bed. I didnae like it," she sulked.

"Yeah, I hate waking up to find Brodyn missing when I expect to find his large, hairy body snoring beside me." Murielle crinkled her nose at the visual of her big, dumb brother covered in hair. "But you were asleep, and Sam didn't want to wake you. You can blame me. Last night, I instructed him to find me when he awoke. I needed his help setting you up for your future with my identity."

"Aye, I've been wondering how ye planned to make that happen."

"The modern world is all about records, and my parents have all of mine. They travel all the time. In fact, they are almost never home. Did you know they didn't even know when I was missing? And when they found out, they were only glad I popped up before they found out... not so they wouldn't worry, but so they wouldn't have to cancel their next vacation. Don't get me wrong; they love me. But they have more money than they know what to do with. Once I went off to college, they set me up with a bank account and took off. They wanted me to be an actress. I know you don't know what that means. When I decided to become an archaeologist, they cut me off, took back all the money in the account, and told me to call them when I was done playing in the dirt. I was never done, so I never talk to them anymore."

Murielle frowned and looked at Lucas. Caitriona was such a doting mother, and it broke Murielle's heart to hear she grew up without the same pure, selfless love. "I am terribly sorry to hear this, Cait." Murielle squeezed Caitriona's hand, but she just shrugged.

"I'm fine, really. It made me stronger. And I never wanted their money. Now, I don't need it. However, it would have come in handy for you. Someday, however, you will inherit a vast fortune."

"I dinnae want yer money, Cait. Ye are already giving me yer identity. I want to make a life for myself."

Cait smiled and nodded. "I know. That's why Samuel loves you so much. You're fierce and independent. You were a feminist before feminism was cool." She waved away her words. "Again, another concept you don't yet understand. Yet. But you will. Anyhow, the point is, you will be just fine. But no matter how strong, intelligent, and independent you are, you will need my birth records, high school diploma, college degrees, and all other records to make it anywhere. That's where my parents come in, or rather, their estate manager, who happens to like me much more than he likes them." Caitriona winked and handed Murielle a sealed piece of parchment. "Here. When you get back to Scotland, have Samuel send this off. It's already addressed, but obviously, I can't buy postage here."

Hesitantly, Murielle took the parchment, but she had no idea what postage was. "What does it say?"

"It's a letter signed by me saying that I am permanently stay-ing in Scotland. I gave Charles, the estate manager, Samuel's address to send all my documents. He is then to burn the note and tell my parents he has no idea where I am. I highly doubt they will ever look for me or care, honestly." She shrugged again, but Murielle saw a flash of sadness in Cait's eyes before she smiled again and gripped Murielle's hand. "It's okay, really. It was meant to be this way. If I had decent parents, leaving them forever would have been painful. This way, staying here with Brodyn was easy. I have no siblings, and my parents were both the only children of wealthy only children. It's a pattern in my family. One and done. Get an heir, pour money on their head, and ignore their existence. But I'm breaking the cycle."

"Aye, ye are. Lucas is the most loved child I've ever kenned," Murielle said, bouncing him on her knee and laughing when he looked up at her with his gummy grin.

"I meant… I'm pregnant again. I just told Brodyn last night. Nobody but him, you, and Emilie know."

"Oh, my!" Murielle yelped, but Cait gave her a look, and Murielle pursed her lips before whispering, "Oh, Cait! I'm so happy for ye and Brodyn! Now, Sam and I must visit every weekend, so I can watch ye expand with child!"

"You better." Caitriona leaned in and hugged Murielle. "I find that all of this works out in the end. Emilie had no parents to miss her when she crossed over because she was an orphan and her adoptive parents passed shortly after taking her in. She had no real family. Anya's entire family died in a war, too. Samuel's parents passed away when he was young. It seems the universe makes certain to close off loose ends. And this letter is my way of tying up yours."

"Ye are the best sister and friend I could have ever asked for. I will miss ye tremendously. But ye said Samuel was also helping. If he didnae write the letter, what is he doing?"

Cait paused and looked around the room, sucking in a deep breath once she knew they were alone. "It seems the book of records has been stolen from the chapel overnight," Cait whispered and waggled her brows. "The monk and priest are in an uproar over it, and they seem to think Samuel, as a former messenger, can spread the word to help locate it. They tried to blame Aldfrith's men, but Brodyn is defending them."

Murielle gasped and clutched her chest. "Is that why all the records are never found? Because the book goes missing?"

Cait snorted and smacked her leg. "No, you goose! It's how

all the records will one day be found—by you and Samuel! It's hidden in my chest upstairs."

She beamed with pride, smiling ear to ear, but Murielle felt the blood leave her face. "Ye stole from a holy man? Och, Caitriona Mac Cull, ye will burn in hell for such a thing!"

"I'll repent later," she said calmly. "Besides, I know what I'm doing. The monk doesn't know that his hard work will never see the light of day, so of course, he is upset. What we are doing is honoring his work. He wants the world to remember the Picts of Fortriu. That's why he is so tedious about his recording. We will make sure it is found."

"But won't that mess with the timeline? If someone finds it before we do, the world will know all about us, ye and Samuel will never go to the cave to seek out Pictish secrets, and ye will never meet Brodyn! And Lucas willnae be born! Och, nay! This is a horrible idea, Cait."

"You forget that Sam and I are archaeologists. It's our job to know which areas have already been excavated over the centuries. I will bury it in a part of the cave where we are absolutely certain no one has yet dug. His excavation was cut short when I went missing. A lot of that cave never got touched. People used the cave for many purposes over the next centuries, but they never built anything that required them to dig, and all the bodies found there by archaeologists were shallow graves near the cave's entrance. The only body ever found elsewhere in that cave was Taylor's, and I'm the one who found it. Trust me, this will work."

"Yer a genius, Cait!"

"I know." Caitriona smiled and stood from her seat, grabbing Lucas from Murielle's lap. "Now, quickly eat your porridge before it gets cold, then meet Sam and me at the longhouse. We have a surprise for you."

"More surprises? I don't think I can take more. I already discovered that you are pregnant and stole from a monk!"

Cait laughed and shook her head. "Oh, Murielle. We will

miss you and your innocence. Sometimes a little dark deed can be a positive thing in the end. You will have proof about the Picts, and his work won't have been done in vain. Win, win. See you soon."

Blowing Murielle an air kiss, Caitriona left the house, and Lucas looked over his mother's shoulder, waving sticky fingers at his Auntie Murielle.

Hastily finishing her tepid porridge, Murielle washed her bowl and wrapped her cloak around her shoulders before leaving the house, curious about what this surprise could possibly be. The wind swept her cloak to the side as she walked, reminding her of one of those superheroes she learned about while in the future. She *felt* like a superhero, taking charge of her own destiny and ready to charge forth into the unknown.

An eerie silence fell over the still village. Where were the little children running in the streets, the women gathered around barrels of dye as they colored swathes of linen, and the men toiling on roof repairs?

Looking around, Murielle found herself to be the only person within viewing distance, and she stopped in her tracks to look around. Nobody was there.

Turning toward the longhouse where Caitriona told her to meet Samuel, Murielle felt tension build in the pit of her stomach. She trusted that her family wouldn't trick her, but she had never seen the village at a standstill in the middle of the day. Even on festival days, villagers ran around in a frenzy.

Approaching the closed wooden doors leading into the long-house, Murielle slowly opened one side, its rusty hinges creaking in her ear. She jumped back with a startled shriek when she found herself face-to-face with Samuel.

Placing a hand on her wildly beating heart, she sighed and looked up at her husband. "Ye scared me! I didnae expect ye to be just on the other side. Where is everyone in the village?"

Samuel smiled and took her hand, leading her into the hall just as he stepped aside. When she looked up, Murielle found the entire village huddled into the room with wide smiles and anticipation glittering in their eyes.

"Surprise!" The crowd of hundreds of people shouted in tandem, making Murielle laugh and jump back simultaneously.

"Wh-what is this all about?"

"Ye dinnae think we'd allow ye to move away without a proper farewell, did ye now?" Her brother said, stepping forward with Caitriona and Lucas.

"I… I suppose I didnae think of it," Murielle whispered, smiling as she looked around the room at all the familiar faces of those she loved. Tears welled up in her eyes as she committed their names and faces to memory, vowing never to forget a single one of them. They might all be dust beneath the ground in Samuel's time, but they were her people—her friends and family. More than ever, she felt a surge of determination to share their ancient world with those in the modern world. Their lives would not be forgotten, and if she had to serve as an accomplice in stealing from a holy man, she now understood that it was, indeed, for the greater good. The Picts would not be forgotten.

"We love ye, Princess Murielle!" Aileen, one of the village's washing women, shouted from the crowd.

Samuel stepped forward with a grin and, standing by her side, took her hand.

"I love ye, as well," Murielle choked. "I love ye all verra dearly. I shall miss each and every one of ye, but I vow to visit as often as possible."

The village believed she was relocating to Dal Riata, home of the Scots, where Samuel was believed to reside as King Domnall's messenger. Nobody from their village, aside from other messengers, would ever visit Dal Riata, and they'd never stay long enough to realize she wasn't there. It worked, though she disliked lying to her people. There was simply no way to offer them the truth.

"We ken ye are ready to leave and willnae slow yer progress. We simply wished to gather as one and tell ye that ye shall be missed and to offer ye our prayers as ye embark on yer new life," Brodyn announced.

Murielle looked up at her eldest brother as tears slid down her cheeks. She often thought of Talorc, Brodyn's twin brother, who'd become power-hungry and betrayed Brodyn on the battlefield. He died that day for his treachery, and though Murielle would never fully forgive Talorc for his actions, at this moment, she wished the three of them could be together for a final farewell.

Rushing into Brodyn's arms, Murielle's small frame managed to knock his large body back a few steps. "Thank ye, Brother. Ye are making it verra hard to leave."

He rubbed her back and squeezed her to him, constricting her breathing. "That just means ye must visit us as often as possible. But dinnae fret over us, Sister. Go forth, follow yer path, and ken we are doing the same. When our roads merge, it shall make it that much sweeter."

Murielle pulled back and shook her head. "I do believe yer wife's wisdom has rubbed off on ye."

"And I believe yer husband's wisdom has only enhanced yers." Brodyn released her from his grip, smiled, and stepped away, addressing his people. "I thank ye all for coming together to bid Murielle farewell. They have a journey awaiting them that we cannae delay."

Everyone shouted their best wishes, waved, and smiled as Brodyn and Cait escorted Samuel and Murielle outside the longhouse, Emilie and Goodwin following in their wake. Ronan and Eva came out, as well, and Murielle braced herself, for she knew she and Samuel must escort Eva home before they could truly begin their new life.

Though Murielle accepted Eva's apology, the woman still left her ill at ease, and she didn't relish the thought of traveling with her.

"Remember to send that letter to my parent's estate manager. He has access to all of our family documents," Caitriona said to

Samuel, who patted the satchel strapped across his shoulder.

"It is safely inside my bag. I will mail it as soon as we return."

Cait nodded. "Are your permits up to date for excavating the cave?"

Samuel nodded. "Yes, I renewed them recently, just in case we gathered our team again."

"Good. In the alcove where I first fell through time, in the farthest corner toward the sea, you will uncover the discovery of a lifetime. Nobody has ever dug in that spot before, so I am assured it will be awaiting you when you arrive."

"I cannot thank you enough, Cait. This means the world to us. You are literally giving up your identity so she can have a life with me."

"Sam, you spend every lifetime stuck in this time loop with a single-minded goal to become my mentor and bring me on your excavation just so I'd fall through time and meet Brodyn. I realize he and I had to marry to correct the timeline and save the future of Scotland, but you do it without fail. You are the most selfless man I've ever known and you deserve your own happiness. I'd do anything for you and Murielle. Anything at all, even steal from a monk." Caitriona waggled her brows mischievously before leaning in to hug Samuel.

"Aye, the man is beside himself," Brodyn grumbled. "That tome is his life's work, so treat it well and put it to good use, aye?"

"Of course, Brother," Samuel said, reaching out to clasp forearms with Brodyn. Murielle's heart swelled to near bursting, watching her husband and brother bond. True happiness blossomed in her heart, warming her insides as if the sun's rays could penetrate her soul. She never considered herself a woman full of such emotions, but Samuel had shown her that there was more to her than the stubborn, willful woman she had always been. A softer side lived within her, and he'd brought it to the surface and nourished it. She'd always be that same fierce woman, but now Murielle had a range of emotions she'd never owned before, and she found that, aside from being more prone to fits of tears, she quite enjoyed this transformation.

Emilie and Goodwin stepped forward to exchange farewells, and wee Anya cooed when her mother took her little arm and made it wave goodbye to Murielle. "You will be missed, Murielle," Emilie sighed. "But I will not drag on. I know you will come back, or I will come and find you."

"Now who will drive me mad every day?" Goodwin asked with a wink. "It was a pleasure to have been your guard before Ronan and, more importantly, be your friend, Murielle. Until we meet again."

"Liar. Ye hated every moment of chasing me down!" Murielle laughed through the haze of tears and fiercely hugged them both, pausing when she made eye contact with Ronan and Eva. She swallowed any lingering bitterness and asked,

"Are you ready to go, Eva?"

Eva looked at Ronan and cleared her throat awkwardly. "We were thinking…" Eva said hesitantly.

"If it is favorable to King Brodyn," Ronan added slowly, "that mayhap Eva can stay here a wee bit and… see where this leads." He grew red as Murielle raised a brow in his direction. She'd known there was a connection between them, but she hadn't expected Eva to stay behind.

Brodyn looked at Eva with scrutiny. "I willnae deny my faithful warrior a chance at happiness, but I must confess, ye didnae come to us over the best circumstances. Dinnae think yer treatment toward my sister in yer time has been forgotten. Ye've apologized, and I am a man who respects humility in people. I will allow ye stay as long as there is no further issue."

Eva crossed her heart and nodded. "I wasn't at my finest then, but I promise that is not my true nature. I will not cause anyone any grief."

"Verra well," Brodyn said with a nod. "Ye are welcome to stay as long as Ronan wishes ye to."

"Thank ye, my king. The safety of ye and yer family has always been and will always be my priority. But, 'tis nice to have someone to share life with that isnae coerced to endure my presence."

"Ronan!" Murielle said with more force than intended. "If ever I made ye feel like yer presence wasnae welcome, then I owe ye the greatest apology. Ye have always been dear to me, even if ye kept me out of the trouble I dearly wished to cause." She cracked a smile and stepped forward to embrace him. "I shall always value yer friendship and appreciate all ye have done to keep me safe over the years."

"It was the honor of my life, and I shall do so again whenever ye visit."

Samuel frowned and addressed Eva. "Don't you need to report back to work? You have classes to teach."

She shook her head and pursed her lips. "I did not mention this before, but I gave my notice to the university. I was arrogant and believed I had the position at the University of Edinburgh in the bag. When they rejected me, I found myself with no teaching position."

"I'm certain the university would offer you back your position. You are a wonderful professor."

"I appreciate that Sam, and perhaps one day I will go back. For now, I'm letting life take me where it will. I did not wake up yesterday morning expecting to end up here. In fact, I didn't wake up believing in time travel or spirits, yet the spirit of the woman you all love so dearly led me here. I must accept that there is a greater purpose for it." She looked up at Ronan, flushed wildly, then looked back at Sam and Murielle. "I am so very sorry for how I treated you, Murielle. You didn't deserve it, yet it led me here, and I am ready for a new adventure."

Murielle smiled and nodded, but she wasn't ready to embrace Eva as she had everyone else. Instead, she put out a hand and allowed Eva to shake it as professionals would. "I wish ye the verra best. Ronan is a wonderful man. I can attest to that."

Ronan grinned ear to ear, and Eva nodded. "Safe travels, you two," Eva added.

With no more words left to say, and a thousand memories, hopes, thoughts, and emotions crowding her mind, Murielle waved one last time as Samuel took her hand and guided her toward a cart strapped to a horse, led by Lawrence, who'd safely accompany them back to the cave. Murielle wasn't sure how much of the situation Lawrence understood, but he'd been there when Caitriona arrived, and he'd been the one to find Emilie wandering the land near the cave. He wasn't the brightest man in the village, and for certain, he'd sustained one too many head injuries in combat, but she'd like to believe Lawrence understood the situation and simply kept to himself as he preferred.

With Samuel's help, Murielle climbed into the back of the cart with him and what little belongings they brought with them, watching her family until their figures became mere specks on the vast horizon. When their figures finally faded into the distance, Murielle sighed and leaned against Samuel, determined to see them again soon enough.

Six months later, Edinburgh 2024

"WELCOME! PLEASE FIND a seat." Silently tapping her fingertips against the podium, Murielle smiled as she watched locals filter into the Burghead Visitor Center to learn more about her and Samuel's recent discoveries about the Picts.

Though she'd been busy traveling around Scotland to do news interviews and guest talks at universities and museums, this particular event had her insides in knots. Burghead was home to her people's descendants, and they were thirsty to learn about their long-lost ancestors. Knowing that she stood upon Pinnata Castra's remains no longer made her wish to cry and flee. She'd accomplished her goal and honored her people today by bringing them back to life through the book they'd "discovered" in a small iron chest buried in the far corner of the cave's alcove. The chest had also contained several types of clothing, jewelry, and baubles. Caitriona had clearly taken proper care to create what Samuel called a *time capsule*.

"Murielle… I mean, Catriona," Callum whispered as he stepped forward to whisper in her ear. "Sorry, I keep forgetting yer new name." He cringed apologetically.

Smiling, Murielle gripped his hand. "I am legally Murielle now that I changed Cait's name to mine, so ye need not worry. Ye have been a good friend, Callum. Thank ye for setting this up."

"It wasnae hard to do. The town's people are pining to learn the forgotten history of their ancestors. All it took were a few posted fliers, and everyone showed up."

Looking around the room, Murielle found Samuel leaning against the far wall with his hands tucked into his jean pockets and a proud grin spread across his face as he winked at her.

The day after Samuel and Murielle traveled back to 2023, they mailed off Caitriona's letter to her family's estate manager in California. Within two weeks, a large, padded envelope had arrived containing all of Caitriona's identification papers, including a social security card and birth certificate. Neither she nor Samuel were citizens of the United Kingdom, so they relied on work visas to remain here while they could, but as long as Samuel remained employed by the university, they were free to stay near the cave and visit her family.

The estate manager had supplied a letter from Caitriona's parents requesting to visit their daughter soon. Samuel and Murielle delivered the letter to Caitriona, and it was decided she would return to her time as needed and stay in Samuel's flat to pretend she lived there. Once her parents left, she would return to Brodyn, Lucas, and now their other child, who would likely be born when Sam and Murielle visited again.

Once her identity had been established as Caitriona Mac Murray, Murielle legally changed her name to Murielle Sullivan.

Caitriona's name no longer existed in this time, and nobody would ever call her out as a fraud. Little would anyone ever know that she was the only authentic Pict alive.

She and Samuel had gathered a small excavation group to explore the cave again. Following Caitriona's instructions, Murielle and Samuel located the monk's tome hidden inside a small metal chest in the far corner of the cave's alcove. Never had Murielle been allowed near the tome before, so seeing its pages for the first time was a genuine discovery for her. Ivan of Iona, the monk, had painstakingly recorded every birth, marriage, and death of her people since her grandfather had adopted the Christian faith and had a kirk built on their lands. Their livestock and crops were meticulously recorded, along with trade, visits from outsiders, their clothing materials and methods of creation—even their symbols were carefully recorded and identified.

It was considered the find of a lifetime, and immediately Murielle and Samuel were thrust into a frenzy of news cameras, interviews, and scientific magazines, and asked to guest speak at universities and museums across the UK. Samuel had been offered more grant funding to continue his work, and Murielle was busy discussing the tome's contents and interpreting them to keen ears, wide eyes, and agape mouths.

Though the 1,337-year-old tome was now safely behind glass at the Museum of Edinburgh, its pages were carefully scanned and replicated so anyone could purchase and read the ancient book. Samuel added his own material to the tome, adding insights and new texts within the margins, and his students used the book in his class, along with students across the world. Together, they published the book and donated the profits to museums and the Scottish Historical Society. Now, with her copy of the tome resting before her on the podium, Murielle smiled at the crowd of eager people, noticing the room was so full that many stood against the walls.

"We have never had a crowd this size," Callum said just before Murielle started, and the crowd roared with pride.

"We've never had the famous archaeologists who discovered Burghead's Pictish roots here before!" one man shouted, making Murielle flush at the compliment. She couldn't possibly be considered famous, could she?

"Thank ye very much for being here," Murielle said with a smile as she glanced around the room. She was still adjusting to speaking to large crowds, but she'd already had plenty of experience since excavating the tome just six months ago. "It's wonderful to be back here, standing upon the ruins of the very place we will be discussing today. I'd like to call my husband, Samuel, up to the podium, for he is the man who led the team. Under his direction, we discovered this wonderous tome, believed to have been created by the monk, Ivan of Iona, who lived right here on this land with the Picts, guiding them in their new Christian faith and recording their daily life."

Samuel approached the podium and modestly waved at the group as they clapped. "Until the discovery of this tome, much about the Picts of Fortriu remained a mystery. Stones found on this very site were left to interpretation for centuries. Now, thanks to the efforts of Ivan of Iona, we know those stones depicted battles fought and won. The most famous battle depicted upon these stones is what we now refer to as the Battle of Dun Nechtan, led by King Brodyn Mac Cuill, the most famous King of the Picts ever recorded. His marriage to his wife, Caitriona of Dal Riata, is well-documented within these pages, and their symbols, the bull and the thistle, are still carved into caves along this coast today. We can thank this tome and Ivan of Iona for his dedication to recording these events and deciphering these symbols." Samuel paused and looked at Murielle, winking before continuing. "It is believed that the marriage alliance between King Brodyn and Queen Caitriona led to alliances that solidified a Pictish victory during that battle. That victory led to more peace and unity between neighboring tribes, which eventually unified the entire land as what we now call Scotland."

Murielle took up the lecture from that point. As she spoke to the crowd, she felt overwhelming tranquility wash over her, as if her family was watching while she told their story to their descendants. Already, Murielle had spent much time with Callum, telling him all about his ancestor, Ronan, and all the trouble he used to cause her. And now, Eva was part of that story.

News had circulated that Eva left Scotland without a trace, and colleagues assumed she was so angry about her rejection by the University of Edinburgh that she returned home to Pennsylvania without a word. Only Murielle and Samuel knew that she remained back in the year 687 with Ronan, where they were married and already expected their first child.

When Murielle spotted a familiar face in the crowd, her heart leaped, and her breath hitched, nearly making her pause as she continued to address the audience. It was a most unexpected face but wholly welcomed, even if it left Murielle slightly shaken. Murielle merely nodded to her surprise visitor and continued talking. To hide her shaking hands, she clutched the book before her and opened the room for questions. Many hands flew up in tandem, and she gladly took the time to answer all of the questions, taking great care with details of the Picts' everyday life, their culture, dress, religion—any topic the people wished to discuss. This was her chance to tell the world about her people, and no question would be left lacking an answer.

After thirty minutes of answering questions, Murielle watched as everyone stood from their seats to applaud her and Samuel for bringing their history and ancestors back to life. But when she scanned the crowd again, the familiar face had vanished despite nobody having yet left the room.

As people began to line up with copies of their books in hand, Murielle leaned toward Samuel's ear. "Did ye see Anya in the crowd? She was there, against that wall. Now, she is gone."

Samuel shook his head and gave her a warm smile. "I didn't see her, but I assume I was not meant to. This was your moment, Murielle, not mine."

"But... she only appears to her family. I amnae blood-related to her."

"Murielle." Samuel creased his brow as he sat beside her at the table, pen in hand and ready to sign copies of their book. "You should know by now that blood isn't the only thing that binds people together as a family. She raised you and your brothers. You are as close to a daughter as she ever had—at least in the lifetime that we knew her. God knows which time period this Anya was from."

"She wore a dress with long, fitted sleeves and many ruffles. A matching hat on her head also had many ruffles and feathers."

"Sounds like Victorian-era Anya," Samuel said with a chuckle.

"I dinnae ken anything about this Victorian era," Murielle whispered in his ear just as the first person in line, a plump woman with rosy cheeks and a puffy green coat, handed her a book to sign. The woman looked strikingly like one of the wash women from Pinnata Castra, and Murielle nearly yelped and reached out to embrace her before catching herself. She'd have to continuously remind herself that Burghead was likely brimming with Pinnata Castra's descendants.

"Thank ye very much for coming," Murielle said to the woman as she signed the book and passed it to Samuel.

"We will catch you up on history, love, one era at a time," Samuel mumbled, only so she could hear it as he signed the book next.

The line stretched far past the visitor center's entrance as photos flashed and people chattered excitedly about Murielle's lecture while awaiting their turn for an autograph.

She had done it. Against all odds and with much help from many friends and family, Murielle had accomplished her goals, not only by moving to the future and marrying Samuel, but she'd also found a way to teach the world about her beloved people. From one village or city to the next, she'd spread that message and make sure the Picts survived the hands of time, just as she and Samuel had.

ABOUT THE AUTHOR

Mia is a full-time mother of two rowdy boys, residing in the SF Bay Area. As a child, she often wrote stories about fantastic places or magical things, always preferring to live in a world where the line between reality and fantasy didn't exist.

In High school, she entered writing contests and had some stories published in small newspapers or school magazines. As life continued, so did her love of writing. So one day, she decided to end her cake decorating business, pull out her laptop and fulfill her dream of writing and publishing novels. And she did.

When Mia isn't writing books or chasing her sweaty children around a park, she loves to drink coffee by the gallon, get lost in a good book, hike with her family and drink really big margaritas with her friends! Her happy place is the Renaissance Faire, where you can find her at the joust, rooting for the shirtless highlander in a kilt.

Website: www.miapride.com
FB: facebook.com/miaprideauthor
Amazon: amazon.com/Mia-Pride/e/B01M6VEWGX
Instagram: instagram.com/mia_pride_author
Twitter: twitter.com/mia_pride
BookBub: https://www.bookbub.com/profile/mia-pride

www.ingramcontent.com/pod-product-compliance
Lightning Source LLC
Chambersburg PA
CBHW061257210726
48293CB00003B/1000